ALSO BY
ALEXANDRA ST PIERRE
THE ORIGIN'S DAUGHTER SERIES

The Origin's Daughter

The Dominion of Sin

THE ORIGIN'S DAUGHTER

ALEXANDRA ST PIERRE

Illustrations copyright © 2023 by Alexandra St Pierre
Map Elements by Josh Stolarz Map Effects
https://www.mapeffects.co/map-builder

Hard Copy: ISBN 9798388614049
Paper Back: ISBN: 9798388649782

To mom —

Stay purple.

A Crisis of Pride

-*Anonymous*

You are mine, said the Prince,
cradling his swaddling of twilight
My Queen, my slave, my lover, my friend the Prince
says as he rocks his shadow, back, back, back
Let us walk through worlds, he whispers
I will teach you to move planets, how to reorder the stars,
to become nighttime itself, how to speak
the language of the dead
I will lay your adversaries at your feet
You have freed me, I will try to free you, says the Prince,
Although your burden is one I cannot bear
I cannot save you from grief, but I can teach you to heal
I can show you how the ground moves beneath your feet
And to slip through the wind, as light as darkness
My salvation, my heart, my friend, my ward,
Let us learn each other's bodies, and
run our fingers through one another's minds
We will dance, leap, writhe and play
As fluently as the cat cuts through grass
I will teach you to be loud as silence, and to
Slip through armies, like a blade through the chest.

1

There was blood on my hands. Thankfully, very little of it was mine.

Mr. Abbey was sitting behind his large oak desk. He was cleaning his spectacles and observing me with tired eyes. The principal's desk was cluttered with pictures of what I could only assume were photos of his family. Stereotypical ornaments that students must have bought for him over the years wove in and out of the frames. His apple-shaped pencil dispenser and his mug which read #1 Principal cheerfully mocked me from his desk. I tried my best not to scowl at the stupid knick-knacks.

My adoptive father, Jeremy, was sitting adjacent to Mr. Abbey and I. Jeremy's cracked leather loafers seemed out of place in the pristine office and his soft worn trench coat fell in uneven folds over his lean, weather-burnt arms. The two men were staring at me with nearly identical expressions. Their tired eyes peeked at me through furrowed brows. Each of them projected affection and pity, haunted with an unmistakable aftertaste of defeat.

"What am I going to do with you, Raven?" Mr. Abbey asked, placing his tiny spectacles back on his nose. His chair squeaked as he leaned forward and crossed his tweed-clad arms across the desk. The question was a sincere one. His tone had no trace of sarcasm, yet I still struggled to find my voice. As much as that little weasel Neil had gotten what he deserved, I couldn't help but feel guilty. I had, once again, pulled Jeremy away from work, and put Mr. Abbey in a position where he felt he needed to make excuses for me.

Behind him, the lights from the ambulance bounced red, blue, then red again against the egg-yolk walls of the office. I fiddled with the silver pendant on my necklace that I had worn for as long as I could remember. The rough carved ring of ravens held onto each other by their talons. My namesake, my adoptive mother, had told me.

"I don't know," I answered honestly. I deserved to be expelled, at least in the eyes of the school board.

Jeremy spoke next, "You hit him with a chair, Raven. The kid might need to have his cheekbone reconstructed." I'd done a lot more than just that. Once he went down, I pinned him to the ground and went medieval on his ass. Somehow it didn't feel like the time to point that out.

I said nothing. What could I say? They were right. Jeremy should never have adopted me. He deserved better. What tore me up the most was that no matter how broken and sad he looked sitting next to me, he would never admit to regretting the decision to take me into his home. On some level, Jeremy knew I couldn't help it.

Mr. Abbey looked at Jeremy, before squeezing the bridge of his nose beneath his spectacles.

"I'm afraid I'm going to have to suspend you for an indefinite period of time." He said. The obvious avoidance of expulsion was noted. I watched Jeremy's shoulders slump, though I wasn't sure whether it was in relief or disappointment.

"Have you enrolled her in an anger management class? Mr. Abbey asked earnestly.

"Yes," Jeremy replied. "She has a session this afternoon."

Normally, I would have been enraged at the idea of being spoken about as if I weren't there, but I bit my tongue. I was simply grateful I hadn't been expelled. Not yet, anyway.

Jeremy stood up to shake hands with Mr. Abbey. The modest principal made eye contact with me over my adoptive father's shoulder.

"Well, maybe this time off will give her time to focus on controlling her...rage."

I felt the familiar twinges of anger nipping at the edge of my vision. I met Mr. Abbey's eyes with the same cool glare I had locked onto Neil Green only two short hours before. Abbey, however, did not drop his gaze.

"Alright, kiddo." Jeremy said, hiking up his jeans and standing. "Let's get out of here. I have to check out a crime scene." He turned to Mr. Abbey and shook his hand. "Thank you, sir, for everything."

Mr. Abbey smiled solemnly at Jeremy and nodded.

"Good luck," he said, as Jeremy ushered me out the door. "To both of you." I was left with the unnerving feeling that he wasn't just wishing me luck in anger management.

We spilled out into the parking lot and I glared at the other kids that had gathered in pools in front of the school. Some of them jeered and called me names. Others just stared at me half in awe and half in fear.

"Ignore them." Jeremy said to me under his breath. I forced myself not to turn and retaliate.

Once we reached the car, Jeremy unlocked the door to his dusty rose Honda Civic by hand and reached across from the driver's seat to unlock the passenger door for me. Wordlessly, he turned the key in the ignition, and the car rumbled to life, however, he didn't put the car in gear right away. Instead, he rested one hand on the steering wheel and the other on the stick shift, watching me with tired eyes.

I ran my fingers through my long black hair and stared stubbornly at my frayed skirt that all girls at St. Bernadette's were required to wear. The blue plaid was worn and stained like most of the things us Fisher's owned. Clair, my eternally optimistic adoptive mother, had always insisted that her belongings were not worn but 'loved.' Clair was forever grateful to be the owner of possessions with so much character.

"Raven," Jeremy spoke my name softly. In the confines of the car, the shouts and jeers of the kids outside were inaudible. I cringed and forced myself to look up at him despite the guilt and regret flooding my stomach. Jeremy reached out and gently tucked a loose strand of hair behind my ear. "You know I love you Raven, no matter what you do." A lump grew in my throat and I tried to swallow past it. I would *not* cry.

"Jeremy, I'm so sorry..." I started, but he didn't let me finish.

"I don't understand why this keeps happening." He admitted, pulling me into an awkward sideways hug and kissing me on top of my head. "But, we will figure it out together, okay? You just have to promise me you won't stop trying." I nodded into his arm, still biting back the tears that threatened to spill over at any moment.

My 'condition' which Clair had taken to calling it, had first reared its ugly head when I was in grade six. I had put another young girl in the hospital for calling me a witch. Jeremy and Clair had put me through counseling, therapy, even hypnosis. Nothing had worked. They had asked the adoption agency for more information about my background. They had assumed that I had been abused before they had taken me in. Perhaps abuse was the reason for the mindless rage that had begun to possess their daughter more and more frequently.

"He just made me so angry. I couldn't see anything."

"I know," Jeremy said softly, dropping one more kiss on my head before releasing me. "Let's get you to that anger management class. I'm sure they'll be able to help you wrangle those monsters in your head better than I can." He smiled at me before putting the car into reverse. I managed a weak smile back and settled into the car seat. I knew that the anger management class would be just as useless as the one I had attended the week before, but I had promised Jeremy I would keep trying. It was the least I could do.

We listened to the police radio in amicable silence on the ride to the recreational center where the classes were held. It was a comforting and familiar thing, to listen to the on-and-off buzz of incomprehensible voices that spoke in numbers and districts to each other.

I had grown up in the front seat of Jeremy's cruiser and before things had started to go sour, I had always imagined him as some sort of hero; off to save the city from certain disaster. Now, I felt as if I were one of the villains in my childhood fantasies. I felt like I probably belonged in the back seat of his undercover cruiser instead of the front. However, I kept my thoughts to myself and we sat in silence for the rest of the drive. I stared resolutely out of the passenger window. I saw Jeremy's reflection in the glass each time he sent a worried glance my way, but I pretended not to notice.

2

Jeremy pulled in front of the disheveled rec center and gave my hand a squeeze as I got out of his Honda.

"Good luck kiddo," I nodded at him and shut the passenger door. Jeremy pulled gently into the slow-moving downtown traffic, and I watched him go.

I had no interest in going to this stupid class. The man who led the seminar was old and balding and he smelled like cats. I had no idea what qualified him to teach people about controlling their rage when it was apparent that he had the emotional range of a wet paper towel. I had promised Jeremy though; so I would go and try my best not to die from the mundanity of it all.

It was rush hour downtown Toronto. The sidewalks were packed. Business women hurried to catch their trains to the suburbs with their high heels held in hand and sneakers on their feet. Men in suits laughed with each other on their way home, ties half-mast. I had no trouble merging into the flow. People had a natural way of avoiding me. It had been this way for as long as I could remember. People around me either physically evaded me completely or lashed out at me. Jeremy and Clair had been the only people I had ever met who seemed able to tolerate me at all. So predictably, I was a tad bitter for my age.

Luckily, because I had taken my trip to the principal's office closer to the end of the school day, I wasn't outrageously early. Just early enough to take a quick detour to the rec's bathroom to scrub the blood off of my hands. I sighed heavily as I watched Neil's blood turn the water a rusty orange before spiraling down the drain. I didn't want to be like this, but I just couldn't seem to stop myself when people got in my face.

In my defense, I had warned Neil a few times to leave me alone, before he made a comment about my mother. The angry creature that seemed to sleep curled around my heart had roared to life instantly at the mention of Clair, and it had been game over.

Finally, feeling like I looked a little bit less like a bad Carrie cosplay, I pushed open the heavy bathroom door and walked by the front desk. The lady behind the counter barely glanced up as I passed, which was fine with me. The less attention I drew to myself the safer everyone tended to be.

I turned into the room reserved for the class and surveyed my surroundings. There was a snack table set up on the far wall with baked goods and a large coffee thermos. Three or four other people were already scattered about sitting in the fold-up chairs. All of them were heavily engrossed in their phones.

Since I was early, the counselor wasn't there yet and I chose a chair at the back of the class. I knew better than to try and sit too close to anyone. It usually resulted in humiliation as they scrambled up to get away from me, muttering excuses.

I was about to pull out my own phone when the smell of the ocean suddenly filled the room. The scent was so powerful that I glanced up in shock to see what had brought on the sudden sensation. No one else had seemed to notice it. Everyone was still checking sports scores or their news feeds. The only thing that had changed was the young man who loped in.

He had cornrows laced tightly against his head and a pair of sunglasses perched on his brow. His skin was dark enough that you had to look carefully to see the tattoos that trickled up both of his arms. As he surveyed his surroundings, he seemed perfectly at ease, as if he were the type of person who could walk into a room on fire and make the best of it.

His shirt was white and crisp, but he wore it open at the collar. Khaki green shorts hung to his knees and thong flip-flops adorned his feet. He looked as if he had just walked right off the beach and I wondered if he had made a wrong turn on his way to paradise. I tried not to snort out loud to myself at the idea. If he was looking for paradise how had he ended up in this shithole?

I watched the young man who smelled strongly of fresh air and salt water as he eased further into the room. He grinned at the table of snacks and sauntered over to pile a paper plate high with cookies and donuts. Holding the plate with one hand, he deftly filled a Styrofoam cup up with the other. Then, to my complete and utter shock, he turned and made eye contact with me. He smiled good-naturedly, flashing white, straight teeth. Sauntering over, he flopped down right next to me and a truly Jamaican greeting tumbled from his mouth.

"*Wah gwaan, Gyaal?*" He grinned. I blanched, and my whole body locked up. The last time someone had intentionally sat next to me, it had been on a dare. I shoved those painful memories back and tried to focus on the situation at hand, considering this insane person was still waiting for me to reply. He occupied himself during my prolonged silence by taking a massive bite of a donut and a gulp of coffee. After, it became clear that I wasn't going to be able to answer, he carried on as if I had.

"I'm Conrad, Conrad Brown; what's yuh name?" He asked though it came out more like '*Mi Conrad, Conrad Brown, wah yuh name?*' His Jamaican patois made everything he said sound warm and friendly. I could almost imagine a rustle of seashells when he spoke, and I almost literally felt a warm breeze and the sun on my skin. I was starting to wonder if Neil Green had slipped something into my soup at lunch before he started harassing me. What was going on with me?

"Um. Raven." Was my beautifully crafted response. *So stupid.* I chided myself. He grinned at me again, as if he could read my thoughts.

"Donut?" He asked offering me his loaded paper plate. I swear my eyes were going to pop right out. I shook my head at him like an idiot. "Really?"

He seemed taken aback. "Mi thought people just came tuh these tings for di free food." Once I'd decoded his easy blend of English and Patois, I shrugged.

"I'm supposed to be working on bettering myself," I replied, immediately wincing at how stuck-up I sounded. I felt awkward and stiff next to him. He was so fluid and easy to be around and here I sat like a dead rock saying things like 'better myself.' He laughed, and it took me a couple seconds to realize that he wasn't laughing at me. He had genuinely thought what I had said was funny. What a strange, strange boy.

"Somehow, mi feel like dis is di type a place dat ruins a person, it no make dem better." Conrad mused. I thought of the bland counselor whom I was convinced had never actually felt angry before in his life and had to agree. If he asked me one more time to take a deep breath and count to ten, I would snap.

"You're not wrong," I responded. Conrad gave me another one of his dazzling smiles.

"Well, let's get out of here, den." He smirked easily, as if he would ditch an appointment with the devil without a second thought.

"What?" I asked, flabbergasted.

"Yuh know. *Ditch*. Let's get out of here." He explained, already standing up.

"I know what ditch means." I snapped. "I just can't, I promised my…er, father." I didn't really want to get into the fact that I was adopted. It was easier to say father than '*honest-to-god saint of a human who took a shit-head like me in*'. Conrad brushed off my excuse as easily as he seemed to do with everything else.

"Yeah, but him not here, is he?" He asked, wiggling his eyebrows, making his sunglasses bounce up and down. I remained silent.

"Fine, suit yuhself." He said, sliding his shades over his dark brown eyes and turning to leave. "Mi nah from here though. Letting me wander around without a local to guide mi could be di death of mi." He called back dramatically. I rolled my eyes and bit back a smile. I tried to convince myself that Jeremy would understand. No one had ever tried to be my friend before.

This guy wasn't much older than me... I thought of all those groups of kids at school, laughing and enjoying each other's company. I had given up on having friends a long time ago, and now the possibility seemed to have come to life before my eyes. I battled with my sense of responsibility to uphold my promise to Jeremy and my teenage desire to have at least *one* friend. The teenager in me won and I shot up from my chair and chased after the boy who smelled like the ocean.

By the time I caught up to him he was passing the front desk. He saluted the lady sitting behind it casually and she blushed, waving shyly back. As I hurried up behind him, he glanced lazily over his shoulder at me, that perpetually lopsided smile still on his face.

"Mi knew yuh wouldn't let me wander 'round dis big city alone." He smirked. I tried not to look annoyed. Guilt at betraying my promise to Jeremy was already welling up in my chest.

We pushed through the smudged glass doors and stepped out onto the street. I again, had the sense that I was horribly stiff and awkward around him. What did normal people talk about? The weather? Local sports teams? I was hoping it wouldn't be the latter. I knew enough about sports to be aware that Michael Jordan used to play basketball, and that was where my knowledge ended. Conrad saved me the trouble of coming up with something to say.

"So, what do yuh all do for fun here? Wheneva mi come tuh Canada mi usually stay wit mi sistah. We dun get up tuh much in di city."

What did people do for fun? Shit, I didn't know. I usually went to the library or the movies; always by myself. Somehow, I didn't think either of those things would appeal to someone like Conrad. I imagined he was the type of person who would hop on a sailboat without bothering to ask where it was headed. I almost smiled at that thought.

"I'm not really sure. I'm usually...pretty low-key." I replied. He rose his eyebrows at that.

"What's a low-key girl like yuhself doing in an anger management class then?" He teased. I glared at him.

"I don't know. What's a tourist doing in a Toronto anger management class?" I shot right back. He shrugged.

"Seemed like someting different tuh do. Wi dun do tings like dat in Jamaica. If you're pissed, yuh fight. When di fight is ova, it's ova." I bit back a laugh at that.

"Really? Well, that's why I was in there. Too many fights."' Conrad chuckled as I pulled my hair back and yanked the hairband off my wrist. It was only May and it already felt like July. A rare hot spring in Toronto.

"That doesn't surprise me," He mused as he gave me a quick once over. "Yuh seem like a fighter. That's why mi figured wi would get along." He winked at me playfully. I allowed myself to smile at him. His eyes widened at my grin and he laid a palm flat on his chest.

"She smiles!" He gasped. "Be still mi heart."

My face flushed, but he punched me playfully in the shoulder. We continued walking down the street, headed in no particular direction. Due to the invisible bubble that seemed to constantly repel people from me, we had no problem navigating the busy streets side by side. "What brings you to Toronto?" I asked and marveled at myself. Look at me go. Making conversation like a human being. I gave myself a mental pat on the back. Conrad was quiet and for a moment I thought he wasn't going to respond. Finally, he told me.

"Mi here on behalf of mi grandmother for some… business."

"What kind of business?" I pressed. He smiled at me wickedly.

"A dangerous, top-secret mission obviously."

I rolled my eyes. "Fine, don't tell me."

"Hey, do yuh like ice cream?" He asked changing the subject. "Mi could use a snack." His eyes gleamed and he rubbed his hands together. I let myself smile again, as I remembered him piling his plate high in the rec center.

"Sure, there's a place we can go around here. I'll take you."

3

Conrad and I had wandered about the city, chatting about nothing for over an hour. I told him about being suspended earlier that day and what had happened with Neil Green. He had laughed so hard when I told him about hitting him with the chair that I worried ice cream would shoot out his nose. I also gave him a subpar tour of the city. I showed him some cool stores to check out and pointed out my favorite haunts. When we passed the Toronto Public Library I paused. I had originally planned to stop by on my way home from the anger management class. I was almost out of reading material and hated to be without a good book. Conrad noticed me hesitating and cocked his head to the side.

"Di library? Really?" He asked. I nodded.

"I love to read." I said, still eyeing the curved stone face of the building. Conrad's curiosity it seems, couldn't be contained.

"What do you normally like to read?" I shrugged.

"Fiction mostly, but I also like poetry," I admitted with a small smile. Conrad laughed.

"Good. For a minute, mi was worried yuh were gonna ask me tuh study wit yuh." I turned to face him, surprised.

"You want to go to…the library with me?" I asked, shocked that something so mundane would appeal to him. I mean, this was the guy who went to an anger management class just to see what it was all about. He shrugged.

"Sure. Mi could be tempted tuh read some fiction." He smirked, wiggling his eyebrows at me again. "Since yuh dun have school tomorrow, yuh wanna meet up here?" I tried not to gape at him. I almost wanted to pinch myself to see if I was dreaming. Not only had he been the first person to approach me of his own volition in well…ever. He actually wanted to hangout a second time. This couldn't be real.

"Uh, yeah. I'd like that." I said smiling up at him.

"Cool." Was his easy response. He glanced at his watch and winced. "I suppose I should walk yuh home though. From what yuh told mi about Jeremy, I doubt he'd appreciate mi taking you home late."

We took the streetcar to the east end of the city and found my ancient home without any trouble. I wondered what sort of place Conrad lived in as I gazed up at my house. My narrow home was built with red brick and the white paint was peeling off my porch. It wasn't much, but it was where I felt the safest. I smiled slightly at our bright blue front door.

I had begged Jeremy and Clair to paint it that ridiculous shade when I was eleven. They had finally caved, and it had remained electric blue ever since. I was just about to turn to say goodbye to Conrad when Clair squeezed through the narrow gap between our house and our neighbor's. She had gardening gloves on and a yellow sundress that matched her short, pale blonde hair. Her grey eyes widened as she noticed us, her delicate laugh lines smoothing out.

"Raven!" She exclaimed, before bursting into one of the most genuine smiles I had ever seen, even on her kind face. "Who is this?" She asked rushing forward and pulling off her soil covered gloves to shake Conrad's hand. I felt my face heat up at her obvious excitement at the fact that I had been socializing with someone my own age.

Conrad had never mentioned it, but I knew he had noticed how people avoided me on the streets. Pulling his heavily tattooed hands out of his pockets, he took Clair's outstretched palm in both of his, grinning in his good-natured way.

"Nice to meet yuh Miss…" He trailed off and I realized I hadn't even mentioned my last name. It was hard for me to believe I had met him just an hour and a half ago. He was so easy to get along with I felt as if I had known him much longer.

"Fisher." My adoptive mother beamed. "But you must call me Clair." Conrad nodded easily.

"Clair it is. Mi just met yuh daughter in… class." He said, not mentioning that the class in question was for people with psychotic rage issues. He needn't have worried. Clair didn't have a judgmental bone in her body. "Raven's been showing mi di city."

"Well, you must be hungry." She said, looking at me, still so obviously thrilled that I seemed to have finally made a friend. "Why don't you two come inside? I have some dinner in the slow cooker." Before I could make an excuse for Conrad, who probably didn't want to spend his evening chatting with my mother, he replied,

"Sure, thanks, mi starving!" I gaped at him. How could he possibly be starving? He had eaten half the snack counter at anger management then gorged himself on an extra-large cone of ice cream.

"Perfect!" Clair said as she turned to lead the way up our sinking front steps. "There's more than enough to go around." I glanced at Conrad, and he just smiled and gestured for me to follow Clair into the house. He fell easily in step behind me.

As I went through my bright blue front door, I was painfully aware that I had never had anyone over to my house before. I tried to see my home as if it were through his eyes. It's not like we lived in squalor or anything, but we certainly did not live lavishly.

Between Clair's double shifts at the hospital and Jeremy's police job, we had a moderate family income, but living this close to downtown was not cheap. A lot of their money, of course, had gone to the various forms of therapy that I needed and wasn't covered by OHIP, or either of their benefit plans.

The foyer was small like most inner-city homes, and I kicked off my hideous school shoes before walking up the two wooden steps into the main hallway. Our walls were a simple off-white and garnished with a few family photos. I felt my back tense as Conrad paused behind me to look at a few of them. A small smile bloomed on his face as he examined one of me on my third birthday; covered in my birthday cake and grinning like a fox with a rabbit. When he turned from that happy moment, documented and frozen in time forever, I could have sworn I saw a flicker of sorrow flash in his eyes. I must have been imagining it though because the sadness was gone almost as soon as it had come.

We continued our way into my small scrubbed kitchen that was attached to our living room. Only a half wall separated the two spaces, which made it easy to watch TV while we ate dinner. For now, however, the TV remained off. I winced as I took in our couches. *Chesterfields* seemed to be a more appropriate term, as their green, floral print screamed that they still belonged in the 80's. Conrad didn't seem to mind though as he passed the living room. He flopped down in one of our wooden, country style chairs, looking for all the world like a Pirate Lord ready to captain his ship. I marveled again at how easily he seemed to adapt to his surroundings.

Clair was busy ladling pulled pork out of the slow cooker and onto some buns. She put the sandwiches on three plates with some pre-made salad and deftly carried all three by herself to the table. A skill she had acquired from her many years of waiting tables through nursing school. I sat in my usual spot which put me beside Conrad and across from Clair.

"So." She began as we all started digging in. "How old are you Conrad?"

"Twenty," he said in between bites. I mulled this over. He was only about two years older than I was. I was about to turn eighteen in a couple of months. For some reason, he felt so much older. So much more in-tune with the world than I did.

"Well in that case, would you like a beer?" Clair offered and I knew Conrad's answer before he beamed.

"Well, yuh just stole mi heart Mrs. Fisha." He said mischievously and she laughed in that open, full-throated way she always did.

Her expression mellowed though as she got up to go get him a beer. She was watching him discreetly, her brows knit together as if she was trying to work out some sort of puzzle.

Conrad met her gaze and there seemed to be a flash of recognition between them for a moment, and Clair's eyes widened just a bit. Mine, in turn narrowed. The strange moment between the two of them vanished and Clair bustled off to the fridge. Once again, I was left wondering if I was just imagining things.

4

The rest of dinner went by without any more odd instances. Conrad had Clair and I laughing so hard that we had tears in our eyes by the time Jeremy came home.

Jeremy entered the kitchen, looking even more drawn and tired than he had when he dropped me off. Whatever scene he had been at must have been a bad one. In fact, he'd been off to more crime scenes than normal lately, and I wondered if work, coupled with the stress of dealing with my constant fighting, were finally starting to wear down his resolve.

As soon as he noticed Conrad sitting at the table, however, he tensed up. I tried to look at Conrad through Jeremy's eyes and registered Conrad's heavily tattooed arms, the easy way he slouched in the chair, drinking one of *his* beers. I suddenly felt nervous.

"Hey Dad." I said carefully. "This is my friend Conrad." I almost choked on the word 'friend.' I don't think I had ever said it out loud before.

"They met in the anger management class." Clair beamed. She was either oblivious to the tension in the room or was choosing to ignore it. My guess was the latter.

"And what sort of things have you done to land yourself in an anger management class *Conrad?*" Jeremy asked tightly. The hypocrisy of it was astounding. I was messed up enough to be in an anger management class and they made excuses for me all the time. Conrad stood up from his chair and ambled over to Jeremy extending his hand politely.

"Oh, I'm not actually enrolled in the program sir. I just come to pick up a friend and ran into your dawta. I'm not from here and she showed me around a little." The small white lie seemed effortless for Conrad, as if he understood the truth would seem less believable to a man like Jeremy. I also couldn't help but notice his accent seemed to melt away when he spoke to Jeremy.

"Well, that's...convenient." Jeremy said, ignoring Conrad's outstretched hand. "I hate to put a damper on your evening, but I am very tired."

I scowled at my father. If he scared away the only friend I had ever made, I would never forgive him. Clair had a similar expression on her face as she eyed her husband from the table. Conrad took the hint easily enough though.

"I should be heading out anyway. I told my sistah I would be home an hour ago." Conrad turned back to the table. "It was a pleasure to meet yuh Mrs. Fisher." He said with that laid-back grin of his.

"Conrad, I've already told you to please call me Clair." She scolded him, returning his smile. Conrad chuckled.

"Night Clair, thanks for di dinnah." He said easily, humoring her. He turned to Jeremy and nodded, his grin never faltering. "Mr. Fisher." He said by way of parting. I stood up from my chair quickly.

"I'll walk you out." I hurried past Jeremy, shooting him a 'don't screw this up for me,' look. Conrad was already at the door by the time I caught up, his hands back in his pockets.

"I'm sorry about Jeremy. He's... had a rough day." Thankfully, Conrad seemed completely unperturbed by it.

"Dun worry 'bout it. If mi dawta brought home some crazy tattooed dude from anger management, mi dun know how thrilled mi would be." The thought of Conrad being anything but relaxed seemed impossible, but I was glad he was being so cool about his unceremonious dismissal. "We still on for di library tomorrow?" He asked.

"Of course, I'll text you in the morning and meet you there." I said, grinning. He gave me a lopsided grin as he turned to open the door.

"*Likkle more,*" he drawled as he sauntered out onto the porch.

"What? I asked to his retreating figure.

"It means 'see you later,'" he called over his shoulder chuckling. He gave his two-finger salute to our elderly neighbor, Mrs. Serafini, who was busy taking out her trash, then he turned the corner and was gone.

I closed the door and leaned against it for a moment. I let out a breath I hadn't known I was holding. My heart was pounding. I almost didn't want to go to sleep in case I woke up to find that everything had been a dream.

Whatever it was about me that pushed people away hadn't seemed to affect him at all. Why had he chosen me to befriend? It was all just so bizarre. I shook my head to clear my thoughts and started to head back into the kitchen but paused in the hallway when I heard Jeremy and Clair arguing.

"You don't find it a little bit *convenient* that with everything going on, *now* she makes a friend?" Jeremy hissed at Clair. I hung back in the shadows. With everything going on? What were they talking about?

"Whatever you think that boy is I can tell you right now that he isn't. We can trust him." Clair retorted. Her tone was soft, quiet. But it was the voice she used when she was about to go to battle for whatever it was she believed in. Jeremy didn't stand a chance.

"And how exactly do you know that after spending, what? An hour with him?" He demanded.

"You better be nice to that young man next time you see him, Jeremy, and that's all I'm going to say about it. This is the first time Raven has spoken to anyone remotely close to her age without it turning violent. She was *laughing. Raven was laughing.*" Jeremy went quiet. Did I laugh that rarely? I thought about it for a moment and realized that they were right. There hadn't been much room for laughter and joy in my life since I had sent that girl to the hospital six years earlier.

"I, of course, want her to be happy," Jeremy said softly, almost sadly. "But I would rather her be safe then —" Whatever he was going to say was cut off by Clair.

"Raven? Honey? What are you doing?" She called into the hallway, and I popped my head in.

"Nothing. I'm going to go to bed." I said, and I knew that they had caught me eavesdropping.

"Ok love." Clair said, her face strained. "We're both working tomorrow so neither of us will be here in the morning. Just text one of us if you need something." I appreciated the update. Their schedules were so sporadic it was hard to keep up with what days or shifts they worked week to week.

"Ok. Night. Love you." I said, heading up the stairs.

"Night Raven." They both replied in unison.

I grabbed my school bag with my laptop in it on my way up the stairs. My room was dark, and I turned on my bedside lamp in favor of the overhead light. Though the days were getting longer, it was already pretty dark out and I basked in the coolness of nighttime. I finally shed my uniform and pulled on my grey sweats and the oversized T-shirt that I usually slept in. It had come as a promotional item with one of the cases of beer Jeremy had bought a while ago.

Curled up in my comfies on my purple duvet, I fired up my laptop. I ran a quick search for the news. I wanted to see if I could find out what Jeremy had been talking about. However, Canadian news wasn't the most forthcoming. Unlike many news stations in the States, Canada liked to be a bit more subtle with the airing of their violent crimes.

The constant effort to exude a sense of security among citizens kept many of the larger crimes under wraps. I knew this for a fact, thanks to my relationship with Jeremy. Over the years, he had investigated murders just as brutal as the ones you would see on Dateline, and never once has one of them been publicly aired. At least not until the perp was caught.

After a couple of minutes of scanning through different newspapers online, I let out a frustrated sigh. Nothing of interest was coming up. What had he meant by *'with everything that's going on?'* I shutdown my laptop and flopped back into my pillows. As I reached over to grab my nearly finished paperback, I resolved to do some snooping through Jeremy's office at some point this week. It wasn't like him to keep me in the dark.

One of the reasons he was so good under the stress at his job was his willingness to confide with his family. It had never before been a burden he had to carry alone… even if some of the stories would make the average person's stomach turn. If Jeremy was keeping something from me it had to be really bad…and I was going to find out what it was.

5

Despite everything that had happened the day before, I woke up in a terrible mood. I had finished my novel then tossed and turned through the rest of the night. I wasn't sure if it was in anticipation for my meeting with Conrad, or because of the conversation I had overheard the night before. Either way, I was left with this clammy feeling that someone had been watching me in my sleep.

After I had lost it on Neil, the clenched fist that lived within my chest had eased, as it usually did, after I had one of my…episodes. Usually, after I had one of my outbursts, I would feel calmer and less on edge for a while. This time, the itchy build-up had already begun, demons clawing at the inside of my skin to get out. The feeling gave me anxiety, especially once it occurred to me that I could possibly lose control around Conrad. I furiously shoved the thought away.

I would not.

I would not.

I would not.

I chanted to myself as I got out of bed and headed for the shower. I stared at myself in the foggy mirror as I got out from under the hot stream. My silver ring of ravens glinted in the steam, and I ran a finger over it, an old habit of mine. There were dark smudges under my eyes from lack of sleep, and my brow had set into a permanent scowl.

I hated that I was like this. Why did I always feel like there was more underneath my skin than just me? It felt like being stuck in an over-packed streetcar, but the streetcar was my own body. It was too much sometimes. I shook my head to try and dislodge the suffocating feeling and left the bathroom to get dressed.

I threw on a pair of black jeans and a matching t-shirt before heading downstairs to make myself a coffee. As it was brewing, I glanced at the clock. It was almost 11:30 am. It seemed like a reasonable time to message Conrad about our library trip. Even though he had been the one to invite me, my hands still shook as I opened a new message conversation on my phone.

My inbox was depressingly empty. Jeremy and Clair were pretty much the only people who texted me. Now, my two open conversations had a third one to hang out with. I smiled, despite the pressure that had been building in my chest since I had woken up.

'Hey, what time do you want to go?' I typed the message and hit send quickly before I lost my nerve. I put the phone down and forced myself to leave it alone while I poured some milk into my coffee. Leaning on the counter while sipping the hot heavenly goodness that was caffeine, I stared at my cell phone and willed it to vibrate. Ten minutes went past, fifteen, next thing I knew it was noon, and I still hadn't received a response. Maybe he was still sleeping. I didn't let myself consider the other possibilities.

Finally, I left my phone on the counter and wandered upstairs. I headed towards Jeremy's office and stopped in the doorway to eye down his neat desk. It would be an invasion of privacy to go through his things. I would *hate it* if he went through my belongings. But…he was hiding something from me. I could tell by the tone of his voice the night before that whatever he was hiding was something big and for whatever reason, it had something to do with me. I had a right to know. *Yeah.* Said a mean little voice in my head. *Keep telling yourself that.*

That fist around my heart clenched tighter and that *thing* that I harbored inside me was slamming against my ribs as I took a step into his office. I clutched a hand to my chest, forcing myself to breathe past the pressure. Whatever it was that was wrong with me seemed to be getting worse.

Neil had been one of three fights this month, though I'd managed not to put any of the other kids in the hospital. I usually got about a week's worth of a break between episodes, but the pressure had been building more and more frequently.

God, it *hurt.*

I did my best to ignore the building discomfort and sat down in Jeremy's black swivel chair. I sat down putting my coffee down on the desk and reached over to the top drawer of his filing cabinet. Locked. I swore vehemently. I had no idea where he kept the damn keys.

I glanced around the office quickly, that pressure in my chest building with each passing second. As the stress mounted, my knees began to curl involuntarily into my chest and I buried my face in them, wrapping my hands around my head to try and dull the throbbing. I wasn't sure if it was from the locked cabinet, the lack of response from Conrad or my impending expulsion, but I couldn't get a grip on myself. The pressure built to a breaking point, and I let out an exasperated scream.

The entire world stopped spinning.

So much energy erupted from me that every drawer in the office shot nearly clean out of the filing cabinet, crashing against their stoppers. My coffee cup *exploded,* and picture frames dropped off the wall. Whatever had come out of me rattled the house to its foundation, traveling through the walls and to the trees outside the window. Startled birds took off from the branches before falling to the ground...dead.

Like in the aftermath of a sonic boom, the air around me seemed to hold its breath. I sat in the wrecked office, staring at the open drawers with my mouth open. That forever-present fist slowly unclenched itself from my heart with a sigh. The prowling beast in my chest quieted.

The world started spinning again.

Just as I thought I would throw up, I heard my phone vibrate downstairs. My head snapped in the direction of the noise, but I couldn't move.

My first thought was that I needed to clean this up before Jeremy came home. If they thought I needed therapy before, they would lock me away in an institution for this. How I was supposed to explain this was beyond me.

Surveying the destroyed room around me, I shakily got to my feet. Still in shock, I bolted for the laundry room. I grabbed cleaning supplies and spot remover for the coffee-stained carpet. High on adrenaline I cleaned up the mess as quickly and as efficiently as I could. I wrapped the broken pieces of my mug up in a cloth and stashed them under my bed. Each picture frame was hung back up and I breathed a sigh of relief once I was sure none of them were broken.

It was the drawers that would do me in. The bolts that kept the drawers closed were warped beyond repair. Not one of them would close properly. I swore over and over again. What was I going to *do?*

As I sat there staring at the wrecked cabinets, panic seeping from my pores, they suddenly seemed to straighten out. I watched in terror. I couldn't be doing that. This wasn't happening. This was a goddamn nightmare... this was like a scene out of a freaking horror movie. But...once the locks were straightened out, they slid to the side of their own accord. The cabinet doors closed themselves, and the deadbolts slid back into place. I gaped; my eyes so wide I felt like they would drop right out of my skull. With a pounding heart and shaking limbs, I glanced around the office.

It was like I hadn't even been there.

6

My phone buzzed again in the kitchen. The house was still so quiet that the vibrating sounded like an alarm. Instead of going to it, I ran to the bathroom and vomited my morning's coffee right back up. I could hear my phone buzzing on a loop as I clutched the toilet bowl, tears stinging in my eyes. They had taught us breathing exercises in anger management class and for the first time in the year and a half that I had been going, I used them. In through my nose, out through my mouth. Count to ten. Repeat.

Finally, I got to my feet. I returned the cleaning products to the closet before walking down the stairs. I felt like I was moving through something thicker than water. Shock. I was in shock.

I picked up my phone to three missed calls from Conrad and a dozen missed messages. I'd barely opened the first one when my phone started buzzing again. I nearly dropped it. My nerve endings were on fire and the vibrations were overwhelming. I slid the bar to the side and answered, more to make the device stop moving than anything.

"*Ray-ven!*" Conrad nearly bellowed on the other end, his Jamaican accent thicker in his apparent panic.

"Yes?" I answered. My voice sounded so far away. I heard what sounded like a relieved sigh on the other end. I was too disoriented to think that it should be strange that he sounded relieved. There was no way he could have known what had just happened... what I had just done.

"Yuh styll wanna meet at di library?" He asked, his normally relaxed tone uncharacteristically tight. Like he was worried.

I heard myself say "Of course."

"Be der in *twenty minutes.*" He said, his accent still stronger than normal, his voice strained.

"Okay. See you then." I said, feeling unnaturally calm. I hung up the phone and walked to the foyer. I had to concentrate to lace up my combat boots. My fingers were shaking so badly that I kept dropping the laces. I went through another breathing exercise. Once I felt a little better, I opened the front door and nearly threw up again. My knees buckled.

Dead birds. Dead birds littered my front yard. A line of dead ants had frozen where they stood on their way to their hill, like some sort of grotesque, dead, still-life. I didn't have it in me to clean up the birds. I couldn't even take a second look at those dead ants. I bolted. I ran from that house. I ran from the miniature graveyard and the, now pristine, office. I ran and wished I could leave my own body behind.

Conrad had said he would be at the library in twenty minutes. I made it there in fifteen. By some stroke of luck, I made it to the streetcar stop exactly as it was arriving.

It was nearly empty as it was one o'clock in the afternoon on a Wednesday. I curled up into one of the hard-backed seats and tried to ease my shaking while staring out the window. Rocking myself gently, I told myself It wasn't real. It wasn't real. It *couldn't* be real. I refused to let myself think about those birds or the way the metal had bent itself back into shape before my very eyes. I had no idea what was going on. If I was insane or dreaming or had died and gone to hell. I didn't care. I didn't want to deal with it.

Once I got off the streetcar, I beheld the curved face of my sanctuary. The library was a blessing. I walked in and inhaled. It was one of my favorite buildings in the entire city. I felt safe here. I felt calm here. There were four stories of literature, all built in a cylindrical shape, towering above me, curving around the open center of the space.

The autumn-colored floors stood out against the soft cream panels that lined each level. When I looked up at the domed ceiling, I felt like I was inside a conch shell, gazing toward its spiral peak from the inside. I shook off the remaining dregs of panic and resolved to choose a book to lose myself into, instead of succumbing to the terror that still threatened to take over.

The thought of whatever had happened before happening again, here in this beautiful refuge, almost made me turn back. I had a sudden disturbing flash of dead people scattering the library the way the dead birds had peppered my lawn. But that fist around my heart was now a relaxed palm, and the beast in my chest was sleeping. I moved forward.

I took the elevator to the next floor where stacks upon stacks of reading material waited for me. The building was nearly empty, and I could almost hear the characters that lived between the pages as they called to me. The smell of paper filled the space as I stepped out of the elevator and wandered like a ghost to the stacks.

Making my way to the back rows, the quietness was like a gentle, peaceful caress. Nothing at all like that apocalyptic silence that had crushed my home only fifteen minutes earlier.

Running my fingers over the spines of the books as I walked, I listened to the tiny voices that always seemed to rise from the text whenever I passed. The written word had always spoken out loud to me, even as a child even before I had learned to read.

I stopped before one book that had a voice clearer than the rest. Usually, that meant it was something I would like. Picking up the small book of poems that had called to me, I turned and nearly jumped out of my skin.

There, leaning against the stacks I had just ambled past, was the most striking human being I had ever seen.

7

He was dressed in pressed black slacks and a deep green collared shirt. Much of his silver hair was pushed back along his head, as if he had run his hands through it one to many times, and it now just grew in that direction.

Some small pieces, however, tumbled into his eyes. The greenest eyes I had ever seen. How had I not noticed him as I had walked past? Had he even been there before?

Fear welled up inside me, egging on my already barely controlled panic as his eyes met mine. Given the day I was having, I couldn't even be sure he was real. I bit down on my bottom lip, forcing myself not to back away.

His eyes slowly made their way down my face and paused at my mouth. I released my lip, suddenly self-conscious. Amusement curled the corners of his mouth as he allowed his gaze to travel lower, before settling on my ring of ravens.

"Don't you just love it," He said softly, his voice like velvet running down my bare arms, "when you find something interesting in the library?"

I nearly stuttered, trying to dig into the snap of anger that had always risen to defend me in the past. But it didn't come. My anger, the one constant

I'd had my whole life, wasn't there to save me. As I reached deep, I suddenly registered the fact that this was the second time in less than twenty-four hours, that someone had spoken to me of their own accord.

This realization slammed into me with such earth-shattering speed and force that it snapped me out of whatever daze I had been in. This had already been one of the strangest days of my life. There was no way it was a coincidence that this stranger had suddenly appeared. Some basic instinct told me that he was dangerous and that I should be very, very afraid.

I relaxed my clutch on the book and forced myself to unwind. I fell back into the easy stance I had seen Conrad use the previous night when things had gotten tense with Jeremy. I would not let this man, this creature, this… *invader* of my library space intimidate me. The dead birds flashed in the back of my mind again, and I wondered if he was the one who should be afraid.

"Where did you come from?" I asked, and his smile widened. He chuckled, and again I had the sensation that someone was rubbing raw velour over my skin.

"I've been waiting for you." He pushed up from the bookshelf and slid toward me. Even the way he moved screamed 'other.' As much as I wanted to flee, I forced myself to hold my ground. I had been so busy counting the inches as he closed the distance between us that I jumped when he reached forward to pluck the book from my hands.

"This is an interesting choice." He drawled, examining the small book of poetry I had chosen from the shelf. "There's a piece in this book that was written by someone who is considered a prophet."

"Who *are you?*"

His eyes creased at the corners as he flipped open the book, and to my utter astonishment, he began to read it to me.

"Let us walk through worlds, whispered the prince," He paused, glancing back down at me, as if he wanted to experience my reaction before continuing. "I will teach you to move planets, how to reorder the stars, to become nighttime itself," He stopped reading as he leaned closer, and snapped the book shut. I jumped, despite myself. He continued to push forward, forcing me to back up into the bookcase.

He pressed his hand on the bookshelf above my head, laughter dancing in his eyes. With his other hand, he curled his index finger under my chin, still holding the small paperback with his middle and ring finger. Looking up at him, I couldn't move. A deer staring down a wolf.

"You, are not a deer," he whispered. Before I had a chance to respond, or even contemplate the fact that this man might have very well have read my mind, the scent of the ocean crashed into the stacks, and there was Conrad.

8

"*Ray-ven.*" He said, his normally calm voice almost a snarl. He stood at the end of the aisle, looking for all the world as if he would murder something. The man before me pulled away, gently handing the book back to me, before turning to face Conrad. He said nothing, just stood quietly next to me, with that small smile still playing on his mouth.

"C-Conrad." I gasped, still reeling from the closeness of the stranger. Reeling from the lines he had read from the book. The same words that had whispered to me from the pages as I had run my fingers down the novel's spine.

Conrad barreled forward, very obviously putting himself between me and the stranger.

"*Leave.*" He said to the strange, beautiful man, as he pressed me farther back away from the intruder. The rolling emotion coming from Conrad smelled so profoundly of salt water that I thought I might drown. I swear the lights in the library flickered. I looked at the silver haired man, my eyes wide, how was he not afraid? Shit, *I* was afraid of Conrad right now. The man chuckled.

"Where is Patricia?" The stranger asked softly. I didn't know who Patricia was. I gaped at the two of them.

"You two…do you *know* each other?" I asked from over Conrad's shoulder. Conrad almost snarled again. The other man merely smirked.

"We're old family friends." The stranger said dryly, as if that explained everything.

"If yuh touch her. Yuh will have Di Board to contend with." Conrad exclaimed. The other man did not look concerned. In fact, he examined the fingernails on one hand before sliding his other into the pocket of his perfect slacks.

Conrad nearly exploded before me in rage at the man's indifference. The stranger with the beautiful green eyes met his gaze. Suddenly, the temperature in the room dropped. When I exhaled, I could see my breath, and that infuriating smile on the stranger's face widened as Conrad visibly wilted before me. The green-eyed man hadn't moved. Someone was going to explain to me what the *hell* was going on.

"Be careful Obeah Man," The stranger said softly, before turning away. "You'll disturb the books." His voice slithered over his shoulder as he slowly exited the aisle that we stood in.

The temperature of the library returned to normal, and I grabbed Conrad's shoulder, spinning him to face me.

"What is an *Obeah Man?* Who is Patricia? What did you mean by *The Board?* What the *hell* is going on, Conrad?" I snapped at him, the familiar feeling of rage finally building in my chest, pushing back the anxiety that had been gripping me since I had destroyed Jeremy's office. Conrad looked so panicked, I almost felt bad for yelling at him. Almost.

He gripped my shoulders so hard it hurt.

"Him touch yuh?" He demanded.

"No, I-I'm fine," I stammered, and Conrad shook me.

"Rayven. Did he *touch yuh?*" He asked again. The desperation in his voice was palpable. I blanched as I remembered how close the stranger had leaned into me, his index finger resting against my chin, tilting my face towards his. As the memory flashed through my mind, Conrad's eyes widened in fear, as if he had seen the image himself.

"Shit." He swore. He grabbed my wrist and began to pull me out of the stacks. "Wi have tuh go. Right *now*." I pulled back against him, ripping my hand away from his.

"I am not going *anywhere*, until you tell me what is happening." I crossed my arms defiantly over my chest and locked him down with one of my worst glares.

"Please Rayven," He begged, glancing around the library, as if the books themselves might attack us at any moment. "Dere's no time. Dey're coming. Dey know where yuh'are now."

"*Who* is coming, and who are *they*?" I pressed, still refusing to move. "And how do they know where I am? Because that guy touched my chin?" Conrad let out the most exasperated sound I had ever heard.

"What happened dis afternoon Rayven?" He asked, the sudden change in topic made me hesitate.

"What do you mean?" I asked, narrowing my eyes. He held my gaze, face serious.

"Why didn't yuh answer yuh phone? Someting happened at home, didn't it?" I gaped at him.

"I have no idea what you're talking about," I said stubbornly, pushing back the memory of the wrecked office, and the birds. Conrad's eyes flashed again, and I could swear he was somehow reading my mind.

"Yes, yuh do. Dat is why dey are coming. It's why dey know where yuh are. Yuh might as well have sent out an S.O.S flare." I was shaking again. My eyes were burning. What was he talking about? I was *not* going to cry.

"We got to go somewhere safe, Rayven. Yuh got to trust me! Please! I will explain everything on the way. But we got to move. *Now!*" The urgency in his tone was mounting. I could almost hear waves crashing against a distant shore, as if a storm were brewing.

"Fine," I said, tucking the library book under my arm. "But I'm taking this book." Conrad nodded his head, grabbing my arm again.

"Take whatever yuh want, just try tuh keep up."

Then we were running.

9

We tore out of the library and spilled onto the street. I hadn't been given a chance to check out the book, and now the alarms were ringing behind us. Conrad quickly scanned our surroundings; I assumed for potential threats, whatever those might be. We took off down the street to the paid parking lot that was tucked behind the library, Conrad pulling car keys out of his pocket as we ran.

We arrived at a dilapidated AMC Hornet hatchback, the red paint rusting around the wheel beds. Conrad put his hand on the back of my head and ushered me into the passenger seat, covering me from behind like some sort of celebrity bodyguard. I watched as he jogged around to the driver's seat and got in, slamming his keys into the ignition before ramming the car into gear.

We peeled out of the parking lot and onto the street. He waved his hand in the direction of the red light ahead and to my complete amazement, it turned green. This pattern continued as we sped down College. Cars seemed to naturally change lanes as we came up behind them, somehow finding space in between other cars that were already crushed in the early afternoon traffic.

"How are you doing that?" I asked in awe, as Conrad forced another light to turn green for us. Now that we were speeding west down College Avenue, some of the panic had left him, and he gave me a quick grin that was the ghost of his usual lopsided smile.

"Doin' wha'?" He asked mischievously. I glared at him.

"Don't play dumb. I'm not stupid, I know you're turning the lights green." He laughed softly at that, keeping his eyes on the road.

"Mi guess di cover pull off di bottle." He said, his smile faltering. "Mi was hoping mi have more time tuh wean yuh into all of this."

"Into all of *what?*" I was getting *really* sick of all my questions being evaded. "Conrad, my life has never been super average or anything, but this day has been out of control. If you don't start explaining things I'm going to snap." I sent a dark glance in his direction, and the beast in my chest twitched. "And trust me, you do not want that to happen." He sighed in response.

"Mi know. Der's just so much to explain it's difficult to know where tuh begin." He admitted as we sped past Bathurst.

"How about telling me who Patricia is?" I prodded. He gave me a curt nod, still keeping his focus on the street ahead of us.

"Patricia is mi grandmother." Well, that was definitely not the answer I had been expecting. So that man from the library hadn't been making it up. They must be some sort of old family acquaintances. He had said *friend*, but Conrad's obvious hatred of the dark stranger made me feel like 'friend' might be a bit of a stretch.

"The one that you're here on behalf of for...business?" I asked. He nodded again. "What sort of business?"

"Mi grandmother is on Di Board." He answered, as if that explained everything. "She is very...respected, but she's getting old. Old enough dat travelling is now difficult. Mi meant tuh take har seat, so mi sent in her place."

"Sent to do what? What is The Board?" The way he said it made me feel like it should be capitalized. He paused before answering, and I saw his throat bob as he swallowed, hard.

"Sent to find yuh." He said finally. I felt the blood drain from my face.

"W-what?" I stammered. "*Why?*" I managed to get out. He glanced at me out of the corner of his eye, putting more pressure on the gas as we shot through Ossington Avenue.

"Di Board has been looking for yuh for a very long time. Where mi taking yuh now, mi sister's house…her father is on Di Board too. He has had suspicions for some time dat yuh were di one wi were looking for and sent word to mi grandmother in Jamaica." With each question he answered I suddenly had about twenty more. His sister's father? Wouldn't that be his father too?

"Why were they - you," I corrected myself "looking for me?" My voice was quiet now. It seemed stupid with all that was going on, but it occurred to me, he hadn't sat next to me the other day because he had wanted to be my friend.

He had sat next to me because I was his assignment. A chore. A job to do. Conrad frowned at me, looking in my direction as quickly as he could before he had to return his attention to the road.

"Mi still want to be yuh friend Raven." He said, answering my unspoken thoughts. My head snapped in his direction.

"How do you keep doing that? *He* did that too. It's like you can read my mind." The corner of his mouth tilted up.

"Mi an Obeah Man. Mi can hear and see what goes through yuh mind most of the time." I don't know why, after everything that had happened to me in the last few hours, it was this that made me suddenly feel nauseous.

"What is an Obeah Man?" I asked, my voice shaking. He had said it like it was obvious what it meant. "Was that other man…the one in the library, was he an Obeah Man too?" Conrad's face darkened.

"Nuh. Prince Amon is not an Obeah Man." Ah. A name to put to that beautiful face. Conrad glanced at me again as we flew through the Dovercourt intersection. How far west were we going?

"Wi turnin' on Dufferin." He said, again, answering my thoughts. I scowled.

"Stop *doing* that." I snapped and he gave me a tight smile.

"Mi can't help it. Until we can teach yuh how to manage yuh aura, yuh thoughts are open for anyone to hear, which is nuh good. Yuh lucky we found yuh first. Der are worse creatures out there than us, and yuh just had di pleasure of meeting one of di meanest of them." He pursed his lips as he drove and then added, "Yuh soon find out, Rayven, that di most beautiful things are di most dangerous." His obvious reference to my impression of Amon made my blood run cold.

"You still haven't told me what an Obeah Man is." I pointed out. We were coming up fast to Dufferin Street, and he turned left, tires squealing against the pavement. We shot like a red streak past the mall, and I marveled at the fact we hadn't been pulled over yet.

"A wizard of Jamaican culture and heritage. Obeah can be traced back to West Africa, Ghana." He explained, and I rose my eyebrows.

"Is everyone on The Board a witch or a wizard?" I wondered what Amon was then, if he wasn't a witch.

"Yes," He replied, as we turned onto a small side street titled Muir Avenue. He parked finally, throwing up the parking brake.

"Quickly." He said, gesturing to the passenger side door, and I got out, turning to face the witch's house.

10

The narrow house before us did not look like what I would have imagined a witch's house to be. It looked a lot like my house if I was being honest. It was made of a dusty red brick and was tucked under a blanket of ivy on one side. A sprawling garden enveloped the front lawn despite the suffocating atmosphere of the city that dwelled just a short distance away.

Fat pumpkins flourished out of season, their vines weaving in and out of the black wrought iron fence that enclosed the yard. There was catnip and saffron, dill, oregano and chamomile all thriving together happily. Among these plants there were several other leaf profiles I didn't recognize, as well as more than a dozen flowers that I couldn't place. If I had been in the company of a human being, my impression of the garden would have gone unnoticed. As it was, Conrad grinned at me again.

"Meredith has a bit of a green thumb," He explained, and led the way to the front of the house, not bothering to lock the car door. As I passed the waist-high wrought iron gate, a shiver ran over my skin, gooseflesh erupting up my arms. I looked at Conrad expectantly, waiting for him to explain.

"Dis property is warded. If dey come here looking for yuh, it will nah stop dem, but it will slow dem down." He told me as he strode down the front walk towards the porch. I swallowed back the anxiety that welled in my throat. The way he spoke, made me feel as if I were being hunted. The concept felt abstract, as we walked through the bright garden on a sunny may afternoon.

A wooden wind chime prattled away next to a bench that adorned the white porch of the house. Before either of us could knock, the door swung open to reveal a tall, blond, young woman. I jumped at her sudden appearance.

I observed the young woman standing before me, who couldn't have been a day over twenty one. She didn't look like she would be a witch, but then again, Conrad didn't look much like a stereotypical witch either. No green skin or warty nose. As inappropriate as it was, I almost giggled at the thought. The witch in the doorway smiled at my thoughts and I realized with frustration that she could also read my mind.

Her blonde flyaway hair was pulled back from her pointed face and her startling blue eyes met mine without hesitation. I took in her long patterned skirt and white peasant top that was garnished with several silver necklaces, each ending with either a pendant or a semi-precious stone.

"You must be Raven," She greeted me. Her voice rang with enough music to compete with the wind chime. She held out a heavily ringed hand and I grasped it instinctively. With a gentle squeeze from her fingers came a curious prodding sensation. I came away with impressions of soft springtime greens and the kind of gold you could catch with an early summer sunrise. I wondered if what I was feeling was the aura thing Conrad had mentioned. Whatever it was, the warmth of it curled around me and I felt the tension between my shoulders relax. It occurred to me that a mere twenty-four hours ago, I might not have even noticed this magickal exchange.

"Pleasure to meet you." She said warmly. "I'm Meredith Abbey."

"Nice to meet you too." I stammered, still reeling from the odd sensation of our aura's mingling.

"Conrad. As always, such a pleasure." Meredith said, greeting the Obeah Man with a kiss on each cheek. She plucked at his black t-shirt with a grin.

"What an interesting choice of color." She said, winking at me. I glanced down at my equally all black attire. What was that supposed to mean? I allowed the thought to slash through my mind before remembering my thoughts were not my own anymore. I flushed red, not wanting to insult her, but she smiled at me warmly.

"Black has a strong correspondence with protection." She informed me patiently. "It is the color used to keep the things that might hurt us at bay. Please come inside. We have much to discuss." Conrad and I followed Meredith into the house.

It felt as if the garden had spilled into the house itself. Plants lined almost every surface and hung from every doorway. Their leaves turned to drink in the warm sunlight that spilled in through the large windows. Shoes and rain boots marched down the wall of the foyer and stopped at the entrance to what appeared to be the living room.

From what I could see, the living room was crammed with squashy looking couches and was littered with literature. Meredith glided down the hall and led us into the kitchen. I was greeted by a mishmash of color that shouldn't have worked together but somehow managed to. Cerulean blue tile floors collided with oak cupboards topped with a charcoal grey granite countertop. On the other side of the counter sat a large, scrubbed oak table surrounded by an uncoordinated assortment of chairs.

There was a narrow bookshelf next to the sliding glass door stuffed with cookbooks and several ancient unlabeled tomes. I glanced around wide eyed as Conrad lounged easily back into a yellow painted country-inspired chair that resembled our chairs at home. Meredith made her way to the stove, which looked like it had been plucked directly from the 50's, before putting a kettle on.

"Please make yourself comfortable." She said pleasantly. The tightness between my shoulders had returned and I couldn't bring myself to sit. Instead, I posted myself at the end of the counter and crammed my hands into my pockets to keep myself from fidgeting. The house seemed to have an aura of its own. I could have sworn I felt it examining me, gently prodding at the beast nestled in my chest, much the same way Meredith had when she had met me at the door. The urban witch turned away from the stove with three cups of tea prepared.

"Don't mind the house," she said, casually, "It loves company." Um. Sure.

One of the teacups Meredith had been holding, to my absolute astonishment, silently glided across the kitchen and sat itself directly in front of Conrad. Meredith handed me mine in the traditional way. I took it with shaking hands. *Holy crap!*

Meredith smiled at me warmly, her aura caressing mine. Again, I somehow felt relaxed almost immediately.

"H-how did you do that?" I asked, certain that if my eyes got any wider, they would pop right out of my head.

"Magick of course." She said, eyeing me up and down. She glanced over at Conrad with an eyebrow raised. "I was under the impression that my brother had explained to you who and what we are. I apologize if I frightened you."

I immediately regretted my question. Of course, it was magick. I knew exactly what Meredith was. Not wanting to get Conrad into trouble I backtracked.

"He did tell me. I know he's an Obeah Man and you're a witch… which from as far as I can tell is pretty much the same thing. I just haven't really seen much… magick. Not real magick like that anyway."

"Easy sistah. Dis only har first day." Conrad said softly from behind his steaming cup. I placed my own cup on the counter. My hands were still shaking, and I didn't want to spill. Meredith was observing me again, a look of concern on her face.

"I see." She said. "You are upset. I can feel your aura expanding in agitation. It is dangerous to leave yourself so open."

"So I've heard." I replied, bristling. I had to learn to get that part of myself under control. I didn't like having myself open like that anymore than they did. My concern was more for my own privacy than safety. Meredith smiled at me and I knew immediately she was listening to my thoughts.

"You two don't look related." I blurted, trying to turn their attention away from me. Meredith smiled kindly.

"We are all children of this planet. In that respect, Conrad is my brother." She explained. I rose an eyebrow at Conrad, but he just shrugged.

"Conrad said you can teach me how to control my aura, and it would keep people from being able to read my thoughts," It was a statement, but I phrased it as a question. I waited, watching her earnestly.

"You are here to learn a great more than that, I'm afraid." She said, her eyes growing sad. "Why don't you have a seat?" She asked. I shook my head.

"I'm fine standing, thank you." I was worried that if I sat down, after the day I'd had, I wouldn't get up again.

"Very well, suit yourself." She glided past me and settled down at the table.

"So," Meredith began, "I'm sure you have a great many questions you would like to have answered. Now is the time to ask. I give you my word. I will do everything within my means to answer your questions honestly."

I took a deep breath, still trying my best to calm down. Her willingness to cooperate with me left me feeling suspicious. I wasn't used to having things handed to me so easily, least of all answers to questions I seemed to have been asking my entire life. It all seemed too good to be true. However, taking in her honest face, I decided to approach this situation like I did most things in life and dive in headfirst.

"What am I?" I finally asked. "Am I a witch too?" I thought of what had happened earlier. Those metal bolts bending back into shape, the animals I had…murdered. Meredith looked at me with something very close to pity, and I clammed up. I didn't need anyone feeling sorry for me. I glared at her, and her summer-fresh aura buckled slightly.

"I'm angry all the time. People avoid me," I continued looking up, meeting Meredith's soft blue eyes again. "What am I?" A terrible coldness was welling up in my chest in anticipation of the answer. I knew immediately I was not going to like whatever it was Meredith was about to tell me.

"You are very powerful, Raven, but you are not a witch," She began. The beast in my chest perked its ears and the hand that was constantly wrapped around my heart twitched its fingers.

"Your body is mortal, much the same way our bodies are," she said, touching one hand to her chest and lying the other hand on Conrad's forearm. "Your soul, however, is not." I frowned at this, not following.

"Witches, or magick folk, if you're looking for a more general term. Our kind goes by many different names and have been gifted our power from the deities we serve. We do not create magick. Every act we manifest comes at a price.

"Every decision for magick folk is based on the concept of balance. Many of us believe that each intention we send out comes back threefold. It is called the rule of three." I nodded, trying to be patient. I shoved my irritation and my burning need for information aside, forcing myself to keep my tongue in check.

"However, there are other creatures that walk this earth who do not need to draw their power from any sort of deity. There are creatures who follow a different set of rules." She explained, pausing to make sure I was listening.

"The shifters, for example, have the power to shift between a human and animal form. This power is not a gift from one of the many gods they believe in but is more of a genetic trait that they are born with. They can shift at will as easily as you can change clothes." Shifters? Like werewolves? I subtly pinched myself to make sure I was awake. If I hadn't seen Meredith float a teacup through the air myself, I would have completely written her off as crazy.

Meredith smiled at my unspoken thoughts, "Not just wolves. There are many different breeds of shifter," she paused, allowing me to absorb what I had just heard.

"Then, there are daemons", she continued. I felt the blood drain from my face. "Daemons do not need to draw power from any source, though they can if they choose to." A great coldness in my chest began to spread.

"Daemons are immortal beings. They transcend time and space. They are darkness and the absence of darkness. They are a power that derives from the very beginning, and a power that will exist until the very end. Their power is not gifted from any diety. Some even consider daemons to be deities themselves."

The world tilted beneath my feet. I couldn't bring myself to ask if I was a daemon. I think, deep down, I already knew the answer.

"You, Raven, are something none of us have seen before. You have the blood of The Origin, the first daemon, flowing through your human veins."

11

I felt like I was going to collapse. Conrad stood but he wasn't quick enough. Instead of rushing to my side he merely glanced at one of the empty chairs sitting around the table and it flew across the floor to catch me. I slumped into it, resting my elbows on my knees, and catching my head in my hands. Running my fingers through my hair, I took three ragged deep breaths.

I heard Conrad rush to the kitchen and then heard running water. Next thing I knew, he was crouching next to me with his warm hand on my back and holding a glass of water. I took it gratefully and took a large sip before sinking into the back of the chair. Conrad looked almost as angry as he had when he had discovered Amon and I together in the stacks.

"Yuh don't have to be so dyamn brazen about it." He growled at Meredith from my side. His accent grew thicker with his frustration. "Yuh gon give di poor gyal a heart attack." I laid a hand on his knee and shook my head. Leaning my head back and closing my eyes as I tried to speak.

"No." I said quietly. "I need to know." I took another small sip of water and met Meredith's eyes once again. Swallowing hard I asked another question.

"Am I...evil?" I asked. Every fight I had ever been in, every time someone taunted me, I would snap. Every fight I had ever gotten into flashed before my eyes. It always ended the same, with my victim's eyes widening as they realized they might die beneath my hands. That had to be evil. *I* was evil.

Since I couldn't yet read minds, I resorted to studying Meredith's facial expressions. Her lips curved downwards sympathetically.

"You are a half daemon Raven. You are not a devil. There is a difference. No being on this planet is purely evil. Sometimes we become possessed with evil intentions. These intentions are often inspired from evils that have been committed against us, or imbalances and imperfections in the maps of matter that make us who we are.

"Every single being who possesses a higher level of consciousness has been gifted with free will. The *choice* to do whatever they wish to do. You are no exception to this rule. It is the choices we make that define who we are. It has nothing to do with our origins."

This was all bullshit. My head was spinning. This day had to be the worst day of my life.

"So, I have to choose *not* to be evil?" I asked blandly.

"I believe you have already made that choice my dear," Meredith smiled. I scowled at her. "The very fact that you are asking me this question, means that you are not evil, Raven.

"The daemon in you both protects and threatens you. Your power is curled around your heart. It is likely that it will fully manifest when you turn eighteen, which is perhaps why you have been feeling more...uncomfortable than usual lately." That was the understatement of the year. I remembered the rising pressure that had built in my chest earlier and had resulted in so many tiny deaths. The guilt I felt about tearing those birds from the sky was overwhelming.

"We have already sent someone to deal with... the mess." She said and I knew she was referring to the miniature corpses that littered my front lawn.

"It is extremely important that you understand Raven, you must get this under control. It is equally important that you know, there are creatures out there who will seek to use you as a weapon. Use you to fulfill their own agendas. I understand that you met such a creature mere moments ago. Prince Amon."

Conrad's fists clenched as he stood quietly next to me.

"Amon? That guy from the library? He was a daemon too?" I asked, already knowing the answer. Meredith and Conrad exchanged looks.

"Prince Amon rules The Court of Pride." She said. "His court is second only to Ash Nevra's Court, The Court of Lust. There are five other courts that rule under The Dominion of Sin; The Court of Greed, Envy, Sloth, Gluttony and Wrath. These courts are named after the Seven Deadly Sins and exist on the other side of The Veil.

"Both The Court of Lust and Pride have been locked in a political power struggle for over three hundred years. Prince Amon will likely seek to use you as a means to overthrow Ash Nevra. She in turn will likely seek to take your power for herself, or outright kill you, to eliminate you as a threat." My tired gaze told her without me having to ask, that I had no idea what The Veil was.

"The Veil is a metaphysical barrier between this world and its parallel counterpart. Daemons can pass between worlds at will. Other creatures may be taken across The Veil if a daemon carries them. This has only been done in the past during times of great turmoil." Her stormy eyes darkened again. "Shortly, I fear, we will all find ourselves in a period of turmoil once again. Your role will be a large one in the events that are to come to pass."

"What's going to 'come to pass?'" I wondered aloud, frowning again. "If you're a witch, can you see the future?"

"The gift of divination is not a strong trait in my bloodline. I come from a long line of green witches. We are excellent healers." She explained. "But I do not need the sight to understand that you are in danger. It has come to the attention of The Dominion of Sin that you exist.

For centuries daemons, witches and shifters alike believed that you were a fairy tale of sorts. The blood that runs through your veins gives you great power while putting you at great risk. There are those who would stop at nothing to destroy you to protect their positions and there are those who would attempt to harvest your power to allow them to advance their courts."

"The Dominion of Sin is like...kind of like... The Board, right? But for daemons?" I asked.

Meredith mulled this over for a moment before answering. "Not quite, but I can understand the comparison. The Board is a governing body run solely by magick folk. The members are composed of the oldest and wisest of each bloodline. Seats on The Board must be earned, and they meet regularly to work towards maintaining the balance between daemons, shifters, and magic folk.

"The Dominion of Sin, on the other hand, operates more like a cluster of monarchies, or a collective group of kingdoms. Each of the seven courts exist within the Dominion, which the Origin founded at the beginning of time. Each court is governed by a daemon powerful enough to claim it.

"The Origin once ruled over all the courts, but he was frozen in stone with his human lover, Elvira, centuries ago. Ash Nevra's court was the only one powerful enough to assume his position. However, now that you have surfaced, you are a direct threat to Ash Nevra's claim.

"Additionally, if any of the other six rulers of the other courts were able to harvest your daemon, it would give them the power to challenge Ash Nevra and bring their court to the forefront of The Dominion."

"So, It's not like I can sign some sort of peace treaty promising not to take over anyone's throne or anything? They're all going to come after me anyway?"

Meredith nodded gravely. "Precisely." A thought suddenly occurred to me.

"What if I just gave my power to one of them? Then they would have what they wanted, and I could go back to my life? Maybe be normal for once?" Something flickered deep inside of me, and an unexplained sadness welled in my chest. The emotion was out of place, and I didn't understand it, so I pushed it aside.

"You do not yet understand the power that lives within you. Perhaps you should make an effort to get to know your daemon before exiling it. Once it is gone you might find yourself regretting it."

"I doubt it."

"Don't be so sure." Meredith cautioned. "If that hasn't convinced you against that plan consider this: giving your power away would be comparable to handing a loaded handgun to someone you don't know. How could you trust them to use it responsibly? Furthermore, such an exorcism would most likely kill you."

"You probably should have led with that last one." I snapped. This situation was beginning to feel impossible.

12

Conrad backed away from me for the first time since bringing me my water. I noticed and did my best to calm down. I tended to lash out when I was stressed or upset. I didn't want to push Conrad away like I did to everyone else. "So, what exactly are my options then?" I asked, doing my best to keep the sarcasm from my voice.

"Your suggestion remains an option, I simply don't advise it. I just wanted you to be able to make an informed decision, no matter what path you choose to take." I rolled my eyes and leaned back off my knees into the chair again.

"Well, what options do I have that aren't suicide?" Meredith, despite my hostility, smiled at my rephrasing.

"I think your best option would be to learn how to control your newly discovered gifts and become acquainted with your daemon. It will take a great deal of time and it will be a challenge to keep you safe while you train.

"However, from what I can discern, this is most likely the best plan of action. We must hurry though. Since you let out that burst of energy today, it is likely the entire Dominion of Sin is hunting for you, and not just Prince Amon."

From the way she said his name, I shuddered. Her voice lowered as if she were afraid he would hear her and show up at her doorstep. Was he really that powerful?

I guess it was also a fair thing to wonder why these witches had tried so hard to find me. Meredith's chime-like voice rang even clearer with my eyes closed. She replied to my silent question about the intentions of the witches first.

"The magick folk on the Board have dedicated themselves to maintaining the balance between species for centuries. You falling into the wrong hands could mean a complete spillover from The Veil. If Ash Nevra were to decide to harvest your power instead of merely killing you, she would not only be in a position to take control of all seven courts, but she could overthrow the Board, and overpower every other being on the planet."

I groaned and curled further into myself. I didn't want to have to deal with any of this. All I wanted to do was finish high school, and maybe enroll in a community college. Then settle into a long eventless career of some sort. I almost snorted at the thought of me wearing a pantsuit and sitting at a desk.

I drew my knees up onto the chair and rested my head on them. All of a sudden, I had a splitting headache. Meredith stood up and flowed around the table, coming to where I sat and Conrad stood next to me.

"This is a great deal of information for you to process all in one day, and I understand that you are overwhelmed." She reached out to touch my chin and lift my face to meet hers, but when her fingers touched that same spot that Amon had brushed against in the library, she jerked her fingers away. Conrad made eye contact with her, and the grave nature of their silent exchange put my teeth on edge.

"What is it?" I sighed. They both glanced at me with matching expressions.

"He touched you," Meredith whispered, clearly disturbed.

"Mi shouldn't have left yesterday." Conrad slammed his hand onto the counter. A muscle in his jaw started to pulse. My own tumultuous emotions suddenly seemed small and secondary. As much as our meeting had been planned and staged by a bunch of old people I had never met, my heart hurt to see Conrad so upset.

"Conrad I'm *fine*," I said as I stood up. I placed a hand on his shoulder. He turned and met my gaze. True honest to God anger was burning through his eyes.

"Yuh might nuh be next time." For the first time since I'd stepped into Meredith's house, I felt a sense of resolve starting to build in my chest.

"It's not your fault," Meredith said calmly. "As powerful as you are, it would take a full coven to keep Prince Amon away from Raven. Even that might not be enough. He has slaughtered armies and burned entire cities to the ground. If he has his sights set on her, the best we can do is make sure that she is prepared."

Her sky-blue eyes dropped to that spot on my chin that he had touched. "And it seems that his sights are indeed set." She finished gravely. I touched my chin gingerly.

"Why is his touch so dangerous?" I asked.

"All daemons, yourself included, use touch in a unique way. Once one of them touches you, they have power over you. They can track you almost anywhere. Prince Amon has left his mark on you, and you have never been more vulnerable." I gaped at her but it was Conrad who spoke up, his voice cracking.

"*Goddess* Mer, could yuh be a little more abrupt?" He looked as nauseous as I felt.

"There are precautions we can take." Meredith continued sagely. She reached around her neck and removed one of her many silver necklaces. The pendant was a perfect circle, with three loops that crossed each other in the middle. She pressed the tiny silver charm between her index and forefinger and exhaled.

The cool metal glowed fiercely for a moment before dulling again. She leaned forward and fastened it around my neck, and it fell slightly lower on my collarbone than my ring of ravens. Her attention fell onto the tiny ravens and she ran a finger over them, much the same way I did when I was nervous.

"I have just given you a *Triquetra*. It wards against the type of power that daemons typically call from. It is not foolproof, but it is the best we can do for now. It will be more difficult for daemons to track you as long as you are wearing it."

The necklace felt heavier around my neck than it should have, and my chin burned at its proximity. Meredith's expression became apologetic as she read my thoughts as easily as I read words from my many books. "You will get used to the side effects... hopefully."

At least she hadn't gone back on her promise to be honest with me. She fingered my ring of ravens again.

"This is the Origin's emblem." She said thoughtfully. "It marks you for what you are as plainly as your aura does," I remembered Amon's cut green eyes as they drifted down from my mouth to my tiny ravens. I moved suddenly to take the necklace off, the necklace that I had worn my entire life. Meredith's hand stopped me.

"This too offers you protection, though the magick is old. Due to your...outburst earlier, every creature on the continent already knows where you are and who you are. It will be more of an aid than a hindrance in the future." It occurred to me for the first time how much these two people, witches, whatever they were, were risking, just to be in the same room as me.

"Speaking of that..." I said, shuddering again at the thought of the dead birds that had littered my front lawn. "Why did that happen? Why now?" Conrad spoke, leaning against the counter.

"Yuh have so much untrained power Raven, yuh human body cannot contain it. Someone as powerful as yuh needs to constantly be using der powers throughout the day, or it will build up an' spill ovah at dangerous times."

He paused as if he were drawing strength from some internal well. "Mi sorry. Mi had no idea how quickly yuh powers have been manifesting. Mi thought we had more time or I would have warned yuh." His normally happy-go-lucky attitude was nowhere to be seen, and I could almost feel the guilt radiating off of him. I touched his hand.

I understood now, why despite what had happened today, I felt better than I had in ages. Years and years of that pent-up energy had finally broken free. That crushing hand on my heart could finally unclench.

"It's ok Conrad. We will figure this out." I gave him a weak smile. I looked at Meredith, understanding how much they were sacrificing by trying to help me. Amon's cut emerald gaze flashing through my mind. I shivered. Conrad squeezed my hand and gave me a half-hearted smile of his own. I stood up.

"Ok. Enough worrying about things we can't change," I stated, determination settled in my chest. "That...*thing* touched me. So what? I'm supposed to be powerful, right? If I learn how to control it, then maybe we can just put this all to bed." Meredith smiled at me.

"I could not have put it more eloquently myself," She stated. I wasn't sure if she was poking fun at me or being completely serious. Maybe both.

I looked at the two of them and the ferocious part of me that lived in my chest growled. I had thought that all of the fights I had gotten into had made me a bad person, now suddenly they made me feel like a survivor. I hadn't sought those kids out and ruthlessly attacked them. They had always been the ones to start it. This didn't feel any different. If the daemon world wanted to pick a fight with me, I would make sure I was ready.

Just then, someone unlocked the front door and I, of course, was the only one that jumped. Meredith turned her glittering gaze towards me and smiled. "Welcome to the Board, Raven." She said before gesturing to the door that was opening down the hall and through the foyer. "I believe you've already met my father, Walter?"

I turned to look at the front door and watched as Mr. Abbey, my principal, entered the house.

13

"Hello Raven, I thought I might find you here." Mr. Abbey said amicably as he hung up his bowler and shrugged out of his tweed jacket. He stepped out of his brown leather loafers and made his way to the kitchen. I stared at his socked feet, slightly weirded out that my principal wasn't wearing shoes. I don't know why I felt like the man slept in his three-piece tweed suit.

"Um, hey sir." I muttered. The pieces fell together smoothly in my head. Conrad had mentioned that Meredith's father had suspected for some time that I was the one they were looking for. Here was the man in question. I had been in and out of his office since I had transferred to St. Bernadette's. My previous school had finally had enough of my...unpredictable behavior and had kicked me out. It suddenly made sense why St. Bernadette's was the only school that would take me in. Mr. Abbey must have known from the beginning.

"Did yuh take care of di...mess?" Conrad asked. His polite avoidance from mentioning my avian massacre was appreciated.

Mr. Abbey settled heavily into one of the mismatched chairs around the scrubbed wooden table and nodded curtly.

"Yes, the birds have been cleared up." He took off his spectacles and polished them on a handkerchief that appeared as if from nowhere, before turning his gaze to me. "I have also warded your home, Raven. It should be safe for you to return this evening."

I glanced at the clock, it was now 3:30. Clair and Jeremy would be returning home shortly. I wondered how I would be able to keep what had happened to me from them. At least there wouldn't be a tiny graveyard waiting to greet them. I glanced over at Mr. Abbey.

"Thank you." I whispered. He smiled at me kindly.

"Not at all Raven. It's the least I could do. I must apologize for not bringing you to light sooner. There was no way I could be sure until your... demonstration this afternoon. I didn't want to bring you into our world unless it was absolutely necessary."

I knew why without him saying it out loud. Once you learn that the monsters under your bed are real, there isn't really any coming back from that.

"I understand," I said blandly. Though it was frustrating to know that all those weeks in anger management was time I could have spent learning to manage my aura instead. Mr. Abbey chuckled at my unspoken thoughts.

"Ah yes. A fruitless but necessary endeavor." He said, referring to the classes I had been forced to attend. His eyes twinkled and he returned his spectacles to his nose. They were just as perfectly round as the rest of him. His large middle and rotund jolly face made him look like a beardless Santa Claus. It was hard to be mad at him for too long.

"You don't seem so shocked to see me." He pointed out as he accepted a steaming cup of tea from Meredith, who smiled at him fondly. I snorted.

"Your grand entrance was far from the most shocking thing that has happened to me today." I responded, leaning against the counter. Conrad returned the seat I had occupied earlier to its rightful place at the table. "I somewhat suspected it when Meredith introduced herself at the door," I admitted. Mr. Abbey nodded.

"You've always been brighter than most." He said thoughtfully, taking a sip from his tea. "Have you put any thought yet into how you would like to proceed?"

Truthfully, I hadn't had much time to process everything, but I already knew there weren't many options, other than dealing with it upfront. I mean, I could always curl into a little ball and have a panic attack. But realistically, that wouldn't help anyone. Least of all myself.

"It is what it is," I said, surveying the small group of magick folk around me. "Before anything else happens, I need to learn how to control this thing inside of me. What happened today can never happen again. If Jeremy and Clair had been home…" I shuddered at the thought. If they didn't die from that blast of power, they might have been seriously hurt. I refused to be responsible for that. Mr. Abbey seemed to understand and nodded.

"That is a wise choice, Raven. Your situation is unfortunate. Young witches are taught how to use their magick responsibly from a young age. I believe even daemons follow a similar practice when they raise their young. Early education minimizes casualties." He met my gaze, his face serious. It didn't go unnoticed that he said *minimized* casualties, and not that it prevents them entirely. "As it is, you have not had the luxury of a teacher in these matters. If you will accept our help, we can begin your training as early as tomorrow."

"You would be able to train me?" I asked doubtfully, "Even though I'm not like you?" Sitting in this bright, scrubbed kitchen, I felt like my power came from somewhere else. Somewhere dirtier, darker. Conrad's clean ocean smell and Meredith's warm gold and green aura were a far cry from the dark shadows that welled up in my chest. I didn't have to be trained to know that they were different kinds of magick. Abbey seemed to mull this over for a moment before answering.

"It is true that you will perhaps need someone of your own kind to act as a mentor at some point. There are depths to your power that even our oldest spells will not be able to make sense of. However, for the basics, I am sure we will be more than adequate."

He smiled then, and the kitchen suddenly felt brighter. "We can figure out the rest as we go along."

At his words, I almost felt like laughing at the ridiculous thought of a *witch* being able to teach a *daemon* how to manage the shadows. I jumped as this aggressive notion tore through my mind. It wasn't mine. That thought *did not* belong to me. I glanced around at the room, panicked, but not one of the witches in the kitchen, for once, had seemed to hear what was going on in my head. Weird.

"We will begin training in the morning. Conrad, I trust you will be able to pick Miss Fisher up. Class will begin at 8:00 am sharp." Mr. Abbey stated, falling back into his role as principal as if it were a second skin. Conrad smiled that easy smile of his.

"Of course, sir." He stated. Mr. Abbey nodded and stood up, extending his hand to me.

"Until tomorrow, Raven." He said, his eyes twinkling as I shook his warm, dry hand.

"Tomorrow." I agreed, shaking his hand firmly. As terrible as the day had been, I was grateful to finally have some answers.

Conrad put his hand on my shoulder and gestured to the front door. I turned to Meredith giving her a shaky smile.

"Thanks. For having me, I mean." I felt oddly shy suddenly. She smiled serenely back at me.

"Not at all Raven, it was our pleasure." I nodded and gave both Meredith and my principal a small wave before turning to follow Conrad out of the witch's house.

14

The sun was setting as we made our way back to his run-down hornet. Mr. Abbey and Meredith stood on the porch as we got into the car. As they waved us off I could have sworn the pumpkin vines waved goodbye with them. Once we were buckled in and Conrad had adjusted the radio to the only station in Toronto that played reggae, he finally turned to me beaming.

"Well, mi tink dat went well." He said, dropping his sunglasses down over his eyes, despite the ever increasing darkness. Conrad threw on the left-hand turn signal once we got to the end of the street and we waited for the light to change.

I watched a young dark-haired man standing on the sidewalk as he took long lazy drags from a cigarette. He seemed to be watching us carefully and I wished Conrad would use his magick to make the light turn green. I was so tired. All I wanted to do was curl up with my new library book and find the poem that Amon had read to me. It had been such an odd encounter. Well, everything about today had been odd.

And those eyes, they had been so green. So piercing. As if he could see that hand that held my heart. As if he knew who I was. I shuddered and scratched the skin on my chest underneath Meredith's *Triquetra*. Amon was dangerous. I needed to remember that.

"Yeah, I guess so," I said, passively. The light turned green, and I watched the dark-haired man get smaller and smaller in Conrad's side view mirror. "I'm a little overwhelmed though," I admitted.

"Mi don't blame yuh. Is nuff tuh take in all at once." He grinned at me out of the corner of his eye. "Yuh took it like a champ though." He said as he took his hand off the gear shift to playfully punch me in the arm. I mustered a smile back.

"Yeah, I guess so. I'm just glad I didn't puke again at Meredith's house." I made a face. Conrad laughed.

"Don't tell me yuh actually puked? When?" He asked. I shrugged.

"At my house, earlier. A lot of…strange things happened, and I thought I was going crazy." I picked at my nails nervously. "I still kind of think I am." I felt Conrad's aura brush against mine, I think as an effort to comfort me. The resulting sensation was comparable to burying your toes in the sand while the tide washed in. I closed my eyes and leaned my head back on the headrest as we drove, Beenie Man's voice drifting through the speakers. Neither of us spoke again for the rest of the ride.

The familiar bounce and flash of emergency lights greeted us as we pulled onto my street.

"What's going on?" I wondered out loud, straightening up in my seat. An ambulance and a police cruiser were parked nearly directly in front of my house. I almost panicked, immediately thinking of Clair and Jeremy.

As we pulled closer, I could see that police tape was wrapped around Mrs. Serafini's house and not ours. Neighbors had started to gather around as Conrad pulled up and parked behind the EMS vehicle. Conrad and I got out of the car and walked over to join the rest of the neighbors.

Two paramedics came out of the house, carrying a stretcher between them. Their slow, somber pace spoke volumes. If the figure on the stretcher had been alive they would have been running down the front steps. I caught a glimpse of Mrs. Serafini's white hair as the paramedics loaded her corpse into the back of the ambulance.

A woman appeared in the doorway of the house. She was in near hysterics, reaching after the ambulance. I recognized her as Mrs. Serafini's daughter. The man who must have been her husband appeared behind her and pulled her gently back into the house, whispering comforting words in her ear. I was so engrossed in the heart-wrenching scene that I almost didn't hear the neighbors whispering.

The neighbors spoke in hushed tones, sharing details of what they knew of the situation. Mrs. Serafini's daughter had come by after work to visit and had found her mother dead on the kitchen floor. The medics had said she had died sometime early in the afternoon. Heart attack. I did the math in my head.

That shock wave of energy that I had let out. That had happened early in the afternoon. The birds. I had killed all of those birds... Conrad grabbed my wrist as he heard the realization pour through my mind.

"Raven no," He growled. I looked at him, feeling hot tears fill my eyes.

"Conrad... did I?" I nearly stumbled over the words. He shook his head.

"Is a coincidence," He murmured under his breath so the onlookers wouldn't hear.

"She lives right next door. She was home when it happened." I hissed. The panic was rising in my chest again. He started to usher me towards my house. I heard someone call my name and turned to find Clair rushing over in her scrubs. She must have just finished her shift.

"Raven, what happened?" Clair's worried face was almost enough to push me over the edge. I stopped to greet her, hot tears sliding down my face. I resisted the urge to completely melt down right there in the middle of the street.

"Mrs. Serafini." I said, my voice shaking. "She's dead."

Clair took in the ambulance and the caution tape that wrapped our neighbor's lawn. She nodded solemnly and frowned at my tears, no doubt wondering why her death had shaken me up so badly.

Mrs. Serafini has never been friendly toward me. I'd heard her whispering about me under her breath more than once. I'm pretty sure the woman thought I was the devil. Now that I knew about my heritage, I guess she had never been far off from the truth. Despite her constant prayers and attempts to ward herself against me, it seems I had managed to kill her anyway. Clair of course knew nothing about any of this.

"She was very old Raven. She had a good life. It was just her time to go." Her frown deepened and she draped her arm over my shoulder, leading me toward the house. "Let's go inside. We can make Mrs. Serafini's family something to eat." I nodded and allowed Clair to steer me onto our front lawn, Conrad trailing behind us. I felt the wards that Mr. Abbey had placed around my home rush over my skin as I stepped onto our property. Clair froze beside me as we walked through the wards, her eyes going wide. She turned her head slowly, staring at Conrad as if she had seen a ghost. I frowned and stopped to stand next to her.

"Mom, what is it?" I asked, but she kept staring at Conrad, who was looking uncharacteristically stiff under her scrutiny.

"Honey, can you run inside quick and let me know if we have any tuna for the casserole? I just want to talk to Conrad for a second." Clair finally turned away from Conrad and looked at me with a reassuring smile. Her eyes fell to the *triquetra* hanging around my neck.

"Uh, sure." I said suspiciously, backing away. I glanced at Conrad who gave me a lopsided grin and a shrug.

"Wi be right der." He said easily, his hands in his pockets. I nodded, still slightly weirded out. Maybe I was just being paranoid. Based on what had happened the night before between her and Jeremy, she probably just wanted to see what his intentions were. Finally, I turned away and went inside.

Once inside the house, I quickly unlaced my boots and scrambled into our dining room. The front windows looked out onto the street and I watched as the ambulance pulled away. Conrad and Clair were still standing on our front lawn, just inside the invisible wards that Mr. Abbey had cast.

Conrad said something and nervously rubbed the back of his neck. I narrowed my eyes. What were they talking about? I wished desperately that I could access some of the power that I knew dwelled within me. There must be a spell to amplify voices... I didn't dare try. The memory of the paramedics somberly carrying Mrs. Serafini on that stretcher flashed in the back of my mind. My power was dangerous, I wouldn't touch it again until I knew what I was doing.

Finally, Conrad and Clair started walking towards the front door. I ducked out of the dining room and slipped down the hall and into the kitchen. I pretended to busy myself looking for tuna as they came in. Pulling two cans out of the cupboard, I turned to greet them.

"Found some," I said, handing the cans to Clair, who smiled at me gratefully.

"Conrad, will you be joining us for dinner?" She asked, before digging through a drawer to find a can opener.

"Sure Mrs. Fisha," I glanced back and forth between the two of them. '*What was that about?*' I mouthed to Conrad, but he just grinned and shrugged again. I frowned at him. Fine. Be that way.

"How many times do I have to tell you to call me Clair?" She asked, as she got started on dinner. Conrad chuckled, and stepped forward, taking the can opener from her.

"Tell yuh what, I'll call yuh Clair if yuh give di casserole to di Serafini's and let mi cook up a real Jamaican jerk chicken dinna for yuh. Yuh Canadians need some spice in yuh life."

Clair laughed and agreed, as they began digging into the cupboards for the various ingredients they each needed. I felt strangely excluded and alone.

The spot on my chin that Amon had touched warmed, as if to remind me that I would always be moved by the darkness. Looking at Conrad and Clair's nearly identical bright, sunny expressions, I wondered if it was true.

15

I woke up cranky again the next morning. Not because of an overwhelming build-up of power, but because it was seven o'clock in the morning and someone was pounding on my bedroom door.

"*What?!*" I snarled, nearly falling out of bed as I scrambled to answer. I ripped open the door to find Conrad beaming at me.

"Rise and shine gyal. Today is yuh first day of training!" I glared at him and ran a hand through the rat's nest that was my hair.

"How did you even get in here?" I snapped. Clair and Jeremy were working day shifts again, there would have been no one to let him in. Even if they had been home, the thought of Jeremy allowing anyone, especially a boy, near my room was laughable.

Conrad just wiggled his eyebrows at me. "Magick." He said. I rolled my eyes at him.

"I need coffee," I moaned, "and I still need to get ready."

He laughed and gave me a two finger salute before turning on his heel.

I closed the door behind him shaking my head. Who the hell was that chipper at seven am? Obeah Men, apparently.

I eyed my cozy bed as I forced myself to get changed.

After pulling on some clothes, I went downstairs and practically snatched the coffee out of Conrad's hands. I gulped down the liquid gold, not caring that it was scorching my tongue. Conrad eyed me with amusement.

"Not a morning person, mi see." He said, poking me in the side. I jerked away and glowered at him over my coffee cup.

"Nothing but sleep should happen before ten," I complained and Conrad laughed.

"Dun tell Mr. Abbey that. He'll give yuh extra homework." He teased. I stuck my tongue out at him as I poured myself another cup of coffee.

Once I had consumed my body weight in caffeine, we made our way back to the Abbey house. The house's energy poked and prodded at me as Meredith greeted us at the door. The fact that an inanimate building had more control over its aura than I did was equally irritating and motivating.

Now that I was more awake, I was looking forward to these lessons. Did I need a wand? Did witches make potions? The idea of Conrad flying around on a broomstick almost made me laugh out loud. The laughter that glinted in his eyes as we made our way through the house and to the back door, told me that he found my thoughts comical as well.

The three of us spilled out into the backyard. I was grateful for my flannel shirt as the world seemed to have realized that it was still only May and us Canadians hadn't quite hit our quota for chilly mornings.

"So, what now?" I asked, turning to face Meredith. Today she was in worn blue jeans and a crisp white t-shirt. Her hunter green spring jacket was all pockets and drawstrings and bunched neatly around her narrow waist. The sunlight glinted off of her many necklaces, charms, and rings as she moved, making her look like a modern day pagan princess.

"We start at the beginning." She said simply. "The first and most important thing, is to teach you how to manage your aura. Once you can do that the rest will come more easily."

"My aura? You guys keep saying that word and I don't think I really understand what it means." I admitted, cocking my head to the side. Meredith nodded and continued.

"Your aura is what has been repelling mortals from you. You cannot feel your own aura yet, but it is a terrifying amount of power. Standing next to you feels like standing on the outside of a magickal hurricane."

My eyes widened at that. "It can't be *that* bad." I grumbled dubiously. Though one look at Conrad and Meredith's tight expressions told me that it was. "Oh." I said, now feeling self-conscious.

"Learning how to constantly keep your aura in check will serve two purposes." Meredith explained. "One, it will make it easier for you to mingle in the human world and will make being around you more comfortable for magick folk. Two, it will be a good way for you to burn enough energy to prevent magical overflow." I nodded.

"Think of your power as water, and your body is the cup. If you keep filling the cup without taking a sip, the water will overflow. By not using your power, you are building up a surplus that needs to be released. You are exceptionally strong, so you will need to use your power more regularly than most.

"It is different for magick folk. We borrow magick, we do not create our own. Daemons are made of power. You are manufacturing energy as you stand here before us, and if you do not learn to use it, it will eat you alive."

"Goddess, Mer... Sugarcoat di damn cookie for once." Conrad breathed, exasperated. "It's gonna be fine, Rayven. Pulling yuh aura in around you should be enough for now. Once yuh get the hang of that yuh will be able to manipulate yuh aura, maybe even take from di auras of others to make yours stronger. Mi heard a daemons who can steal talents and skills from other creatures and use them as der own."

I didn't like the sound of that.

16

"Does it hurt? Other people I mean, if I steal their… energy." I felt cold, and it had nothing to do with the brisk morning air.

"It depends. If you take a little at a time and are gentle about it, it can form a bond between you and the other participant. They will retain the skill themselves and you will be able to call on it as you please. If you forcibly tear what you want from them, it can be painful, even deadly." Meredith explained.

We were back to me being a monster. I shook my head in an attempt to rid myself of doubt. This is why I was here. To learn how to control this strange new part of me, and hopefully keep anyone else from getting hurt.

"Do you think learning to use my…gifts, will help with the rage?" I wondered out loud. Meredith looked thoughtful at this question. "It is possible that your bouts of rage are a side effect of magickal build-up."

"Well, let's get started. I'm freezing." I chattered, rubbing my hands up and down my flannel-clad arms. Meredith smiled gently and the air around me seemed to warm a little.

"We shall start small, the first step is being able to feel your aura. Even humans have auras, they, however, lack the ability to physically become aware of them."

I nodded, wondering what Jeremy's aura was like. I almost giggled. It was probably stiff and orderly. "Close your eyes," the witch continued. "You must put yourself in a state of mind that witches call '*Eirene.*' It is a meditative state."

I did as I was told. I attempted to feel for my aura. As much as I tried, I couldn't feel anything, except maybe a little bit silly. Finally, I sighed in frustration. "This isn't working." I complained opening my eyes.

"Yuh trying too hard, man!" Conrad said chuckling. "Close yuh eyes and try again. Mi help this time." I scowled but conceded. With my eyes closed I tried to relax. I could hear the wind rustle through the trees and the buzz of far-off traffic.

As my mind cleared, Conrad brushed his aura against mine and suddenly I couldn't just feel it, I could *see* it. With my mind's eye I could see the seafoam blue cloud of Conrad's aura mingling with Meredith's earthy greens and golds. Both of their energies were so light they seemed to dance. Conrad's rocked and bowed like the ocean's tide and Meredith's seemed to bob and sway like leaves caught in a stray breeze.

Mine was much different. It was such a deep black that it seemed to pull at the very air surrounding it. I was so startled at first I almost didn't notice the tiny pinpricks of light that speckled the midnight energy that surrounded me. I marveled at what almost looked like galaxies twisting in a night sky. It was as if the whole universe exuded from me and I gasped.

My eyes sprang open in wonder. "It's…beautiful." I said.

Conrad and Meredith exchanged glances. As I watched my aura expand and brush against theirs, they both shuddered uncomfortably. I immediately drew it back and away from them. Now that I was conscious of it, it felt like an extra limb. A muscle I could flex and move at will. I grinned.

"This…this is unreal." I breathed, reaching out a hand to brush it through the translucent dark energy that surrounded me. The stars that peppered the yawning blackness twinkled as I ran my fingers over them. I felt a thousand bursts of warmth as if they really were tiny burning suns. "Is mine so different from yours because I'm a half daemon?" I wondered out loud. "Both of your auras are warm. Mine is cold. Except for the stars…"

"Mi don't pretend tuh be an expert." Conrad replied. "Mi only met a few daemon's in mi day, but mi have never ever met one with an aura quite like yours."

Meredith offered a hypothesis, "It is just a theory my father and I came up with, but we think that your aura is a personification of the universe because you are born of the blood of The Origin. The Origin is rumored to have been the creator of all things. Other daemon's auras also draw from aspects of the universe. They can connect with and play with the very ingredients that make up the reality around us."

"What about magick folk?" I ran my hand through my stars again, smiling as they burned brighter for me.

"Magick folk embody elements of the planet we live on. Most of us tend to associate strongly with one specific element. Conrad's power, for example, is heavily based on water, mine is connected very closely to the earth. Fire mages are rare, and there are also magic folk, that can easily control the wind and the weather."

"So, what you're saying is that because my power affiliates itself with the universe, in theory, I should have access to all elements, and maybe even more?" I wasn't sure if I was excited or terrified at the thought. Meredith smiled.

"My father was right," She mused, "You do catch on quickly. Once you know what you are doing Raven, there is almost no limit to the things you can accomplish. That is why it is important that you always remember who you are and where you came from. You can tip the scale in the war that is surely brewing both here and beyond The Veil. You must stay true to your principles and ensure that you have a very strong moral compass to drive your choices."

"That sounds like a lot of responsibility," I grumbled. Meredith smiled, but there was no joy in it.

"Yes. It does." She said softly, almost apologetically. Resolve built again and I flexed my aura. I watched, dazzled as it bent easily to my will, as if I should have been able to do this my whole life. I looked up, locking eyes with Meredith.

"Well then." I said. "We had better get to work."

17

Work we did. Over the next couple of days, Conrad woke me up banging on my bedroom door.

I dutifully went to the Abbey house each day and practiced the exercises they had provided for me. The first lesson was learning how to keep my aura from touching humans. The trick was to force myself to believe that human auras and my own were akin to oil and water. Two things that just didn't mix. Over time, my energy avoided human contact as if it were second nature.

We practiced this by walking through Yonge and Dundas square at lunch time. By the end of the practical, I was being jostled around by the crowd as if I were just a normal person. For the first time in my life, people didn't trip over themselves to get away from me. I had slept more soundly that night than I ever had before.

The next lesson consisted of crossing into the minds of others and picking through their thoughts. This lesson doubled as a defense class, where I alternately learned how to throw up barriers and prevent someone else from reading *my* thoughts. In my opinion, this class hadn't come quickly enough. I went home with Conrad that day feeling more at ease than I had in weeks. It was nice to be able to have a thought that I knew no one else could hear. Something I had taken for granted my entire life.

I was so caught up in learning how to control this whole new part of me that I forgot about being suspended and my pending expulsion. I forgot about Mrs. Serafini's death. The fist seemed to have permanently unclenched from my heart and I was almost happy.

One afternoon, I was sitting at Meredith's scrubbed wooden table, slurping chicken noodle soup and trying to make a flower grow out of a pot when Mr. Abbey came home. The lesson of the day had been drawing power and talent from another person. Meredith had volunteered to be the guinea pig. I didn't look up at Mr. Abbey as he came in. I was too engrossed in my project. I had opened a tiny black hole in my portable universe. Carefully I drew a thin line of power from Meredith, using it to urge the potted seed to crack and grow. I almost jumped out of my chair and cheered as the first green shoots started to break free from the soil.

My premature celebration weakened my control and the black hole in my aura became unstable. It stretched and grew, sucking more and more of Meredith's aura up until she cried out in pain. The flower in the pot shot toward the ceiling, and its roots began to spread at an alarming rate. The pot shattered and soil spilled over the table. The roots knocked over my chicken soup and I cried out as the hot liquid burned through my jeans. Panicking now and worried about what I was doing to Meredith, I tried to cut off the connection. It didn't work, and more and more of Meredith's power continued to be drawn into me. I felt almost drunk on it, until Mr. Abbey intervened and severed the link with a few choice words.

Meredith had nearly slid right out of her chair. I, on the other hand, was impregnated with her power. I needed to let some of it out. *Now.*

Mr. Abbey rushed me outside and I fell to my knees, pressing my hands into the cold ground. The energy spilled out of me and suddenly the backyard sprung to life. Green shoots of grass erupted around me. The cherry blossom tree in the corner bloomed spontaneously. The browned plot of herbs erupted and flowed out of its garden walls. I could feel the roots expanding beneath me. I was extremely aware of every living thing that crawled and the intricate balance that allowed the world to spin. Everything had a purpose, everything had a job to do. If one tiny piece of the puzzle failed, the entire world could crumble because of it.

Finally spent, I fell onto my side, gasping. I could vaguely hear Conrad rush out the back door and Mr. Abbey saying my name. Everything sounded like I was hearing it from underwater. The galaxies that constantly spun around me were out of orbit. Dust-sized planets crash into each other and exploded. Several of my stars went supernova and I shuddered with each miniature eruption.

I don't know how long I lay on the cold, green earth; nursing my billions of solar systems back to health. Mr. Abbey and Conrad stayed with me the whole time and I suddenly remembered Meredith.

"Is she okay?" I croaked. Mr. Abbey looked relieved that I finally seemed able to use my words.

"She will be fine. There is always a risk when training a novice. Meredith is strong and we have ways of healing her."

"I'm so sorry." I murmured dumbly, trying to sit up. Conrad rushed to help me and a couple more planets collided at the sudden movement. My head was throbbing.

"Noh gyal." Conrad said softly, helping me to my feet. "Don't be sorry. It happens to the best of us." Then he smiled at me mischievously. "When mi was five, mi almost set a tsunami on Jamaica."

"No you didn't." I tried to laugh. "That's crazy." Conrad put the hand he wasn't using to support me over his heart.

"If mi lying, mi dying." He chuckled. "Mi granny had to come out and stop it. She did pretty impressed though." He winked at me.

18

We came inside and Meredith was no longer in the kitchen. She was curled up on the couch in the den. Holding an ice pack to her head, she was sipping something that looked hot and smelled sweet. I brushed Conrad off and rushed over to her.

"Meredith I'm so sorry!" I exclaimed, dropping to my knees next to the couch. She looked at me and smiled. Up close her complexion was so pale it was almost grey. I kicked myself for being so careless. "I could have killed you." I breathed, worry overwhelming me. If Mr. Abbey hadn't stepped in, I was convinced I would have drained her dry.

"Raven, it happens. You will get the hang of it." She reassured me warmly. Mr. Abbey chuckled in the doorway.

"Luckily you didn't attempt that little experiment with Conrad. I feel like the house would have flooded and our neighbors would have been out of water for weeks." He commented comically.

Meredith gave him a weak smile. "Precisely why we started with a tamer element."

I gaped at them. How were they all so cool about this? Was it always so dangerous to train someone in magick? You'd think they would have come up with a less volatile lesson plan by now. I felt guilty for thinking that way and was grateful they could no longer read my thoughts.

Mr. Abbey cleared his throat and all three of us looked at him. "I have some news."

The way he said it made me feel like I wasn't going to like it. "I received an email today from the school board Raven." My galaxies, which had just started to stabilize began to wobble again. "Unfortunately, Mr. Green's father has threatened to sue the school board if we permit you to continue your education. As an attempt to keep the peace, they have ordered your expulsion."

"No…" I whispered, sitting back on my heels. My hands fell to my lap and I felt myself deflate. This couldn't be happening. I was just starting to get a handle on myself. My hopes and dreams of attending school as a normal girl flew from my head. I would never have the chance now to see if my new skills would allow me to make human friends. I had thought for sure that if I had worked hard, Mr. Abbey would have been able to get me back into class. What was Jeremy going to think? What would Clair say? My mind was racing and my aura began to act up around me again. The fist in my chest which had been relaxed since my explosion at the house started to tighten again around my heart.

Then, peculiarly enough, that odd spot on my chin started to burn and a cool voice slithered through my mind. *'Calm,'* it whispered to me, *'Breathe.'* It was as if someone had taken my hand and helped me reign in my ricocheting planets and stars. My little universe was at peace again. What the hell was up with *that?* I thought in alarm, glad that my mental shields were still in place.

I glanced up at the magick folk around me to see if they had also heard the strange voice in my head, but none of them had seemed to notice. I touched my chin. It was colder than the rest of my face. It was also where Amon, the daemon Prince of the Court of Pride had touched me. That altercation in the library now felt like it had happened eons ago. I had nearly forgotten about him. The book he had read to me still sat, untouched, on my end table.

"Raven?" Someone was talking to me, and this time, it wasn't a voice in my head. I jerked my head up to find the magick folk staring at me. Had someone asked me a question?

"Sorry," I murmured, dropping my hand from my face. "That was just a lot to take in." I lied, curling deeper into my barriers. Mr. Abbey was looking at me sympathetically.

"It is what it is." I said. The callousness of my tone was forced and I stood up.

"Rayven —" Conrad's voice was filled with compassion and he reached out to me as I moved to walk past him. I dodged his touch and slipped past Mr. Abbey.

"Don't worry about it. I think I just need to walk it off."

Mr. Abbey frowned behind his spectacles, but thankfully he nodded and stepped back to let me pass.

"Maybe mi should go with yuh," Conrad suggested. I shook my head at him and attempted to smile. I realized, I hadn't really had a lot of alone time since Conrad had come into my life. I was grateful to finally have people that I called friends, but it was a big adjustment, especially for someone as introverted as I was.

"I really just want to be alone right now Conrad. I need to think about what this means for my future. If I can't go back to St. Bernadette's to finish the year, I'll fall behind. It'll be hard for Clair and Jeremy to get me into another school on such short notice, especially with my track record. I just need a second to think…ok?"

Conrad nodded minutely, though he did not look at all pleased. He and Mr. Abbey made eye contact and I knew they were having a private conversation about me wandering off unprotected. I had a feeling that Conrad would probably be following me at a distance. If not just for my safety, then for the safety of anyone who crossed my path. I resisted the urge to growl at the thought of being tailed and bit my tongue.

I could understand the paranoia. If the daemon world was really after my blood, then wandering around by myself to work through my teenage angst was probably not the best idea I'd ever had. Nothing had really happened since my incident. Even the episode with Amon in the library had been anti-climactic.

He never ended up pursuing us as we had raced to Meredith and Mr. Abbey's house. As far as I knew, there hadn't been a breach in the barriers surrounding my home. So, I apologized again to Meredith and slipped out the front door, my boots clomping on the steps of the front porch as I left.

My shoulders slumped almost immediately as I slid through the wards that marked the perimeter of Mr. Abbey's property. I hadn't realized how much I'd really missed just spending time by myself.

I did small exercises with my aura, as I made my way home. I tried to expand it at will and retract it whenever I approached another person on the street. Once I made it onto the streetcar, I practiced holding it tightly against my skin for the entire ride. Playing with my aura was a lot like working out an under used muscle. By the time I got off at my stop, I was tired, hungry and my skin felt raw. I arrived at my house and though I couldn't see Conrad, I had a very strong feeling that he was somewhere nearby, making sure I had gotten home safe.

I picked up the stack of flyers sitting on the welcome mat and leafed through them as I pushed open the front door. It was unlocked which meant Clair was probably home early from work.

"Hey mom," I called out, kicking the door shut behind me. "It's me. What's for dinner −" I stopped dead in my tracks, the flyers tumbled from my hands and scattered across the floor.

There was a stranger in my kitchen.

19

He was wearing scuffed motorcycle boots that he had propped up on my kitchen table as he leaned back in one of the chairs. His whitewash blue jeans were shredded at the knees, and his leather motorcycle jacket was all straps and silver buckles. The buckles on his jacket matched the trail of silver earrings that marched up his left ear, standing out against his dark olive skin and ink-black hair.

You would think the most shocking thing about him was the knife that he was tossing lazily into the air, then catching it effortlessly by the hilt. It wasn't. The most shocking thing about him were his eyes. They were golden... so much so that they were almost yellow. The pupils were slit vertically, like a cat's. As alien as he was, and as much as he did *not* belong in my kitchen, he seemed vaguely familiar.

"Hello, Kitten." His mouth curved into a smile. "I've been wondering when you would come home." My heart was beating so loudly, I was sure he could hear it. My mind was racing, where were Jeremy and Clair? Were they at work? I couldn't remember what their schedules were for the week. Had this man hurt them?

"Where are my parents?" I managed to get out. He tossed the knife in the air and caught it again by the hilt. He studied it and ran his finger along the blade as if checking it for sharpness.

"Don't worry luckily for them, you came home first."

My blood ran cold. He glanced back up at me. "You're the one I'm interested in. If you cooperate, I promise I won't hurt them."

"Why don't I believe you?" I snarled and his smile just widened, showing off slightly pointed canines. He shrugged and slid his boots off the table, letting the chair fall back down onto all fours. He unfolded himself with a sort of effortless ease. It was as if he had muscles in places that I didn't. When he came to his full height, he towered over me. I felt insignificant compared to him, even from across the room. Everything about him was lean, deadly, and his stance screamed 'killer.'

I slowly angled my body away from him, glancing down the hall behind me. I wondered if I could make it out the front door before he caught up. Almost as soon as the plan entered my mind, something whizzed by the front of my face - so close that I could feel the rush of air as it passed.

Startled, I looked back to see the knife he had been tossing into the air embedded into the wall, inches from where my head had been. I turned, as slowly as I could, back to face him. My hands came up of their own accord, I think to reassure him that I would not make any sudden movements and that I was unarmed. My entire body was vibrating with shock. I was terrified.

"Don't even think about it, Kitten. I would skin you alive before you made it down the hall." He purred and began to stalk toward me. I made eye contact with his eerie eyes and wondered how a daemon had gotten through the wards without alerting Conrad. I brushed my aura against him and realized with a shock that he wasn't a daemon. His aura was as different from mine as Conrad and Meredith's, but he wasn't magick folk either. That left one more creature that I knew about. He must be a shifter.

The more I focused, the more information I could gather from him. He didn't seem to be aware as I poked and prodded, which I took as a small blessing. His aura was constantly changing, from deep rich greens to browns and cool shades of grey. He smelled like the rainforest. There was a humidity about him and I was starting to guess that he changed into some sort of large cat from the way he moved.

I blinked and he was in front of me. I gasped.

Damn, he was fast.

20

He hadn't been kidding. There was no way I would be able to outrun him. It was frustrating and scary coming up against a creature that was more monster than I was. I was used to being the fastest, the strongest, and even the meanest.

By the way this shifter was looking at me, I knew I had been bumped from my long-standing seat at the top of the food chain. This was not some teenage asshole looking to bully me to show off to his friends. This man was a professional.

I tried to call out to Conrad with my mind, but there was no answer. Had he even followed me home? Had he left once he realized I'd made it here safe? I swallowed and forced myself to stop shaking. No one was coming to my rescue. I had to get out of this myself. I had to get this *thing* out of the house before Jeremy or Clair came home. I had no doubt he would kill them on the spot if they interrupted whatever it was he was planning to do with me.

"Who the hell are you and what are you doing in my house?" I growled. My voice was low and to my pleasure, steady. He was now so close I could smell his aftershave. He was inches away and he kept eye contact with me as he reached behind me to pry his knife out of the wall. I thought for a second he would do something lecherous, but he surprised me by taking a step back. He flipped and rolled the knife nimbly through his fingers without looking at what he was doing. I hoped he would cut himself.

"I'm here to kidnap you," he said with a smile that I think was meant to be charming. "Now be a good girl and turn around so I can tie you up." I scowled at him.

"You honestly think I'm just going to *let* you tie me up?" I forced a laugh and spat at his feet. "Go to hell." He looked at the spit on his boot for a second before glancing back up at me.

"Now…why did you have to go and do that?" He asked, his voice soft. I suddenly regretted being a smartass, just in time for him to slam me against the wall by my throat. I cried out as he plunged the knife into the wall by my head with the hand that wasn't suspending me several inches off the floor.

Wrapping both hands around his wrist, I clawed at his skin as I struggled to breathe. He didn't budge. He leaned in and whispered in my ear, making me shiver with revulsion.

"Don't make me hurt you, Kitten, not before I have to." He inhaled deeply, then exhaled against my neck. "I don't know if I'll be able to stop myself once your blood starts flowing." He said, nuzzling into my throat. I kicked at his shins and bucked against the wall trying to get him away from me. "You smell like… *power.*" He breathed against me, and then to my complete and utter horror, he licked my neck. I thrashed in fury as he pulled back, chuckling at my efforts. I couldn't speak with his hand crushing my windpipe, so I settled for hissing into his mind. *'I'm glad this is amusing you.'* He grinned, his yellow eyes twinkling.

"Kitten, you have *no* idea," he purred out loud.

Finally, I gave up struggling and let myself hang limp. I wanted him to underestimate me, then when he was least expecting it, I would take him out. I wouldn't be able to do that if I struggled until he strangled me to death.

Unfortunately, I was too terrified to fall back on my usual rage. His touch sent waves of fear through me. The skin beneath my *triquetra* was on fire and the spot on my chin where Amon had touched me was so cold it almost hurt.

Was this about him? Had he sent this creature to collect me? I felt tears well behind my eyes and I blinked them back. I would *not* let this monster see me cry.

After what felt like an eternity, the nameless shifter seemed convinced that I was done fighting him. His grip loosened on my neck and he made soothing sounds as he lowered me gently to floor.

"That's my girl." He murmured, "Shh, there you go. Sorry it had to come to that…" Once he let me go, my hands flew to my throat, massaging it where I knew a bruise was already blooming. I kept my head bowed and watched him through my hair. He didn't step back or give me any room to maneuver.

"I'm not your girl." I croaked, cringing. He just chuckled in that condescending way of his. He pulled handcuffs out from somewhere and grabbed me by the shoulder, spinning me around to face the wall.

"Put your hands behind your back," he demanded, and I forced myself to obey. The cuffs felt cold against my skin and he tightened them enough that the metal cut into my wrists. I hissed at the pain.

"Sorry Kitten, can't take any chances with you." He deftly pulled his knife out of the drywall again and helped me turn to face the back door on the other side of the kitchen. "We're going to go out the back. You will keep quiet or I will gag you. And Kitten…" He grabbed a fistful of my hair and yanked my head back so he could look me in the face from behind. "I would love an excuse to gag you, so it would be in your best interest not to give me one."

My heart was hammering in my chest again. I had no idea how he planned to spirit me away in broad daylight, though I didn't really plan on finding out. The second he let go of my hair I leaned forward, putting all of my weight on my left foot and pivoted, kicking my right heel directly into his groin. It was a move Jeremy had taught me when I was younger. I had never had to use it until this moment.

My captor swore loudly and doubled over in pain, just as I knew he would. I didn't stop to marvel at my work… I ran. I was at the back door in seconds, but I immediately realized I would lose precious time opening the door with my hands tied. Whipping around, I started to fumble with the knob behind my back, all the while watching as the shifter cursed and shouted, trying to push past the pain to stumble after me.

Finally, I heard that lifesaving '*click*' and the door flew open. I slipped through it and sprinted into the backyard. As soon as the fresh air hit my lungs, I opened my mouth to scream. Before I could even get a syllable out there was a thump and a crack followed by a blinding pain in my head. Then, everything went black.

21

The first thing I was aware of was the pain. I felt like someone had hit me on the head with a hammer. Probably a concussion. I groaned out loud and tried to touch the thudding pulse in my skull. That's when I realized that my hands were tied up. I peeked through my eyelids, wincing at the dim light. Nausea roiled through my stomach, and I bit back bile. Yep. Definitely a concussion. It took a second for the horrifying events of the afternoon to come back to me, and even longer than that for me to get my bearings and take in my surroundings. It wasn't looking good.

I wasn't sure how long I had been out, whether it had been a couple of hours or a couple of days, but it was nighttime. I seemed to be in some sort of motel room, lying on my back on a bed that had been dragged into the center of the floor. My hands and legs had been tied to the four posts of the bed so tightly that the only thing I could move was my head.

My kidnapper was standing in front of the desk where he had a laptop set up. Its bluish-white glow was harsh against my eyes in the dimly lit room. I pulled against my restraints again and sighed in frustration when they still didn't budge. I had to think. What would Jeremy tell me to do? What would Conrad do?

"Ah, you're awake," my captor said without turning away from his computer. "I was worried I'd hit you too hard. I thought you would be a little bit more resilient. Apparently, you're not as strong as everyone has made you out to be." God, he was chatty. I decided to keep him talking. The longer he was talking the more time I had to figure out how to get out of this mess.

He pulled his phone out of his pocket, and scrolled through as he spoke.

"You do have quite a bit of fight in you for someone so fragile." He chuckled, "You kicked me pretty damn hard, I have to say, *bravo.*"

I scowled at him. "What do you want with me? Why am I here?" He cocked his head to one side and grabbed the chair from the desk and brought it to the side of the bed, sitting down next to my head.

"You must know. How could the daughter of the good old detective be so ignorant?" He mused out loud. He looked down at me and waited for my response. When I said nothing, he continued. "Your little magick friends didn't tell you that you were being hunted? I find that hard to believe. Magick folk are always meddling in business that doesn't concern them."

I sensed a note of prejudice in his voice, and I wondered what had happened between him and the magick folk in the past to make him dislike them so much. Hopefully, Conrad would come soon and give him another reason to hate them.

"So Amon sent you? Is that it?" I asked. He looked surprised for a second, then he threw his head back and laughed.

"Prince Amon? You think that arrogant prick would ever hire someone to do his dirty work? Of course not. My employer is a little bit more...sinister, unfortunately for you." He looked thoughtful for a moment, then turned his phone around, to show me what he had been scrolling through.

"Would you like to see photos from the case your father has been working on for the last couple of weeks?" The abrupt change in topic startled me, but he didn't wait for a response. He held the phone up for me to see.

It took a moment for my eyes to make sense of what they were seeing. When the mind knows it's seeing something horrible, it tries to protect itself by simply not understanding it. However, I couldn't look away.

The photos were crime scene pictures of three different girls, all brutally gutted and murdered, and tied down the way I currently was. Their flesh was covered in webs of intricate cuts and scars. However, the part that shook me the most was that all three of the girls looked like me. They all had dark hair and pale skin, and they all had my build.

It hit me like a ton of bricks. Jeremy had been playing this case close to the chest, more so than any other case he had worked on. Now it made sense, Jeremy hadn't shared this case with me because *I matched the vic's profile*. This psychopath was going to gut me just like these poor girls in the photos. These girls were dead because they had been mistaken for *me*.

I was going to die.

My mind was screaming, but I forced myself to remain calm. Panicking would get me nowhere; easier said than done. I took deep breaths, in through my nose and out through my mouth. If I could just avoid going into hysterics I could get out of this. I knew I could. I remembered my earlier plan…keep him talking.

"Where did you get those?" I demanded. He shrugged, pulling the photos away so I could no longer see them. Thank God.

"I've been hacking into the police system since I was fourteen. This case is everywhere right now. Big news. Whoever Ash Nevra hired before me was fucken useless, let me tell you."

My eyes snapped to him. So Ash Nevra had hired him. That wasn't good. He continued, oblivious to his slip.

"All I had to do was find out who was working the case. Turns out, the detective leading the investigation is your father. I broke into his office a little over a week ago to do some snooping, and wouldn't you know? He had pictures of his daughter on his desk who matched the description of the girl I was supposed to find." He paused for dramatic effect and met my eyes.

"Now I don't know about you, but I'm not one to put too much stock in coincidence."

The idea of this monster being that close to Jeremy made my skin crawl. I had to get the hell out of here. But how? I was supposed to be this all powerful daemon. I should be able to take this shifter on with nothing but magick or power or whatever the hell it was daemons used, right?

I flexed my aura and it brushed against my captor's mind. I pressed a little harder than I normally would and his name came to me. His name was Rycon, and he was a shifter from the Olkuyrbe Tribe in South America. He was the son of the chief but had abandoned his birthright to become a mercenary after... Rycon slammed the door shut on his mind and grabbed my face.

"That is *rude,* Kitten. You shouldn't go prying into people's minds. Especially when they're trying to tell you a story." Well, I guess he wasn't as oblivious as I had originally hoped. He hadn't noticed until I started pressing. Maybe if I went gently...

"Anyway, where was I? Oh yes. Coincidences." He let go of my face and leaned back in the chair. "Once I discovered the detective had a daughter, I decided to go check you out. It wasn't hard to find your address. Unfortunately, the magick folk had gotten to you first. As annoying as that was, it meant that I was on the right track." He plucked an invisible piece of lint off his t-shirt and flicked it away.

"I followed you to that house that's warded three ways from Sunday. It didn't take me long to realize that your own house wasn't warded against shifters, which was obviously a mistake." He said, gesturing to my prone state. "All I had to do was wait for you to come home. That Obeah Man rarely follows you into the house anymore. Even if he had today, I'm sure I would have been able to remain undetected until he left."

That's when I realized where I had seen Rycon before. He had been the dark haired man smoking on the corner that day in Conrad's beat-up Hornet.

I remembered earlier what I had done to Meredith. I absorbed her energy and took it into myself. In fact, if I focused, it was as if I still had a piece of her inside me. I knew if I tried hard enough, I could make something grow.

Rycon was fast and strong. He was probably strong enough to snap the restraints.

What if I did to him what I had done to Meredith? Drain him until I was strong enough to escape and he was too weak to follow me? It seemed like the best chance I had. I would just have to go slowly so he didn't notice what I was doing until it was too late.

22

I concentrated until my aura shimmered before my mind's eye. I opened up one of my tiny black holes and shuddered as it started to slowly draw in Rycon's humid energy.

His nostrils flared and he narrowed his eyes at me. "What are you doing? You smell like you're up to something." Shit. How could I *smell* like I was up to something? I asked him another question to distract him from the metaphysical siphon I had just installed.

"So you're going to gut me like those girls in the photos then?" I asked, and he shrugged.

"That remains to be seen." He answered, still eyeing me suspiciously. "You're worth a shitload of money right now, Kitten." He said, leaning back in his chair. "I was thinking; now that I have you…contained, I would open up the bidding floor for the other courts. I know the Court of Greed would pay a pretty penny for you." Power started trickling down the line connecting us, and I felt my muscles immediately react to the raw energy. I hoped Rycon wouldn't notice, but his nostrils flared again.

"I know you're up to something, Kitten." He frowned and checked my restraints. "It's just a matter of figuring out what…" My heart was thudding against my chest, likely giving me away even more. I hoped he chalked it up to me being understandably terrified. I just had to keep him distracted until I had enough power to break free.

"You don't think Ash Nevra will be pissed off that you're selling me to someone else? From what I've been told she doesn't seem like someone you would want to double cross." Realistically, being sold to another court was probably in my best interest.

He paused from his work tightening my restraints and leaned in as if he were going to tell me a secret. "You see, I still have a tiny bit of my father's blood from when he died." He pulled at a black cord that was tied around his neck and a glass vial full of blood tumbled out from inside his white cotton t-shirt. *Gross.*

"I mixed his with my own when I signed the blood oath with Ash Nevra. It gives me a little bit of wiggle room. Normally blood oaths are bound by magick and the participants are physically unable to break them. She won't be expecting me to screw her over until it's too late. By then you'll be sold, I'll be a great deal richer, and I can spend the rest of my life happily on the run." He said it as if the idea of living his life running from a daemon hell-queen was his idea of a grand old time.

"I see," I said doubtfully. "So if no one offers you enough money you're still going to kill me?" Rycon leaned back and made a 'this is awkward' face.

"Well… yeah," he folded the stack of papers over and stood up. "Speaking of which, I should check and see if we have any offers." He winked at me before ambling back over to the laptop. The invisible line of power connecting us followed him to the computer.

Despite my situation, I was starting to feel *fantastic*. The throbbing in my head was quickly disappearing and I was able to see much more clearly in the dimly lit room. My hearing and sense of smell seemed to be heightened as well. I could hear well enough to know we were in an old, abandoned building. There wasn't another person for miles. I could scream and scream and no one would hear me.

I continued to draw energy from Rycon as he busied himself on the laptop. Using my newly adopted capabilities, I explored my surroundings. I could see things more clearly than I ever had in my life. I could almost see each tiny movement my captor made before he made it. I could hear earthworms wriggling in the dirt beneath the floor and the mice scurrying through the walls.

Along with my new powers, I also had this primal instinct to hunt. I was beginning to understand Rycon's shameless demeanor towards me. I was prey and he was a predator. I was food. I was meant to be hunted and eventually killed. That was the way things were.

Rycon was not human. As much as he resembled one, I would need to remember that he was not. Begging would never work on him. He craved violence. It was in his nature to kill. The cat does not feel remorse for the death of the mouse.

As more and more of his energy slid through the siphon, I stretched and flexed against the restraints. The bedposts groaned with the effort and a small smile bloomed on my face. It wouldn't be much longer now. I watched as Rycon shook his head sharply. He put a hand to his forehead and turned away from the computer. His eyes crushed closed and he looked pale. My smile widened. Finally, his eyes snapped open and he looked at me, realization dawning across his face.

"I knew you were up to something," he snarled. I shrugged innocently. *Shit.* It was too early to be discovered. I needed more power. I opened my little black hole wider and he staggered as more energy burst from him and flowed down the line toward me. "You little bitch!" He roared and moved to take a step in my direction. I pulled at my hands a little harder and reveled in the sound of the bedposts splintering.

Suddenly a chill rolled through the room, and we both froze. We simultaneously looked to the door as a scraping sound met our ears. It was as if someone or some*thing* was dragging their nails down the wood of the motel door on the other side.

'*What the hell?*' I asked into his mind, not daring to breathe a word out loud. He glanced at me, then back to the door, his fists clenching and unclenching at his side.

'*We have company.*' He responded and frowned. '*I don't think either one of us is going to like it.*'

23

Rycon grabbed his knife off the desk next to the laptop, just as a childlike giggle sounded from the other side of the door. The sound made the tiny hairs on my arms stand on end.

"Rycon cut me loose," I demanded, my voice low. He looked conflicted for a moment, as if it might be a good idea to have me fight whatever it was with him, especially in his weakened state.

"Knock, knock." The sickly sweet voice said through the wood. "Rycon, my pet. Do not leave me in the cold." The thing dragged its nails down the wood again. Then the voice changed to something deeper, darker, more sinister. "I will not ask again." It echoed through the room and I jerked as the door exploded into a million tiny splinters of wood, revealing what stood behind it.

The thing looked like a little girl, but it was not. Where the whites of its eyes should have been, there was only black, black as deep as the dark hair that fell in strings to the creature's shoulders. It wore a white nightgown, and its feet were bare. The most disturbing part of the creature was its hands. Whereas the rest of it was proportionate and shaped like a human girl, its fingers were so long that the tips of them nearly grazed the floor. It seemed to have extra joints and the spindly appendages were bent like spider's legs. I stared, a scream frozen in my throat. I pulled more at the restraints and thrashed, fracturing the wood, but was still unable to break completely free.

'*RYCON!*' I bellowed into his mind. '*LET ME GO!*' Some basic instinct told me I did not want the monster in the doorway to touch me. Rycon glanced at me but did not respond. I could see the wheels turning in his head, planning, trying to figure out what to do and why this creature was here.

He leaned casually against the desk, tossing the knife into the air and catching it again, much the same way he had done in my kitchen.

"Hello, widowmaker." He drawled, and the creature slowly turned and fixed its all-black eyes on him. It smiled, and what looked like black ink shined in its mouth, staining its teeth. The monster took a step forward, its nails scraping against the carpet as it walked. Every single cell in my body was screaming for me to run. I thrashed again but quickly stopped as the creature turned its face towards me at the sound. Thankfully, it turned its attention back to Rycon.

"You have been a *bad, bad kitty.*" It said. Its voice was small, feminine, and childish once again. "Mistress says you signed a bad deal."

It cocked its head to the side and raised one of those long, bone-white fingers toward him. He casually sidestepped the finger, moving closer to the bed. Closer to *me*. Rycon shrugged.

"A male has gotta look out for himself," was all he said. He pushed his thoughts down the line of power that I still had attached to him. '*You're going to have to kill it, Kitten.*' He thought to me, and I gaped at him.

'*Are you crazy? I don't know how to fight that…that* thing.' I felt his rage bubble at that comment.

'*Well, you should have thought of that before you stole from me. I am too weak to defend us now. I'm going to give you whatever I have left and then you are going to slaughter this little bitch.*'

'*How?*' Was all I asked, and a small smile twitched on his face.

'*Kill it with fire.*' He said before he shoved an enormous amount of energy down the line.

My back arched against the sudden flood of power. My muscles sang and my bones shifted from the force of it. My entire body contracted, and I pulled my hands and feet toward my core inadvertently. The bedposts gave way and ripped apart beneath the rope as if they had been made of cardboard. I sprang from the bed faster than I had ever thought I could move. The amount of strength that coiled beneath my skin hammered to the beat of an ancient drum and an inhuman snarl escaped my lips.

Rycon fell to his knees but somehow remained conscious. As the last bit of energy drained from him, I felt a strange 'click,' and a pull. Our minds melded in what felt like a very permanent way. I cut off the siphon and filed the strange 'togetherness' that I was feeling away. I resolved to examine it more closely later if either of us made it through the night.

The widowmaker cocked its head again with a jerk. Its skull pivoted on its neck in an unnatural way until its ear was parallel with its left shoulder and its chin with its right. The creature's movements were erratic and abrupt.

"The raven has talons, it seems." It sang, an eerie smile painted across its black, dripping lips.

'Do not let it touch you,' Rycon said in my mind.

'No Shit. What is it?' I asked, glancing at him before fixing my gaze back on the monster that stood before me. Rycon's eyes darkened.

'A widowmaker. They feed on fear and nightmares,' He replied. *'Lighting it on fire is probably your best bet.'*

'How? I don't even have a lighter.' I snarled at him without taking my eyes off the widowmaker.

'You mean to tell me you don't know how to conjure a flame? What kind of useless piece of shit daemon are you?' I sent an image of a vulgar hand gesture to his mind and he sighed out loud.

"Catch," he said. My heightened reflexes allowed me to easily catch the metal lighter that he tossed to me from behind. "It's better than nothing. Make sure it doesn't catch you in its web."

"What web?" I asked just as the widowmaker opened its mouth and fired wet, inky, strings in my direction. I barely had time to get out of the way as the jet-black substance slammed into the wall where I had been standing. The widowmaker licked its sticky lips and jerked around to face me.

"I have eaten flies bigger than you, half-breed!" Its voice bubbled through the tar dripping from its mouth. The next thing I knew, it was on all fours. It scuttled towards me like a spider, faster than I had expected.

I dodged it, using my new speed to leap over the bed and away from it before tucking and rolling as it fired more black web towards me. I barely made it out of the way in time. I jumped to my feet and spun around, looking for the spindly creature. I couldn't see it anywhere, which was terrifying considering the size of the room. How the hell was I going to light it on fire if I couldn't see it? Would lighting it on fire even kill it? Where the hell had it *gone?*

'Look up, you idiot!' Rycon snarled into my head. I glanced up to see the widowmaker crouching on the ceiling directly above me. A gob of black tar dripped from its mouth as it smiled.

"The itsy bitsy spider went up the water spout…" The vile creature sang from above before it opened its mouth, and thick ropes of web exploded toward me. I watched in slow motion, and it came down around me. I had noticed the fiend too late.

"Down came the web and wrapped the Raven up…" *How creative,* I thought as I fought against the sticky strands. It lowered itself down from the ceiling upside down, its long fingers reaching toward me. The web was heavy and thick and seemed to have a life of its own. It wrapped around my neck and wrists and anchored me to the ground, holding me still as the widowmaker slowly came down from the ceiling.

As the web crushed and spread between my fingers, it forced me to drop the lighter. I stared at it and knew I was going to die. No matter how hard I pulled against the web, I couldn't move. It was almost as if there was something in it that drained my strength. The more I struggled, the weaker I felt.

"Out came the sun and dried up all the rain…" It cooed as it reached out its index finger. I went cross-eyed as I watched the sharp tip reach closer and closer to my face. *Don't touch me, don't touch me, don't touch me.* I chanted in my head, a sob choking at my throat as the web wrapped itself around my mouth, silencing me.

"And the itsy bitsy Raven, *never woke up again...*"

24

I had accepted that I was going to die, when every shadow in the room came alive and swirled together, forming the shape of a man. The monster jerked its hand away as it spun on its ebony thread to confront this new intruder.

The shadows settled and solidified, and there stood Amon. He was holding a sheathed sword in one hand. The sword seemed out of place, considering he was dressed in slacks and a crisp collared shirt. It was almost as if he had left whatever he had been doing in a hurry, and grabbed the sword as an afterthought.

I never thought I would be happy to see him, but here I was, nearly sobbing with relief. The monster screamed an inhuman cry and lashed out at him with its deadly fingers. He unsheathed his blade, which was unlike anything I had ever seen before. The blade itself seemed to be made of midnight. He used it to cut the widowmaker's hand clean off its wrist. The hand jerked and danced on the floor, spraying putrid black blood on the carpet. The fiend screamed louder, launching thick ropes of web at him from inches away. He did not try to dodge the attack, but merely held up a hand, and it seemed to hit an invisible wall, before boiling and steaming away.

Amon made quick work of its second hand, severing it with his midnight blade, before grabbing the widowmaker by the throat and ripping it down from its venomous thread. He held it up before him effortlessly as it thrashed in his grip, bloody stumps streaming stinking blood.

"Mistress will kill you for harming me!" It shrieked. Black ink bubbling down its chin and onto his hand. He didn't seem to notice the filthy substance staining the cuff of his shirt. His expression was cold and filled with a silent rage. I watched from my stranded place on the floor as his grip tightened around the creature's throat. I heard a crack and pop that made me wince as bones broke in its neck.

"I doubt Ash Nevra will shed a tear for something that has demonstrated such incompetence." His tone was cold and unforgiving.

"You cannot kill me." The creature spat. "I was a god before you were even a twinkle in this young planet's eye." Amon rose an eyebrow at this and smoke began to billow from where he had his hand wrapped around her neck.

"I have yet to come across something that I could not kill," he growled, his lips curling into a smile. "If you prove to be as immortal as you claim, well, there are worse things than death." The smoke became thicker, and the widowmaker screamed again as it caught fire. Amon just held it until nothing but a blackened skeleton remained. I gagged against the smell, especially with my heightened senses. The entire room smelled like rotten eggs.

He dropped the skeleton to the ground. It still jumped and twitched along with the two severed hands, which were now crawling slowly towards me. I struggled against the web to try and get away. Amon noticed and was suddenly by my side.

"Hold still. I'm going to burn the web away," he said, and my eyes widened. I really had no desire to end up like the widowmaker. He seemed to understand my reservations. "I will not let the fire touch you. Just the web. You must trust me." I stared up at him silently. The web still wrapped tightly around my mouth.

Trust him? That was a tall order. I glanced over at Rycon who just shrugged at me. He seemed to be in no rush to intervene. I suppose this was the best offer I was going to get. Amon nodded at my silent consent and went to work carefully burning away the web.

When it was all finally gone, I got to my feet uneasily. Most of my hard-won strength had been sucked away by whatever had been in that black, tar-like substance. I wobbled on my feet, but neither the shifter nor daemon moved to help me. I was more than okay with that.

Amon turned his attention to the widowmaker's remains. He waved a hand and it disappeared.

"Where did you send it?" I croaked, rubbing at my freshly bruised neck. Its web had tightened around my throat in the struggle, and it ached again. He met my gaze with those green eyes. He seemed surprised by the question.

"I sent her back to my court," He explained. "If it is truly immortal, it will heal from what I have done and needs to be contained. My court will take care of that."

Finally, Rycon piped up. "So, have you come to make an offer for her then?" He asked, gesturing toward me. The shifter leaned back against the wall, though I noticed he was careful to avoid the puddles of tar leaking from the ceiling. Amon turned his attention to Rycon, his movements slow and dangerous.

"You do not seem to be in a position to be making any sort of bargain with me." Amon's tone was deadly.

"Hey, fair is fair," Rycon said. "She is mine by right. I have claimed her. It's a magickal contract that you cannot break."

Amon looked for a moment as if he might murder the shifter where he stood. I wasn't surprised Amon was angry that Rycon had gotten to me first. I backed away from both of them, glancing at the open doorway. Maybe I could get out of here while they were occupied with each other. As I eyed the darkness beyond, all I could think about was crouching spiders waiting for me in the dark. I began to tremble. I wished Conrad would find me. I was tired, scared, and hurt.

Amon sneered. "I believe that has changed. You both now owe me a life debt. You know the rules. You are mine now to do with as I wish." Both Rycon and I gaped.

"That's bullshit." Rycon snarled. "Sure, you saved that little brat's life but I was completely fine before you showed up. I owe you nothing."

The smile Amon gave Rycon was more sinister than anything the widowmaker could have pulled off.

"I've forgotten how blind your kind can be," he said, his voice low. "Can you not see it? You are now bound to The Origin's daughter. She has claimed you as hers to call. If I had let her die, you would have died with her."

25

I felt Rycon's terror before I saw realization spread across his face. That 'click' I had felt when I had drained the rest of his power. This 'togetherness' that I felt. I remembered Meredith mentioning something like this. She told me that this could happen.

"That's not possible," Rycon breathed. Amon just smiled at him then grabbed my wrist so fast I couldn't have possibly dodged it. He drew his strange blade across my forearm. I cried out in shock and pain just as Rycon swore, cradling his own arm to his chest. Blood welled in the wound on my arm and I tried to pull away from Amon, but he held me in place.

"Let go of me, you sick piece of shit!" I snarled at him, throwing my entire weight against his grip. Rycon hissed from the other side of the room, rage and hatred smoldering in his eyes. I didn't know if it was directed at me, Amon or the both of us... until I felt the panic clench around his heart as if it were my own. His dreams of freedom fled from his mind. He was bound to me—a prisoner. The hatred was for me. Definitely for me.

Amon frowned slightly at the wound he had carved into my arm, he seemed almost confused for a moment as he watched my red blood drip into the dirty carpet. Then his gaze found the *triquetra* around my neck, and his eyes darkened.

"Remove that charm, *now*," He ordered, still holding my arm. I spat in his face and attempted to kick him in the groin, much the same way I had done to Rycon earlier. My spit never made contact. He magicked it away before it could land. The daemon simply chuckled and blocked the kick with his leg, all the while maintaining his grip on my wrist. His anger quickly melted away into amusement.

"So feisty," He purred, smirking at me.

"Go fuck yourself," I snapped at him, enraged that he seemed to find my futile attempt at escape amusing. His smile just widened.

I heard a car pull up outside and knew from the familiar squeak of the brakes that it would be Conrad. Relief flooded through me. He would know how to get me out of this mess. Sure enough, within seconds, he was in the doorway. I watched the blood drain from his face as he took in the scene before him.

I tried to see it through his eyes. Black sludge dripping from the walls and ceiling; the Prince of the Court of Pride holding me by the wrist and a murderous shifter lurking in the corner.

"Let her go," Conrad said. His voice was darker than I'd ever heard it. He came to my side and pulled me away. Surprisingly, Amon did as Conrad asked and took a step back.

"I was wondering when her bodyguard would get here," Amon mused. Rycon snorted.

"Some bodyguard." The shifter snickered, and Conrad looked so angry I swore he would call a tsunami to drown us all. Rycon just laughed.

"I'm just saying, it wasn't exactly hard to kidnap her. You must be new."

"Shut up, Rycon." I snapped, and to both of our surprise, he did. Maybe this binding thing would turn out useful if I could order him around like that. Conrad had been observing the interaction and his eyes widened as he to, noticed our connection to each other.

"Rayven…what have yuh done?" He asked softly, and I sighed.

"I was hoping you could tell me. It's been a long night. What took you so long?"

Guilt spread across Conrad's features like wildfire. "Mi sorry." He said. "Mi did a tracking spell as soon as mi found out yuh were missing. Yuh parents worried sick. Jeremy thinks mi murder yuh, it all mi could do to keep him from arresting me long enough to track yuh down." Rycon sniggered in the corner at this. Oh right. My parents. I groaned, putting my face in my hands. How was I going to explain this to them?

"Yuh bleeding!" Conrad gasped as he noticed the huge gash in my arm that Amon had cut, just to make a point. I snorted and pointed to the daemon in question.

"You can thank *him* for that."

Conrad whirled on Amon.

"The Board will have yuh head for this," Conrad warned him.

Amon just shrugged. "I really doubt it, considering she owes me a life debt. Her and her new pet."

Conrad physically staggered with the blow of the news. He looked at me, devastated, as if his worst nightmares had just been realized.

"*What?*" His mouth was hanging open. He pulled me into him and hugged me. *'Dis is all my fault,'* he whispered into my mind. *'Mi should have been here sooner.'* Out loud he asked, "How di hell do yuh owe him a life debt?"

I sighed again and pulled away. I explained what had happened. By the time I was finished, Conrad's eyes were so wide I thought he might faint. Rycon was the first to pipe up.

"Well, I don't know about all of you, but I would like to go and wash some of this ... tar off of me." He said, gesturing to the black sludge that was now starting to harden in scabby patches. He glared at me, resentment saturating from each and every pore of his body. "I guess I need to ask your godsdamned permission for that now?" He snapped.

Did he? I shrugged, "Sure, go ahead."

He mimicked me, mocking my tone, like a child. "*Sure, go ahead...* Try not to get us both killed while I'm gone." He grumbled and left without a backward glance. I could have sworn I heard him mumbling something about 'now having to follow around a whiny child for the rest of his life.' I bit back a smile. I wasn't exactly thrilled to be attached to him either, and maybe we could find a way to reverse it. But for now, revenge was sweet.

I felt more than saw Amon's eyes trace over me. His hands were in his pockets and that cocky little smile still perched on his lips. Every time I felt his eyes on me, I felt like I was naked. I shuddered uncomfortably. "Go home Raven. Pack some things. Spend some time with your loved ones. I will come for you in seven days' time."

"Come for me? And take me where?" I demanded. He just gave me a dark look, one that promised nefarious things. Then he wrapped the shadows around him like a cloak, and he was gone.

26

The walk from the trashed motel room to Conrad's Hornet was tense. I couldn't shake the feeling of the widowmaker's sticky black web. Gooseflesh erupted on my arms, and I searched the shadows relentlessly for spindly fingers and black, soulless eyes. The full moon hung like a pearled orb in the sky and cast wisps of nighttime across the cracked parking lot. I jumped every time a twig snapped beneath our feet and my aura expanded around me.

"Yuh alright?" Conrad asked quietly. I felt like he was trying to keep his voice low and steady so as not to startle me.

No. I absolutely was *not* alright. That monster had been seconds away from killing me; and now I was now stuck with some sort of shape-shifting mercenary who also tried to kill me. On top of all that, now I owed Amon a life debt, which he seemed bent on me paying with my freedom. I had never been so *not* okay in my entire life. I didn't bother to answer. Instead, I ripped open the passenger side door and checked the back seat for monsters before slipping in and buckling up. Conrad got into the driver's seat and switched the car into gear.

"We'll find a way to get yuh out of this." I could hear the empty promise in his voice. I could tell from his tone that there was no getting out of this. I stared out the window into the darkness and my reflection stared back; a ring of bruises coiling around my neck like a string of black pearls.

What was I going to tell Jeremy and Clair? I glanced at the clock; it was almost midnight. I had never come home this late in my life. My clothes were covered in black goop, and my hair smelled like smoke from when Amon burned away the web. I looked like the mess that my life was. Conrad seemed to notice and mumbled a spell under his breath. Suddenly, I looked like I had that morning. Fresh and clean.

"How did you-?" I asked, startled. He shrugged.

"It's called a glamour. Yuh still need a shower when yuh get home and yuh should probably throw away that outfit. At least you'll look alright coming in the door."

"Thanks." I sighed, burying my face into the heels of my hands. I was so *tired*. I was so *scared*. I didn't know what to *do*.

"Mi already sent word to Meredith and Mr. Abbey about yuh life debt, Raven. They've alerted the rest of the board. Wi *will* find a way to get yuh out of this." I looked up at him and frowned.

"Maybe this is a good thing. You said yourself that at some point I would need to learn from my own kind. I almost killed Meredith earlier today. It would probably be safer for everyone if I just went with him." Even as I said the words, I knew I didn't mean them. I didn't want to be Amon's slave. I didn't want to leave my parents, my home.

"Raven, yuh have no idea what yuh saying. Amon is one of di most ruthless beings tuh exist on dis plane. He has tortured and killed innocent people tuh get what he wants. He did nuh save yuh out of di goodness of his heart. He saved yuh so that he could control yuh. So dat he can *use* yuh to overthrow Ash Nevra. He wants to rule over the seven courts and yuh are his ticket to doing that."

My arm throbbed where he had sliced it open in response to Conrad's claim. I tried not to let my imagination run wild. Where would Amon take me? To the other side of The Veil most likely. Where the daemons and creatures like the widowmaker cajoled each other and fought for power on a burning field, scorched with their greed. I imagined a dark cell that smelled of sulfur, and chains that cut into my wrists and ankles. What kind of humiliating stunts would he have me perform?

"Rayven-?" Conrad cut through my waking nightmare. I shook my head and surfaced from my dark thoughts, watching the lights on the highway flash as we sped by.

"Have you ever been across The Veil?" I asked softly, hoping that he would be able to quell my fears. Conrad shook his head.

"No mortal alive has crossed The Veil. Centuries ago, when The Origin still walked, daemons would carry magick folk, and sometimes shifters across The Veil to join their armies." He glanced over at me apologetically, "Mi know that's not what yuh wanted to hear, but mi don't want to lie to yuh either." He turned onto the next off-ramp. We were almost home.

"What do you think it's like?" I asked. My question had been so quiet and he had taken so long to answer that at first, I wasn't sure he had heard me.

"Let's figure out what we gonna tell yuh parents. Yuh don't need to worry about what's on the other side of The Veil, Rayven. Mi noh let him take yuh dere."

I wanted to believe him. But the worried pinch in his tone was enough to convince me that all my nightmares were about to come true.

I stared at our family's electric blue door. The lights were on, and I hesitated, before going inside.

Of course, they were still awake. I don't know why I even bothered hoping that they would have gone to sleep.

"So yuh have di story down?" Conrad asked quietly. I nodded. We had decided to tell them that I had fallen asleep in the stacks and no one had noticed while closing up. It was a bit of a stretch but realistically, what else was I going to tell them? Conrad put a hand on my shoulder.

"Yuh can do this." I nodded and held my breath before finally opening the door.

As soon as I stepped over the threshold, I heard chairs scrape back from the kitchen table.

"Raven?! Raven is that you!?" Both Jeremy and Clair came running down the hall. Jeremy brushed against some of our family pictures in his hurry and they tumbled to the ground. I watched them shatter on the floor and tried not to see symbolism in the destruction.

Jeremy seized me by the shoulders and frantically checked me over. "Are you alright? Are you hurt?"

"No dad, I'm fine." I said, shame and guilt welling into my chest. Clair pushed forward and held my face in her hands, tears streaming down her cheeks.

"Raven..." Was all she said and pulled me into her. I wrapped my arms around her narrow waist, and she buried her face in my hair, her shoulders shaking with relief. "I'm fine, I just fell asleep at the library," I lied.

Jeremy pulled both Clair and I into him and kissed the top of my head. He held us for a heartbeat before stepping away. I watched as relief drained from his features and was replaced with a hot and suspicious rage.

"Why didn't you call?" He demanded. I resisted the urge to glance back at Conrad.

"I forgot my phone at home. I didn't expect to be out that late." Jeremy narrowed his eyes on me.

"The library has been closed for hours now. How did nobody notice you sleeping there?" I shrugged.

"I was all the way back in the stacks, no one ever really goes back there so I guess they assumed it was empty." Jeremy did not look convinced, and I could hear his thoughts as clear as day. He didn't believe a word I was saying. He thought I had been out with Conrad at a party or something ridiculous like that. I was spared having to come up with a rebuttal for his next question by Clair.

"Well thank goodness you're safe." She said, giving me and Conrad a watery smile. "Thank you, Conrad, for finding her and bringing her back all in one piece."

"Nuh problem Mrs. Fisha," Conrad said. "I'll let you guys get to bed, it's late. Night Rayven, mi talk to yuh tomorrow." He gave us his usual two

111

finger salute and left. As soon as the door closed, Jeremy whirled back to me.

"You're hiding something from me Raven, and I don't like it." He snapped. I raised my eyebrows at him. I understood that he was upset but he had never raised his voice at me like that before.

"Excuse me?" I gaped. "You're the one that's been hiding what's been going on from *me* for months now!" I shot back, unable to keep my own sense of indignation from bubbling up.

"What are you talking about? You've been acting differently ever since you brought that delinquent home." Jeremy retorted.

"You don't know what I'm talking about? You didn't think it was worth mentioning that I match the vic profile of a major serial killer?" Jeremy looked as if I had slapped him.

"How did you find out about that?" He asked, his voice much lower.

"Not from you." I snapped. I knew I wasn't being fair, but I couldn't help it. I was hurt that I had heard about it from my kidnapper, and not my own father. Clair was watching me carefully, her brows pinched together. I thought she would interject, but Jeremy beat her to the punch.

"That's it." He snarled. "You're grounded. You're not to leave the house. No more Conrad, no more going to the library. You're staying right here where I can keep an eye on you." My eyes widened. Stay here? That was impossible. There was no way I could stay here. Not with all that was happening. How was I supposed to train? How was I supposed to get out of the life debt with Amon?

"Dad- that's not fair..." My tongue nearly tripped over my words.

"Do you know what's not fair? Having your mother and I comb the streets looking for you until midnight when you would obviously rather be off hanging out with that *stranger* than come home!"

My hands clenched into fists. I closed my eyes and forced myself to take a deep breath through my nose. I let the air out slowly from my mouth and started counting backward from ten. Maybe anger management had taught me a thing or two after all. When I opened my eyes again, Jeremy was still standing before me, his stance mirrored mine. Fists clenched at our sides, both of us glaring at each other.

"I'm going to bed." I said. My voice was strange, even to me. It sounded otherworldly, and when I met Jeremy's eyes he blanched a little bit.

I realized I had scared him and felt my heart break. No matter how angry I was, I didn't want Jeremy to be afraid of me. Was this what it meant to be a daemon?

Maybe, I was just a monster to be feared. Maybe, I belonged in a cell with the widowmaker. Maybe my family would be safer, if I just went with Amon across The Veil.

27

I forced the beast in my chest to settle down and turned on my heel to head upstairs before I did anything I would regret. I heard Clair angrily hissing at Jeremy in hushed tones as I closed the door to my room. Every inch of me wanted to slam it, but I closed it gently and flopped down onto my bed. Look at me, making progress with my temper.

I looked at myself in the wall-length mirror opposite to me. Conrad's glamour flickered in and out as I unbuttoned my pants and slid them off. I peeled the still-wet jeans off each leg and wrinkled my nose at the now crusty black goo that coated them. My t-shirt came off next and it looked like someone had tried to tie-dye it in a vat of tar. Streaks of the stuff marred my flesh and I held my breath as I balled my clothing, and tossed it all into the trash under my desk.

Finally, I wrapped myself up in my fluffy black bathrobe and made my way into the bathroom.

Every part of my body ached. I turned on the tap and started to fill the tub with water before turning to face my reflection in the mirror. I frowned. The marks around my neck were still covered up with Conrad's glamour, but

I could still feel them. The pain was already considerably less than it had been at the motel. I could still feel a dull throbbing across my throat and clavicle like some sort of grotesque necklace was draped around my neck and down my chest. They shouldn't have been healing as quickly as they were.

I scratched under my *triquetra*, which seemed to be annoying my skin. Scowling at the small offending piece of jewelry, I considered taking it off for some relief. The bruises hurt enough as it was, I really didn't want to be scratching away at my chest because of some allergic reaction.

'Remove that charm, now.' I shivered as I remembered Amon ordering me to take it off. That alone was enough reason for me to leave it exactly where it was. I got into the tub gently. My muscles screamed at me as I lowered myself into the steaming water. With my hair piled on top of my head, I leaned back and sighed. I could still hear Clair and Jeremy arguing downstairs. Their voices were muffled, but the tone of their conversation traveled through the walls.

I shouldn't have lost my temper, not when I only had such a short period of time left with them. They were just worried about me. If they were this upset about me being a couple of hours late how were they going to handle it if I disappeared? Maybe Conrad could put a spell on them and make them forget I had ever existed in the first place. In the privacy of the bathroom, I let the tears well in my eyes and fall silently down my face.

I don't know how long I sat there, but my fingers were like prunes, and Jeremy and Clair had long since gone to bed when I decided to finally get out. I dried off and stepped into my usual bedtime outfit, cotton shorts and an oversized t-shirt.

Grabbing the book of poetry I had taken from the library, I headed downstairs. I tiptoed as quietly as I could and made a cup of Chamomile tea, making sure to remove the kettle from the stove before it started to whistle.

Taking my tea outside, I crept out the backdoor and curled up on the bench swing that Jeremy had installed on our deck. It was well past midnight and the ebony velvet sky hung over the city like a blanket. I could barely make out any stars because of the city's lights, but the moon beamed down on me, lighting the deck enough for me to see my book. I flipped it open to the page that Amon had read to me from. That day in the library now felt like it had been months ago; not just a few weeks.

'You are mine, said the Prince,
cradling his swaddling of twilight.'

As my focus narrowed in on the words on the page before me, I could almost hear Amon's voice as if he were standing next to me, whispering in my ear.

'My Queen, my slave, my lover, my friend, the Prince
says as he rocks his shadow, back, back, back.'

I was beginning to wonder if this poem was indeed about a prince or if it was about Amon himself. What was it that he had said about this poem in the library? That a prophet had written it? What did he *want?*

"Raven?" I nearly jumped out of my skin and the paperback went flying. I yelped as I spilled the hot tea down my front and immediately pulled my now wet t-shirt off my skin to keep the burn to a minimum. "I'm sorry, I didn't mean to startle you!" Clair exclaimed as she rushed forward to take the teacup from my hand.

"It's fine, I'm fine," I reassured her, flapping my fistful of t-shirt back and forth. The fabric cooled quickly in the balmy springtime air. I glanced up at Clair. "I hope I didn't wake you up," I mumbled. Clair shook her head and offered me a solemn smile.

"No, I was up anyway. Mind if I sit?" I shook my head and gestured to the cushioned seat next to me on the bench swing. She looked invincible in her lavender ankle-length nightgown and her bare feet. She folded herself onto the bench so gently that the swing barely moved.

We sat in comfortable silence for a moment, both of us enjoying the peace and quiet of the nighttime. Finally, Clair spoke up.

"Do you want to talk about what happened today?"

"Not really," I said. "You wouldn't believe me even if I told you," I explained.

"Why don't you try me?" Clair asked, and I sighed.

"I'm not ready to talk about it," I shuddered, remembering what it felt like to wake up in that strange room, tied down. I could still feel the phantom web suffocating me as the widowmaker slowly lowered itself from the ceiling. Death on a thread. Clair nodded in understanding. She reached out and put her hand on my knee.

"Raven…" I glanced over at her. Her brow was pinched together again, and she looked like she was unsure about something. After a long pause, she spoke again.

"When I was your age, my father put a great deal of pressure on me. I was very gifted for my age. When I was young, I was arrogant, almost proud to be the prodigy that everyone kept telling me I was." I held my breath.

Clair had never spoken to me about her childhood before. I had never met the grandfather she spoke of, and I wondered what had spurred on this particular story. "As I grew older, I began to realize that things weren't always black and white. The things my father expected me to do for the family name stopped making sense. Sometimes, the things he asked me to do were downright cruel." I frowned at her.

"What kind of things did he ask you to do?" I whispered. She smiled, but there was no joy in it.

"That is a conversation for another day. The point I'm trying to make is that although I knew following in my father's footsteps was not the right path, it did not make leaving him and everything I had known easy.

"Sometimes the hardest thing is the best thing for you to do. You may not believe me, but I understand what you're going through more than you think I do. I know it's difficult for you to talk about, but I want you to know that you can come to me about anything, at any time."

"I know, mom." I said softly. I thought for a moment that if anyone would believe all the crazy shit that was going on in my life, it would be Clair. She smiled at me and pulled me into her. She kissed the top of my head and I allowed myself to rest my head on her shoulder. Just for a minute, just for this one second, I would let myself be a little girl again. I would let my mom hold me and tell me everything was going to be alright, and I would believe her.

"Promise me you will be careful. People who sometimes seem like they're friends can turn out to be the bad guys. Promise me you won't forget that." I frowned.

"What do you mean?" I asked, pulling away to look at her. Her expression was grim, the most serious I had ever seen her.

"Just promise me Raven."

"Mom, what-" I asked, but she stood up and brushed my hair back out of my face with a smile. She glanced down at my neck and frowned.

My hands flew to my throat, but I could still feel Conrad's glamour shimmering beneath my fingers. Had she seen the bruises? No, I was sure she would have said something if she could see them. Instead, Clair floated into the house as silently as she had come out, and I was left staring after her.

28

I dreamt of Amon that night. He was standing in my bedroom, looking at the framed photos from my childhood that were propped up on my desk. He was draped in a black cloak that brushed against the floor and blended into the long shadows. His silver hair competed with the moon, and his too-green eyes reflected the soft light from the stars, piercing through the darkness. He was nighttime incarnate.

"How did you get in here?" I murmured, my voice thick with sleep. The corner of his mouth tilted upwards in a small smirk. He seemed to glide to my bedside, leaving the hot scent of cinnamon in his wake. Leaning casually against the wall to face me, he ran one of his elegant hands through his hair. Hands that had severed the widowmaker's fingers from its arms. Hands that had not hesitated to slice open my own arm... just to make a point.

"I'm not really here. This is a dream." He explained. "Even the Obeah Man's wards can't keep me from your dreams."

I eyed him warily from where I had sat up in my bed. He was watching me carefully, and I couldn't decipher the look on his face. I was so tired and I was so sick of riddles and games. It was bad enough that he would be tearing me away from my family, I didn't need him haunting me in my dreams. I just wanted to *sleep*.

"What do you want with me? Why don't you just kill me and get it over with?" For a short second, I thought I might almost welcome it. A quick death would almost be a mercy… if all I had to look forward to was more terror, more violence. My subconscious twisted Amon's normally cold features into an expression of something that almost resembled concern.

He moved as if he were about to reach out to touch me, but the *triquetra* flashed, and I jerked away. I remembered how he had touched my chin in the library and everything Conrad had told me about daemons and their touch. I wondered if it worked the same in a dream.

Amon dropped his hand; the pained look in his eyes deepened briefly before quickly morphing into his usual mask of mild amusement. He turned away to look out the window into the night.

"You would not serve me well dead, Raven."

"I don't want to serve you," I retorted. He let out a low soft laugh, though there was no joy in it.

"Yet, you serve the magick folk. You follow them and have committed yourself to The Board's agenda without learning about each of the options available to you." He didn't phrase it as a question, but I answered it as if it was one anyway.

"Conrad and Meredith have done nothing but be kind to me and they are trying to help me. They have not tricked me into a life debt and forced me to serve them." Amon sighed and turned away from the window, his midnight cloak moving like a living shadow with him. He leaned back against the sill and observed me carefully.

"And if I had asked you to hear me out, and consider my side, do you think you would have?"

I pretended to think about it, but I knew he was right, I wouldn't have given him the benefit of the doubt. I just couldn't trust him. He nodded. As if to say: *That's what I thought.* Instead, he said:

"The charm that you wear with such pride dampens your powers. Its hold on your aura increases with each passing day. Your new friends will never be able to teach you the things you will need to know to protect yourself. Your powers are manifesting; if you continue to follow them, you will die."

"Is that a threat?" I snapped, though deep down, I knew it wasn't meant to be one. I thought of the rash that had formed on my neck beneath the pendant and wondered. Did Conrad know that it was hurting me? Or was that just a necessary side-effect I would need to endure to keep Amon and the other courts from the Dominion of Sin from touching me? I shook my head. Conrad would never do anything to hurt me. He was my friend.

"The Obeah Man is a very small representation of The Board," Amon said darkly, echoing my thoughts. "There are powers at work here that you cannot possibly fathom." He pushed up from where he leaned against the sill and gathered his cloak around himself. The shadows rippled along its edges, and he seemed to fade into the darkness. "If you're ever looking for some answers, all you need to do is ask."

I will teach you to move planets,
how to reorder the stars,

The words whispered through the space between us, and I felt myself drift away, exhaustion finally taking over. Amon's form seemed to dissolve into the shadows as I settled back into my pillows. *'Sweet dreams, Raven.'* He whispered into my mind. Then there was nothing but the warm scent of cinnamon in the air and the soft brush of velvet on my skin.

29

I woke up the next morning feeling terrible, with the taste of cinnamon in my mouth. My head was pounding and the rash on my neck had spread. Happily, the bruises were nearly gone. Amon's face swam before my vision, and I struggled to remember the details of my dream the night before. I could barely remember what had been said. I was just left with a heavy sense of foreboding, which added to my miserable state. Pulling on an oversized knit black sweater and leggings, I headed down the stairs, my hair sitting on top of my head in a messy bun.

Jeremy was sitting at the kitchen table reading the paper while sipping on his coffee in his O.P.P mug. My shoulders tensed, and I braced myself. I was unsure about the terms we were on. However, I needn't have worried as Jeremy tipped his head at me and lowered his paper.

"Morning." He said as I made my daily beeline toward the coffee machine.

"Morning," I responded coarsely as I poured myself some coffee. I took a long deep sip, completely foregoing the milk. My headache receded slightly, and I turned to face Jeremy.

"How was your sleep?" He asked carefully, and I shrugged.

"Shitty. How was yours?"

"Mine was shitty too." He sighed, pinching the bridge of his nose. "Listen, Raven, I know I lost my temper yesterday. I don't want to coop you up, and I'm sorry that I kept what has been going on from you." I waited, watching him from over the rim of my coffee cup. "I'm just worried about you. I don't want you to get hurt. I tend to assume the worst when I don't know where you are. I thought I had lost you last night." He looked up at me, dropping his hands to the table. My throat tightened at the fear and love in his eyes.

"I understand, dad. I'm sorry too." I said. He smiled at me.

"So, can you just humor me then? Can you stay indoors until I can put this case to bed or until your suspension is up?" My heart sank. Right. I hadn't told him about my expulsion.

"Umm. Sure, dad. Just, there's something you should know." My heart was pounding, and my face flushed red.

"What is it?" He asked.

"Um, apparently, Neil's parents threatened to sue the school board if they allowed me to return to St. Bernadette's." It felt like Mr. Abbey had broken the news to me weeks ago. It was hard to believe it had just happened yesterday.

"What?" Jeremy exclaimed, his face blanching.

"Mr. Abbey had no choice but to expel me." I bit my lip to keep it from trembling. Guilt welled up in my chest. I had just been a couple of months away from graduating. Jeremy shook his head; his eyes were furious.

"I will talk to Neil's father. I knew him in high school, I'm sure we can work something out." I frowned. The way Jeremy said 'talk' made it sound like there wouldn't be much 'talking.' The last thing I needed was the added guilt of Jeremy losing his job because of something I had done.

"Don't worry about it dad I can get the rest of my credits online. It sucks, but it's not the end of the world. I don't care about graduating with any of those kids anyway. It's probably better this way." Jeremy didn't look like he was going to be so easily convinced. I watched him battle with himself internally when Rycon appeared in the window behind him. My eyes widened, and I tried to control my expression to keep Jeremy from turning around.

'What are you doing here!?' I snapped into the shifter's mind. He grinned at me mischievously, his exaggerated canines pressing slightly into his bottom lip. The shifter shrugged and pretended to knock on the window, as if he were going to get Jeremy's attention intentionally.

'Don't you dare.' I growled telepathically. His laugh floated through my mind in response.

"Dad, it's nine o'clock; you're going to be late for work," I said suddenly. Jeremy glanced at the clock and nodded, getting heavily up to his feet. I glared over his shoulder at Rycon, who was making stupid faces through the window at the back of Jeremy's head. I pushed up from the counter and went to meet my adoptive father as he made his way to the front foyer. He rested his hands on my shoulders, leaned forward to kiss my forehead, then pulled away to look me in the eyes.

"We will figure something out, Raven, don't worry. In the meantime, please stay in the house and spare me from an early grave." He smiled at me. "I'm too young to die from a heart attack." I smiled up at him as sincerely as I could.

"I promise."

"Good," he said, patting my arm before brushing past me. "Your mother will be home around six. I'll be a bit later." He called over his shoulder before slipping out the door. I waved after him before spinning around to find that Rycon had already let himself in through the back door.

"Morning Kitten," The shifter said with a mischievous grin before heading for the coffee machine. He poured himself a cup and dug through the fridge for the milk as if he had lived here his whole life. "Got any sugar?" He asked with his head still in the fridge. I tried to slam the door shut on him, but he pulled out of the way too quickly for me to do any real damage.

He was out of the fridge and leaning against the counter faster than I could blink and had somehow managed to keep from spilling a drop of coffee. Not only should it not have been possible, but it sure as hell shouldn't have looked *easy*. He smiled at me lazily and poured some milk into his cup. He watched me the whole time with those eerie yellow eyes, slit pupils dilating with mirth.

"What are you doing here?" I asked again, this time out loud. He shrugged and crossed his jean-clad legs in front of him as he took a sip from his mug sans sugar. The jade hilt to his knife winked up at me from where the blade disappeared into his scuffed motorcycle boots. It was carved into the shape of a panther. I hadn't noticed the night before how ornate the handle had been. Though I supposed that was understandable, considering I had been more concerned with keeping him from gutting me with it than the dainty details.

"I'm here to see you, Kitten. You didn't think I would just disappear, did you?" He raised an eyebrow, that infuriating smirk still on his face.

"I suppose that would be too much to ask," I grumbled. He ignored me.

"In case you weren't listening, Kitten, you and I are bound now. My survival depends solely on you not *dying*. So until I can get rid of you, I guess you have a new bodyguard...and trainer." He said, the latter almost as an afterthought. I raised an eyebrow.

"Trainer?"

"Well, if last night was any indication, all anyone has to do is send someone with basic motor skills, and you're pretty much a goner. Watching you try to battle that spider-bitch was one of the most pathetic things I've ever seen." He drained the last of his coffee and dropped the cup in the sink with a clank. "So yeah, I'm going to train you." My face flushed red at the insult.

"Well, I didn't see you jumping in to help at all." I snarled at him. He rolled his eyes.

"And what? Risk this handsome mug? I don't think so," He preened, gripping his chiseled jaw. He looked me up and down and made a face. "Go change into something, you'll feel more comfortable getting your ass kicked in. I'll meet you out back." Before I could come up with anything witty to say in return, he was gone.

I debated locking the door behind him and curling up to watch TV, but thought better of it. Knowing him he would blow the door right out of the hinges and drag me outside by my ankles. Maybe it wasn't such a bad idea to try and learn how to fight with him. Maybe, if I got good enough, I could kick his ass right back. So, with that cheerful thought in mind, I dragged myself upstairs to change.

30

I walked out into the backyard in black joggers and a t-shirt. I had to dig through the closet to find a pair of Clair's old Nike's that, thankfully, fit just fine.

Rycon looked at me critically as I ambled outside. My feet felt heavy, and my head was swimming. I almost felt like I was coming down with a cold. I shook my head and a wave of nausea roiled through me, but I forced it down. I was not going to puke in front of this asshole.

"That'll do," Rycon grunted. He had shrugged off his leather jacket and was standing before me in his boots, jeans, and white cotton t-shirt, smoking a cigarette. I wrinkled my nose at him.

"We're about to work out and you're smoking a cigarette?" The smell of the smoke was doing nothing to help my nausea. He took another pull, the ember burning red between his blunt fingernails, which were coated in chipped black polish. When he spoke, plumes of smoke escaped with each syllable.

"Correction, *you're* going to work out." He smirked.

I snorted at him. "I thought you said you were going to teach me how to fight? Aren't we going to spar or something?"

I had learned to spar in gym class, where I reigned undefeated in our boxing unit. Until, of course, I had been told that I was 'too aggressive' and was excused from participating in future matches. I mean, it was boxing. The whole point of the sport was to knock the other person out. I hadn't understood all the backlash at the time. Now that I had been expelled, yet again, for fighting, I guess it made sense. I could understand why people were uncomfortable with me learning to be even more deadly.

Rycon literally laughed out loud. "Spar? You look like a strong gust of wind would knock you over. You probably couldn't fight your way out of a wet paper bag."

I crossed my arms and glared at him. "If you're trying to piss me off, it's working."

"I'm not trying to piss you off, Kitten. Pissed off just seems to be your natural state. I'm telling you the truth. You look like shit. You're too skinny, and you probably couldn't run a mile without collapsing. When was the last time you did a sit-up?"

I gave him a vulgar hand gesture, and he rolled his eyes. "Fine." He said, flicking away his cigarette. "You want to spar? Come at me. Give me your best shot."

I started moving before my mind even registered what I was going to do. I had barely made a step, and I knew he was right; I was much too slow. He was so fast that he was barely a blur. Before I knew it, he suddenly had me in a chokehold with one arm twisted behind my back.

"Whoops. You're dead. Which means *I'm* dead." He let me go and kicked me between the shoulder blades, forcing me forward. I whipped around, catching my balance at the last minute.

"Again." He said, standing there with that infuriating smirk on his face. I lunged for him, and he hit me in the stomach this time, hard enough to send me to my knees. I nearly threw up right there and then. Panting on all fours in the grass, I spit up the bile that had begun to gather in the back of my throat.

"This is serious, Kitten." He said as he began to circle me slowly. A great cat, closing in on its prey. "The people you're going to come up against aren't going to care that you're a girl." He didn't wait for me to get up, he kicked me in the side, and I grunted, gritting my teeth. "They will murder you without a second thought. This is not a game." He grabbed me by my hair and dragged me to my feet. I hated him, I hated him, I hated him!

He threw me away from him and beckoned for me to try him again. I clutched my side, trying to discern whether or not he had cracked a rib. I limped forward, pretending I was more hurt than I was. His eyes flashed. I feigned right, then went left, only to earn myself an elbow to the nose. I cried out and hit the ground again, this time on my back. I curled into a ball, cradling my face. I could taste blood.

"Lesson number one, Kitten. Never try to trick a shifter. We can smell a lie a mile away. I knew you were going to go left before you even did." My eyes were slammed shut, but I could hear him pacing around me.

"Except I was able to trick you yesterday." I gritted out, head still between my hands.

"I knew you were up to something. I just didn't know exactly what."

I let the world fall away, and my aura shimmered in my mind's eye. I forgot about the fact that I could feel my pulse in my lip and that my nose might be broken. In this state, I could trace Rycon's movements from where his humid rainforest energy whispered past me. The shimmering trail of power that bound us to each other glinted and whipped between my tiny planets like a muscular tail, and I drew strength from it.

When I felt he was close enough, I struck. I whipped my legs back and blasted myself off the ground to my feet faster than I thought would have been possible. I was setting up a roundhouse when he kicked me hard enough in the chest to wind me. Before I could think, I was on the ground again, gasping for air. Rycon chuckled.

"Lesson number two, don't get up once you've obviously been beaten down; your opponent is less likely to hurt you. That was actually pretty good, though. If you weren't so damn slow, you might have been successful. Who taught you how to do a kick-up?"

I couldn't answer. I was still trying to breathe past the vacuum in my chest. I had no way to tell him I had never done anything like that before in my life and had no clue where it had come from.

Still, on the ground, I closed my eyes again and reached deep down into that part of me that I knew bubbled with power. I felt it seep up from its cold bed in the pit of my chest and flood through my veins. As the darkness rushed through me and I readied myself to attack, I heard a small *'click,'* and something told me to open my eyes. I was staring down the barrel of a handgun that Rycon had pointed directly at my head. The power that had been building dissipated immediately with my shock and terror. I tore my gaze away from the muzzle of the gun and met Rycon's golden stare.

"Now, for the third and final lesson, Kitten." He said, his voice deadly quiet and his stance unearthly still. "Bullets are faster than magick. Don't ever forget that."

31

Rycon uncocked the gun and spun it in his hand like a cowboy from an old western movie. The firearm disappeared under his t-shirt to wherever he had originally pulled it from. I stayed where I was, shaking. I hadn't expected him to have a gun, but honestly, I wasn't surprised.

"You're tough, I'll give you that." He said before offering me a hand up. I eyed it suspiciously, still trying to breathe. He rolled his eyes.

"I think I've made my point, Kitten, I won't hit you again... today." I narrowed my eyes at him but grabbed his hand anyway and let him haul me up.

"How can you 'smell a lie?'" I asked, my voice rough. I coughed with the effort and sprayed blood all over my t-shirt. You could barely see the stain on the black cotton. One of the many upsides to an all-black wardrobe. Rycon shrugged.

"Mortals and daemons, alike, secrete hormones and pheromones. They all have different scents that spike at different times, depending on what the person in question is up to. You grow up smelling a certain scent every time someone lies, you start to put two and two together." I didn't like the sound of that.

"So, have I gotten through to you? From now on, we're going to train, and we're going to do it my way. I'm not going to bother sparring with you until you can at least beat me in a sprint, which is not something that is going to happen overnight." He said. I scowled at him, though I knew he was right.

"And for godssake *eat more*. Carbs, protein, and more carbs for you. You're skin and bones." He shook his head at me as I wiped more blood off my chin with my wrist.

"Rayven?"

I turned, mid-wipe, to see Conrad stroll into the backyard. "Mi rang di doorbell, but nobody answered...wha' gwaan here?"

Rycon watched the Obeah Man approach with his usual air of superiority.

"Hey, Conrad," I said, spitting more blood on the grass. "You're late today." Conrad's eyes widened at the blood that was still leaking from my mouth and nose. I was sure I looked as bad as I felt.

"What di hell did he do to yuh?" Conrad exclaimed and rushed forward, putting himself between us. Rycon rolled his eyes and bent down to pick up his jacket.

"Calm down, Obeah Man, I was just proving a point." He said, digging into his jacket pocket and pulling out a pack of Camels.

"And what exactly was yuh point? That yuh can easily beat up a seventeen-year-old girl? I think yuh already made dat point when yuh abducted and tried to murdah har yestaday!" Conrad snarled. Rycon shrugged before putting a cigarette in his mouth and lighting it.

"Essentially, yes. That was my point," He took a long drag and exhaled the smoke in Conrad's direction. The Obeah Man hissed in rage and with a flick of his wrist, a jet of steaming hot water shot toward Rycon's lit cigarette. Rycon stepped out of the way easily, narrowing his eyes at Conrad.

"Okay, that's enough." I snapped. "I don't have the energy for the two of you to have a pissing contest." Conrad looked at me with a 'he started it,' expression and Rycon just shrugged.

"Rycon's going to teach me how to fight." I had been fighting my whole life, but there was a bit of a difference going up against a bunch of teenagers and a professionally trained shape shifting mercenary.

Conrad snorted, "Do yuh really think dat's what yuh need tuh be focusing on right now? Yuh still need to get a stronger grip over yuh powers. Di closer yuh get tuh turning of age, di more dangerous they're going tuh be."

The truth was I felt quite the opposite. I was drained, and my aura felt dull. A far cry from the rich tabloid of brightly colored planets that normally blinked in and out of my mind's eye.

"It wouldn't hurt to do both," I said. "Not that any of it will matter when Amon comes to take me away."

Conrad frowned. "Mi working on dat last one. Meredith is on har way over here, wi need to talk about our plan and how wi going to get yuh out of yuh life debt. In de meantime, we should really work more on yuh powas than han' to han' combat. Magick will win every time."

"Care to put that little theory to the test?" Rycon asked, his hand drifting towards the spot on his waist where I now knew he had a concealed weapon. Conrad flipped him off. I rolled my eyes.

"I'm going to go take a shower and wash the blood out of my hair," I murmured. "Try not to murder each other." As I walked back to the house, I could hear the distant crash of waves and the cry of gulls that always seemed to emanate from Conrad when he was pissed. I knew Rycon would be sneering at him, daring him to make a move. This was going to be a long day.

32

By the time I got out of the shower and headed back downstairs, the glaring party had moved into my living room and had increased by one. Meredith's tense gaze turned to a smile as I entered the room. Dressed in a long, flowing, earth-green skirt and a billowy white blouse, she glided over to me and hugged me tightly. I felt miserable next to her light flowery energy. She caressed her aura against mine in an attempt to soothe me. However, when she pulled away, she was frowning. She laid the back of her hand on my forehead and clucked her tongue.

"Are you feeling okay?" She asked, "You seem...off." I shrugged.

"I've felt better. I guess that's to be expected. Last night was...stressful." I shot a dark look at Rycon, who was leaning against the far wall with his booted legs crossed in front of him.

"Aw, come on, Kitten, that was just a regular Tuesday night for me." He drawled while managing to look excessively bored with us all. Meredith turned towards him, disapproval radiating from her. He winked at her and blew her a kiss. "I'd love a chance to tie *you* up, sweetheart." He purred.

"Shet up your mouth!" Conrad snarled, leaping from where he had been perched tensely on the couch. I tugged on the line that connected me to Rycon in an attempt to get him to shut up, but the metaphysical effort made my head swim. I stumbled and Meredith caught me.

"Maybe you should sit down." She said kindly, leading me to the couch Conrad had just vacated.

"Are you okay?" He asked, forgetting about Rycon.

"Yeah, I'm fine, just a little bit dizzy." I sunk into the couch heavily and rubbed my temples. When I opened my eyes, both Conrad and Meredith were watching me carefully, worry etched into their faces. Rycon, on the other hand, was watching the magick folk hover over me, his eyes narrowed.

"What's wrong with her?" He asked suspiciously. Both Conrad and Meredith ignored him.

"I'll make you some tea," Meredith said before gliding into the kitchen to put on a pot of hot water.

"Wi need tuh talk 'bout last night," Conrad said, sitting on the couch beside me. "Wi need a game plan."

I shrugged. "I don't see what there is to do. You said yourself that there's no way out of a life debt."

"Not dat wi know of, but Mer and mi reached out tuh di other members of Di Board last night, an' one of di senior representatives mentioned dat he might have a solution."

Rycon scoffed. "That's the most ridiculous thing I've ever heard. There is no *solution,* to a life debt. All you can do is pay it. Sorry to break it to you Kitten, but we're going to the other side of The Veil to fight that prick's war whether we like it or not."

"Yuh cyaan *shut up!?*" Conrad exclaimed. I could tell by Conrad's increasing use of patois he was obviously at his wit's end with Rycon.

However, if I wanted to be perfectly honest with myself, it felt like a good thing to have an opposing opinion around for this conversation. It occurred to me that all the information I had received up to date had come from the magick folk. As good as their intentions were, it was bound to be biased.

"It's okay, Conrad." I said calmly, "Please continue. Who is this senior member?"

"His name is Kieran. He is a very powerful wizard from a very old bloodline." Conrad explained. "He lives in England, but he said he could be in Toronto within the next day or two with some coven members. Maybe with Mr. Abbey, miself, and Meredith, it be enough." The pot started to whistle, and Meredith went to tend to the tea.

"Hold up," Rycon said.

Conrad let out an exasperated groan. "Wha' now?"

"Which bloodline, exactly, is this Kieran from?" I glanced over at the shifter, who seemed more interested than he should have been in the conversation. Conrad hesitated and glanced at Meredith before answering.

"Nightshade," he said, and Rycon's skin rippled with pricks of what looked like hair rubbing at his skin from the inside. Meredith passed a cup of tea over to me. I wrapped my hands around the warm surface and watched Rycon warily over the rim of the mug.

He pushed up from the wall, his feline pupils dilating. "You guys are insane." It came out low and controlled; the animal-like growl that laced his words raised gooseflesh on my arms. It was easy to forget how dangerous he was when he was constantly making fun of everyone around him.

A memory came shooting down the chain that anchored him to me. I reeled back from the freshness of his pain, though I knew what I was seeing had happened long ago.

A tiny house was on fire. Its pastel paint was peeling off the walls under the white flames. I was seeing the memory through Rycon's eyes and I was screaming, the salt from my tears flooding my mouth.

"Mami! Papi!" Rycon cried until his voice broke and he ran for the burning house. A young girl who I immediately knew was his sister, grabbed his chubby infant hand and held him away from the flames. The fire was so hot it burned his face from where he stood on the cobbled street. I heard his thoughts as if they were my own. He would murder the magick folk that were responsible for this. He would kill them for what they had done.

"You can't save them, Rycon." His sister choked past her sobs. "They're gone. They're gone."

I snapped back to the present as Rycon snarled at me. His eyes flashed, and I knew he was horrified that I had seen that memory. I guess I now knew why he hated the magick folk so much. My stomach churned at the violence. It was hard to imagine the scuffed renegade as a chubby toddler screaming for his dead parents, but my heart broke at the thought of it. I saw him register the pity that welled in my eyes and understood his resentment of it. I averted my gaze and pretended I hadn't seen the painful moment from his past.

He flipped us all off.

"You're all godsdamned, batshit crazy. Talking shit about Amon and his cronies and then enabling a psychopath from *Nightshade?*" Rycon shook his head and sneered. I suddenly realized that he seemed like his usual self to Conrad and Meredith. They hadn't seen the memory. I wondered what went on through his head on a day-to-day basis. Was his personality just a defense mechanism? After enough years of therapy and counselors telling me that's why I acted out, I felt disinclined to believe that. But maybe they had been onto something.

"The Nightshade line has been politically neutral for centuries." Conrad argued. I glanced at him, noting that his tone was off. It sounded as if he was trying to convince himself, not just Rycon and I.

"Really?" Rycon asked, taking another step forward. "For centuries? There's never been *one* incident to make you question their position?"

Conrad stood up. "Who is you to chat 'bout positions? Yuh just do whatever the rass yuh want without consideration fah nobody else. Yuh was going to murdah Rayven without a second thought except for how it would benefit *you.*"

"Yeah, and I still would if I thought it would save me from having to deal with you three idiots for the rest of my life. Let me tell you something *Obeah Man,* the only person you should ever look out for is your godsdamned self. Want to know how I learned that? From your piece of shit friends, the *Nightshades.*" Rycon turned to me. "This will endanger us. Stay away from them."

"I'm going to need more information," I said blandly. "Who are the Nightshades?" I ran my hand through my hair, massaging my scalp. My headache eased a bit, and Rycon laughed out loud. It was one of those laughs that you just knew was fake. I crushed my eyes shut.

"Oh-hooooo." Rycon sneered, "So you haven't told her?"

"Told me what?" I snapped with my eyes closed, my fingers pinching into the inner corners of my eyes.

"They haven't told you *why* you're being hunted? You didn't think to ask? You really *are* an idiot."

"Say what you mean, you insensitive asshole." I snapped, finally dropping my hand from my face and forcing myself to focus.

"There's a prophecy about you," Rycon said, and the madness in his eyes caught fire.

33

Conrad and Meredith exchanged a glance again, and I felt a familiar finger of rage catch hold in my own chest.

"What do you mean, there's a prophecy?" I stood up. "Why haven't either of you told me about this?"

"We were waiting for the right time. Things have been happening so fast… we didn't know how to bring it up." Meredith said as she came toward the couch.

'*You know we don't mean you any harm. We're here to help you.*' She whispered into my mind. I shook my head, nausea passing over me again, but I held my ground.

"Tell me the damn prophecy."

Conrad glared at Rycon, who returned the look with a curl of his lip. The shifter gestured to the Obeah Man to proceed.

"Di story says that yuh are di daughter of Di Origin, Aleites."

"Yes, you've told me that before. What does Aleites have to do with the prophecy?" I asked, unsure if I wanted to hear about my supposed daemon underworld father that had left me to fend for myself in the human housing system.

"Tell her." Rycon hissed, and the magick folk once again exchanged a glance. I felt a growl rise up in my chest.

Conrad buried his face in his hands and Meredith reached out to touch me. I ducked away, forcing what little strength I had to intentionally reject her efforts to soothe me. Clair's warning about being careful who I trusted was ringing in my ears. Why were they hiding things from me? I couldn't tell if I was being paranoid or genuinely had reason to be concerned.

"A'right." Conrad said into his hands. "All dis is going tuh do is make yuh hate dis plan."

"If you're hiding a detail from me because it will make me hate this plan then it's a shit plan to begin with. Tell me or neither of you are welcome in my home again." I wasn't sure what rules they had woven into the magickal boundaries around my home, but the wards groaned against that command and both of them looked panicked.

"I am trying to tell yuh, please just let mi talk." Conrad pleaded.

"Hurry up," I grumbled. My faith was unraveling. I wasn't sure if it was Rycon's prejudice that was influencing my feelings toward the magick folk or if it had been Clair's warning that had planted a seed of doubt. Either way, it made me uncomfortable that they kept information from me when they promised me the truth. Conrad pinched the bridge of his nose like Jeremy sometimes did. Remembering the happy-go-lucky Conrad I had met not even a few weeks ago, I wondered dryly if I just had that effect on people.

"First, yuh must undarstan' who Aleites is for this story tuh mek any sense at all. Aleites was di first daemon, hence him title, 'Di Origin.' The story goes that he has walked the Earth since it came into being. His footprints marked the molten crust as our planet crashed through di solar system. He was alone, fah much of di beginning. Though over millennia, creatures began tuh evolve and he came tuh share di Earth with dem in peace.

"Howeva, ovah time, him silent life no longar fulfilled him. Him become lonely and created otha' creatures in him likeness." Conrad had taken on a storyteller's voice, and I was enthralled. Rycon rolled his eyes.

"Don't you think you should let a daemon tell her this part of the story?" He grumbled, "Somehow, I doubt the magick folk will get it right; it's already way different from the version I was told as a cub."

"The whole idea is to keep her out of the hands of the dark ones." Meredith pointed out. "If we have anything to do with it, she will never be around a daemon long enough to hear the story." I frowned at that. An uncomfortable swirl of emotion welled in my chest. Did I truly never want to know my heritage or learn about my kind and where I had come from? I wasn't sure if I cared. It definitely wouldn't help me to achieve my goal of one day leading a normal life. Though at this point, I was so far past normal, my dream felt out of reach.

"Well, can we speed it up then and get to the part about the Nightshades?" Rycon took over the story, brushing an increasingly annoyed Conrad out of the way. "So, long story short, the powerful Aleites founded the Dominion of Sin and populated it with daemons. There's this whole part about daemons trying to co-exist with humans, shifters, and magick folk. Some versions even suggest that Aleites created them as well.

"The daemons were feared, especially by the magick folk. The daemons quickly became concerned that they would need to eradicate the magick folk entirely or live in a state of constant war. So, they cut through The Veil and set up camp on the other side."

"Dat's a pretty important part a di story dat yuh just glaze over-" Conrad tried to interrupt, but Rycon bulldozed on.

"In the early days, Aleites didn't believe in muddying daemon blood with something as weak and pitiful as a human. That changed, however, the day he met Elvira." Rycon explained. Both Conrad and Meredith looked annoyed.

"How did he meet Elvira?" I whispered, and Meredith picked up the story quickly before Rycon could resume.

"The Court of Lust had grown unhappy in their position and wanted more. the queen of The Court of Lust at the time was Anjoilie Nevra. Ash Nevra's mother.

"Being queen of the Court of Lust was not enough for Anjoilie Nevra. She wanted to be queen of the Dominion, she began to attempt to seduce

141

Aleites. She hoped he would mate with her, and she would rule at his side. Aleites had created the Dominion of Sin to alleviate his boredom and loneliness. Consequently, he found Anjoilie's advances amusing in the beginning. He would entertain her in his palace from time to time and enjoy her company when she offered it. However, he never intended to share his throne with her.

"When Anjoilie's games became tiresome, he would often leave the Dominion to wander the human realm in peace." Meredith paused to take a sip of her tea before carrying on.

"Then, one day, while wandering through the pastures of England, he found her, his life mate. She was the daughter of a farmer, working in the fields. She had long dark hair to match his own, black as the raven, and a smile that eased the crushing loneliness he had been plagued with since the beginning of time." That must have been my mother. My mind was spinning. How could that be? If this story was true and this had happened hundreds of years ago, how was I here now, about to turn eighteen? Conrad picked up the story again.

"There are many versions of di story dat retell their courtship, but each version ends di same. Aleites making Elvira his mate and taking har back across The Veil wid him to rule at his side. As yuh can imagine, dis did nuh go over good with Anjoilie."

Meredith interjected, "Of course, Anjoilie was not the only one who was unhappy with the pairing. Many of the other courts believed that a human had no right to rule them, especially when many of them had been denied the taste of the fair species for so long by Aleites himself. The tension was felt even on the other side of The Veil. The magick folk and the shifters all knew a revolt was coming.

"Everyone could see it, except for Aleites, who was blinded by his love for Elvira. Knowing that she was mortal and she would die in a short period of time by a daemon's standards, he impregnated her, hoping for a more permanent piece of her to remain by his side." Meredith met my eyes. "He impregnated her, and you were conceived, Raven."

"So wait, you're trying to tell me that I was conceived three hundred and sixty years ago?" I tried to laugh at the silliness of it, but everyone in the room was dead serious. "Jesus," I whispered.

Rycon snorted. "That guy has nothing to do with it, believe me."

"*Anyweay*," Conrad said loudly, "De news dat dis mortal woman was pregnant with a half-breed infant, who would one day rule de Dominion of Sin, enraged Anjoilie. Dis was unacceptable, and she would nah have it. She alone was not strong enough to stand against Aleites. She would need an army to back har up if she were going to usurp di throne. As unhappy as di rest of di courts were with di arrangement, dey did not feel personally slighted as Anjoilie did, and dey would not join har in her vendetta. Dey feared Aleites enough tuh deny her deir swords.

"Finding no allies in Di Veil, she was forced tuh look elsewhere, and traveled to di mortal world, where she had heard of a powerful line of magick folk, di Nightshades." I was starting to get where the story was headed, and my blood began to run cold.

Conrad continued, "It was a dangerous time for magick folk and shifters alike, all over di globe. Enslaved Obeah practitioners in Jamaica were often blamed for tings like hurricanes and were hanged by slave owners as 'punishment.' Di British at the time worried dat Obeah would be used against dem after slaves were liberated, so dey prohibited it. Di practice of Obeah is still technically banned in Jamaica."

"Things in Europe were not much better." Meredith added. "There were regular witch hunts, especially in Scotland, where women were captured, interrogated in unwinnable trials, and burned at the stake. Men were not safe either, as they could just as easily be accused of being a shapeshifter or werewolf that the devil sent. Usually, the humans never caught a true witch or shifter, and it was their own kind who was burned at the stake, but all the same. Covens and tribes alike were lying low, doing their best to keep attention off of themselves."

Rycon's skin rippled again, and I wondered if the beast that lived within had been awoken at the thought of being hunted. "My sister and I learned about the witch hunts in our lessons as children." He said, his voice a low growl. "Many innocent lives were killed in horrific ways. Shifters were often mistaken for witches, caught and then tortured to death."

Conrad nodded in a rare display of agreement with the shifter. Meredith picked up the narrative, her eyes haunted.

"The Nightshades were even more influential in the magick community in the 1600s than they are today. They resented being hunted and hiding out like animals. So when Anjoilie approached the head of their coven and promised them power beyond their wildest dreams, it was not a hard decision for them to make. They followed Anjoilie across The Veil and into the Dominion of Sin. A rare privilege for any mortal being. It was unheard of for a daemon to allow passage to someone who is 'other.'" She glanced at me with sympathy in her eyes.

"Anjoilie knew that she would not survive her attack against the throne. As she took on Aleites, she knew that he would kill her. She just needed to keep his attention long enough for the coven to work their magick. There is no known way to kill The Origin, so they froze him and his mate in stone, doomed to live for eternity bound and separated. As the curse began to set, and Aleites realized what was truly happening, he created a curse of his own. A curse on the Nightshades and the Court of Lust.

"He vowed that one day, a Nightshade with a pure heart would emancipate themself from the cursed family. By doing so, they would undo the curse on Aleites' mate, and his child would be born from her womb of stone. He cursed Anjoilie's entire line with your existence. Anjoilie was killed by one of Aleites' guards shortly after he turned to stone." I gaped at Meredith, my mouth hanging open.

She pressed on, "With no one to stand in her way, Ash Nevra rose to take her mother's place as head of the Court of Lust, and she assumed control of The Dominion of Sin. As long as you exist, Raven, you are a threat to her. You are the one true heir to the Dominion of Sin. You are The Origin's daughter."

34

I sat in my mother's out-of-date chesterfield and tried to process all this. Nearly eighteen years ago, a member of the Nightshade family had emancipated themselves from the line and triggered my supernatural birth. I was the heir to some daemon throne that I did not want. I was the only thing standing in the way of an evil daemon who wanted to rule over an entire world of godlike beings.

It took several long moments for me to realize that everyone was staring at me, waiting for my reaction. I surprised myself and managed to remain calm. As overwhelming and impossible as this information was, it felt right in some strange way. Somehow, I knew in the depths of my bones that it was all true. Now I just needed to decide what to do next.

Every fight I had ever gotten into happened because someone attacked me first. They would put me down and berate me for no reason other than the fact that they were afraid of me. I hadn't understood why, but I knew now they were picking up on something neither they nor myself could have possibly understood. For the first time in my life, I knew why I was being attacked, and I would be damned if I would stop fighting back now.

I had a family that I had to somehow protect from the mess I had been born into. I wasn't about to let this evil queen ruin my life any more than I was going to let Neil Green humiliate me in front of a room full of my peers. If Ash Nevra wanted to pick a fight with me, I would approach it the same way I always did, head on.

"Alright," I said, my voice calm. "So, with all that being said, please explain to me why we're trusting this Kieran person if he's a Nightshade."

Conrad and Meredith looked relieved at my obvious acceptance of the tale, and Rycon looked relieved.

"Kieran claims that he is the one who emancipated himself from the line," Conrad explained. I mulled over this bit of information.

"Do you believe him?" I asked. Conrad bobbed his head back and forth as if mulling over the question himself.

"Mi nuh know. When someone separates demselves from deir bloodline, it sends a shockwave through di world, and dey normally leave di name behind. Mi remember feeling a surge of power when mi was very young, and yuh're here, so di emancipation definitely happened. However, mi nuh di only one who thinks it is strange dat Kieran has kept di name 'Nightshade' despite his supposed denouncement of di line."

"So he could be lying." It wasn't a question, it was a statement. Conrad nodded.

"Yeah. He could bi lying. However, he claim dat when he stepped away from di coven, he kept di name tuh encourage other Nightshades tuh follow him down di path of di goddess." I remembered Meredith's earlier lesson about how some magick folk believed in a goddess who held them to the rule of three.

Whatever you send out into the universe comes back to you threefold. Maybe this Kieran was getting sick of the bad karma generated by his bloodline and wanted to make amends with this diety.

"Even if he were lying, it would have made more sense for him to change his name to maintain the integrity of the lie." I was thinking out loud. "So, the question is, do we take a chance and trust him? Where does Amon fit into this whole story?" I asked. Meredith took a sip of her tea and sighed.

"Amon is a wild card." She ran one of her silver-ringed fingers around the rim of her cup. "By a daemon's standards, he is a relatively new player in the game. His father was a cruel leader whose loyalty to Ash Nevra was unshakable. A little less than a hundred years ago, his father was blindsided in a small rebellion from one of the other courts, Greed, I think it was. He was killed, and the Court of Pride went to Amon. Amon is now arguably the most powerful daemon to exist next to Ash Nevra."

"So what's his motive then? Is he not loyal to Ash Nevra as well?" I asked, and Meredith shrugged.

"That *is* the question, isn't it? Before his father's death, there was talk that the two of them would be mated, and Amon spent a considerable amount of time in the Court of Lust in earlier years." That did not sound promising. The spot where he had touched me on my chin flared, and my *triquetra* burned in response against my already sensitive skin. I tried to contain my wince so as not to disrupt the flow of information from the magick folk.

Rycon stretched his arms over his head lazily and grinned. "That's the thing about Amon, though; he left the Court of Lust as soon as his father died. I don't blame him. He's strong enough to rival Ash Nevra, he might even be strong enough to take her throne."

"So why doesn't he?" I asked. Rycon shrugged, and Conrad answered.

"Wi nah sure. If he still loyal to har, dat would explain it. Amon's always been a politician. He fill whatever role is needed tuh survive. It could be dat he's after yuh so dat he can hand yuh over tuh Ash Nevra himself, or he could be using yuh as a weapon to usurp di throne."

Meredith picked up, "Ash Nevra's army is ten times the size of Amon's. You most likely are the winning piece. Much like a human mob can take out the strongest of our kind, Amon is concerned about attacking a court with such a powerful army, no matter how strong he is." Meredith explained. She got up from her seat to bring her empty teacup to the sink.

Conrad stood up. His eyes were devoid of the joy that had been there when I had first met him, and my heart broke. The charm on my neck flared again, and another roll of nausea coursed through me.

"Either way, der is nah trusting him. He's done unspeakable tings in di name of Ash Nevra and his father. He's made it painfully clear dat he nuh care who he hurt, as long as he get what he want. In di few times dat he has shown mercy or kindness, it has been done tuh further his own political agenda. Yuh will be no different. Wi must keep yuh safe from him, Rayven. Der have been rumors dat he's entertaining Ash Nevra at his court as wi speak. Wi can'nuh allow him tuh take yuh across The Veil."

As we speak? It was such an obtuse thought to have. It was one thing for everyone to talk about The Veil and the history of creatures. It was a completely different thing to think of a court that was active and functioning as we sat in my living room. Was Amon there now? Was he holding court with Ash Nevra. Were they plotting out all the horrible things they would do to me once he took me across The Veil? This was suddenly getting real and my mind was whirling.

Finally, I nodded. I wanted to put off my acquaintance with Ash Nevra as long as possible.

"Alright, then," I said decidedly. "I see no other option than taking a chance on this Kieran. If he is who he says he is, maybe he'll be able to get me out of my life debt." Rycon rolled his eyes at that. "If not," I continued, shooting a meaningful glance in his direction, "We will deal with him accordingly." Conrad smiled at me.

"Giving orders suits yuh, Rayven." He said. I shrugged.

"Just let me know when he'll be here." I looked at Rycon, my lip still throbbing from when he had elbowed me in the face. Rycon nodded at the determination in my gaze.

We would make sure I was ready.

35

The magick folk left. Conrad made a fuss about how late it was and how Rycon surely had something else to do. The shifter had responded to this with his usual infuriating sneer.

"I'm not going anywhere, Obeah Man. Jealous?" Conrad swore at him in patois before being ushered out by the ever-patient Meredith. When the door closed behind them, I turned to face Rycon.

"You know you can't be here when Clair comes home in…" I checked my phone, "twenty minutes."

"Do you know what you're doing?" He asked softly in a rare display of sincerity. "If Kieran is lying, you're putting yourself in a great deal of danger."

"I would be flattered if I thought your concern for my well-being extended beyond your own self-interest." I snapped. I pushed past him to return to the kitchen, where we had seen the magick folk off at the front door. He grabbed me by the arm and spun me back around to face him.

"You're right. I don't give a shit about you or your perfect little life here with your perfect little family. Sue me for wanting to survive this *mess* that you've trapped me in. But I'm the only person you should trust right now.

Maybe my motives are selfish, but you know that I'm not manipulating you when I say this is a bad idea. You know it is because if you die, I die."

'If someone is touching you and you want them to let go, stare at their hand.' Jeremy had instructed a younger me. I believed it would repel the bullies. It had not. However, it proved especially effective in this case. I stared at his fingers as they gripped my arm. I then raised my gaze to meet his golden eyes. He buckled first. Rycon ripped his hand away.

"What else would you have me do?" I snapped. "You said it yourself that I don't stand a chance. I'm pretty sure you referred to my fighting skills as 'pathetic.' It'll take time to train me. I can barely come against you, let alone the queen of the underworld. We need help."

His skin rippled, and his pupils dilated, which I was starting to recognize as a sign that I had hit a nerve with him.

"This situation is impossible," he growled.

"You need to put your prejudice behind you and try to work with the magick folk if we're going to get out of this."

"My prejudice?" He asked, his voice dangerously soft. "When they kill someone you love, and trust me, they will; I'll ask you to put that aside, and we'll see how easy it is for you."

I opened my mouth to retort, but nothing came out. That chubby, screaming toddler flashed across my mind, and when my eyes refocused, Rycon was gone. The electric blue door to my childhood home was swinging on its hinges. For the first time since I had met the shifter, I felt like I was more heartless than he was.

Clair came home around six thirty and found me on the couch with Amon's book in my lap. It was a sure sign that summer was coming, as the sun had barely started its descent in the sky this late in a Canadian evening. The light had started to turn a soft pink as it filtered through the windows, and it reflected off of the silent tears on my cheeks.

"Oh honey," Clair whispered, the smile falling from her face as she walked into the living room in her scrubs. "What's wrong?" She put her shoes down by the counter and padded over to the couch in her socked feet. Just seeing her made me feel better, and I scrubbed at the tears on my face, embarrassed that she had caught me crying. It was such a mom thing to be able to do. To take the pain away just by being there.

She sat on the couch next to me and pulled me into her arms. She was strong and warm, and she smelled like lavender. How a woman worked a sixteen-hour day and finished smiling while still smelling like a spring flower was beyond me. I curled into her embrace and closed my eyes as she kissed the top of my head.

"Everything's a mess," I whispered. She laughed softly and stroked my hair.

"Well, thank goodness for you, cleaning up messes is my specialty."

"I don't know if you can clean up this one. I think I need to handle this one myself." I murmured. She patted my shoulder and pulled back to really look at me.

"I feared this day would come!" She exclaimed dramatically, laying the hand that wasn't holding me against her forehead in mock drama. "The day you no longer need your mother is one I've been dreading." She smiled at me and used her thumb to wipe the tears from my cheeks. "Why don't we go out to the garden? I have to clear the weeds to make sure the perennials can breathe. Then you can tell me all about your mess that you don't need me to help you with." I nodded into her hand while trying to imagine a way to explain my predicament without sounding like a crazy person.

"Alright," Clair said matter-of-factly. "Let me get changed out of these clothes, and I'll meet you out back."

Fifteen minutes later, we were both in the backyard, kneeling in the dirt. I felt like a child again, helping Clair with the gardening. She had always kissed away the bruises other kids gave me at school. She taught me about plants and different leaf profiles. Like which plants had healing properties and which ones would give me a rash.

Clair knew more about gardening than anyone I had ever met, maybe even more than Meredith. We pulled weeds together in silence. I waited for her to ask me why I had been crying. I waited for her to ask me why there was a hole in the kitchen wall where Rycon had thrown the knife two days ago. I waited and waited, but she never asked. I think she knew I couldn't tell her even if I tried.

Instead, she told me that she was late planting sunflowers this year, and was worried they would strangle the rest of the plants. She told me that Tammy from her work was fighting with her husband. She told me that she had spoken to Jeremy, and yes, I matched the vic's profile, and no, she wouldn't allow anything to happen to me. I didn't have it in my heart to tell her it was too late. Things had already happened to me. Instead, I told her I was fine.

She used her wrist to brush her hair out of her eyes, her floppy gardening glove dropping soil around her face. She met my gaze, and when she spoke next, her tone was serious.

"Raven, you're a fighter. You always have been. Whatever you're going through, just know, I'll always be here to fight with you." Then she threw a huge chunk of dirt at me. I watched as she picked up and ran, and I knew, as I grabbed a huge handful of soil, that if she would fight for me, I would fight for her too.

We had a dirt fight in the backyard before eventually heading inside to collapse on our ugly couches, exhausted.

"What about the sunflowers we were supposed to plant?" I asked, thinking about the little sac of forgotten seeds that sat in the aftermath of our dirt war.

"A couple more days won't do any harm. I'd much rather make us dinner. I'm starving." She said before getting up to make us something to eat.

Jeremy came home much later, scratching his head at the two exhausted, dirt covered women in his life, who had crashed haphazardly on the sofas in the living room. He tucked each of us in with clean blankets and shook his head as he made his way upstairs to shower.

36

Amon stood in the middle of my living room, his face white with fury.

"What do you think you're doing?" He demanded. I was dreaming, I had to be. There was no way Amon could have gotten past the wards, could he?

My aura was sickly. It was nothing more than a bleeding pulse collected around the *triquetra* at my throat. The charm's daemon-repelling blanket had spread like ivy, and I could now see its metaphysical fingers digging into my skin. I moved to touch it, but the charm burned white, and I tore my hand away. *What the-*

"Do you see what you're doing?" Amon snarled. "You're being careless and stubborn. You need to take that thing off before it's too late."

"It protects me from beings like you." I snapped. I suddenly realized that Clair was still asleep on the couch. I inched closer to her, intending to put myself between her and Amon. I wasn't sure if he could hurt her from my dreams.

"You *are* a being like me, Raven." He hissed. His usual amused mask was gone. "On top of that, you have invited the Nightshades? Are you trying to get yourself killed?"

"How do you know that?" I asked suspiciously, my eyes narrowing. He watched me, unnaturally still, as only a daemon could be. I knew that if he had been human, he would have nearly screamed with exasperation.

"If I was not currently hosting Ash Nevra and her...court, I would come to collect you right at this moment and you would thank me." He growled, his lips barely moving.

"Don't act like you're doing me any favors. We all know you just trapped me so you could use me," I snapped back. I knew I was being bold, but this didn't feel real, and I wasn't afraid of him.

"Use you for what?" He asked, his voice velvet and dangerous, "What is my motive? Please, enlighten me." I didn't appreciate being spoken down to, as if I knew nothing.

"If you're not using me to take over the throne, then you're just going to hand me over to Ash Nevra yourself." I retorted. He cocked an eyebrow.

"You have me all figured out, don't you?" He seemed to have caught himself and realized that he had let his mask slip. He schooled his features and slid his hands into his pockets before allowing himself to drift closer to me, that dangerous smile returning to his lips.

"Stay away from me," I seethed, inching closer to my mother's sleeping form. He ignored me and pressed closer, the scent of cinnamon wrapped around me as my aura bucked against the magick of the *triquetra*. It felt as if my power were straining against the stifling energy of the charm, trying to get to him.

"I am not here to attack you," he said, though he continued moving toward me, forcing me to step further back. "You think that charm will protect you from your own kind? It won't. Was I not able to touch you the other night? Just to make a point?"

He had me there. I glanced down at the already healed cut on my arm where he had sliced me to prove that I was now bound to Rycon.

"What do you want from me?" I asked, looking up at him. He was so close I could almost feel his breath on my cheek.

"I want you to stop pretending you are something that you are not," He was almost whispering now.

I could feel it. The press of memories that he was trying to show me. The *triquetra*. It was burning. Somewhere in the darkness, I could hear a baby crying.

> *I will teach you to move planets,*
> *how to reorder the stars,*
> *to become nighttime itself,*
> *how to speak the language of the dead*
> *I will lay your adversaries at your feet.*

37

"Wake up." Someone was shaking me. 'Wake up for fucksakes, wake UP!" Coldness poured over my entire body, and I shot out of bed, drenched. Rycon stood over me in my bedroom, bellowing with laughter, holding an empty glass. I swung at him clumsily, gasping for air. He dodged and continued laughing.

"You should see your face!" He cried, doubling over and holding his stomach as he laughed.

I glowered at him, my hair dripping wet. My rage seething hot. I swear the water he had dumped on me was steaming off of my body. How did I get to bed? I had fallen asleep downstairs. I looked down at myself. Yup, still in my filthy clothes from the dirt fight with Clair. I shook my head. Why could I taste cinnamon? I couldn't remember anything.

"Ok Kitten, get into your sorry excuse for workout clothes. We're going for a run."

I was still sputtering mad. "GET OUT!" I screamed at him and chased him out of my room, slamming the door behind him. I could hear him laughing downstairs as I tried to get my bearings. I sat on the bed, my hands on my knees and my head bowed until I heard the bubble and hiss of the coffee machine, followed by the lilting scent of heaven's nectar brewing.

I felt like something important had happened. I just couldn't remember it. It danced in the periphery of my mind, slightly out of reach. I rolled my head back into my shoulders and inhaled. I would get it back, whatever it was.

I pulled on the same outfit as the day before and headed downstairs. Rycon handed me a coffee, and I eyed him suspiciously.

"You're being...weird," I said skeptically, glancing down at my cup. "Do I need to check this for poison?"

He rolled his eyes. "Don't be lewd. I would just slit your throat if I wanted you dead."

I took a sip and watched him incredulously. We hadn't separated on amazing terms the night before. I didn't want to talk about it, and thankfully he seemed pretty into the idea of burying his feelings about it as well. He shrugged and sipped his own coffee. He was wearing black joggers, running shoes, and a white t-shirt.

"Nice shoes," I said, eyeing the expensive-looking footwear, my own hand-me-down tennis shoes flashing in the back of my mind.

"About that. You can't wear those to run." Rycon said, reading my thoughts. I quickly realized that the uncomfortable thought-sharing went both ways with him now.

"I bought you some new shoes." I choked on my coffee at the sheer unexpectedness of the statement. Was this his weird attempt at an apology?

"Stop. That's...nice...of you."

"Running isn't just pick up and go." He stated, oblivious to the fact that buying me footwear was weirding me out. "People make that mistake all the time. You can't just start running in the spring after doing nothing all winter and be shocked when you suddenly get shin splints. You need to take it slow and wear the proper footwear. I could sprint in combat boots and be fine, but your little human-ass legs will need some proper support. So here."

He passed me a pristine new box. I lifted the lid and gazed upon the pair of brand new running shoes. They were purple, with little green accents, and probably worth more than any item of clothing I had in my closet.

"Did you steal these?" I asked. His sudden generosity still felt questionable.

"No. Do you have any idea how much money a mercenary makes?" He snapped. I guess he had me there.

"Put them on, and let's go. I don't want to hear any complaining."

"Rycon, I'm grateful for this gift, but I promised Jeremy I wouldn't leave the house. I can't go for a run. Can't we just do laps in the backyard?"

The shifter shook his head. "You can't run on spring grass. That shit is so soft you're going to break an ankle. We're going for a run out front. I promise I won't let anyone abduct you. Ask your dad for permission if you need to, I'll wait. But you are running today, with or without his blessing." I thought about it. One lap around the block wouldn't hurt. I would talk to Jeremy about it when he got home. I figured it was better to ask forgiveness than permission.

"What if we get ambushed? Conrad isn't here, I don't have any control..." Rycon pulled out his gun and spun it in the palm of his hand before sliding it back into his waistband.

"What is lesson number three Raven?" He asked, his golden eyes crinkling.

"Bullets are faster than magick," I sighed, and we were off.

I felt like I knew what I was doing when we set off. Cool. Calm. Collected. It didn't feel cool for long. We barely made it to the end of my street before I was gasping for air.

"Don't stop. Push through." Rycon shouted back to me, in an infuriatingly steady voice.

"Can't...I... Can't need...holy...STOP - "I slowed my gait to a stop, resting my hands on my knees and panted. We had barely made it a block. God, I was embarrassed.

"Gods Kitten, you should be embarrassed." He said, echoing my thoughts. Well, that pretty much killed any warm feelings I had towards the new shoes. "Your cardio is shit." He continued.

"No," gasp, "Shit," gasp, "Sherlock."

"Hmm, yes, so witty. The 90's called, and they want your poorly executed joke back. Try and keep up." He took off at a very respectable, very *normal* human pace that I could barely match. By the time we made it around the block and back to my house I was more than winded. I was in pain.

"You're lucky you have a high metabolism. You would be a massive tub of lard otherwise." Rycon commented casually as he rolled into the kitchen to pour some waters. He was right. Where had my inflated ego come from at school? How had I destroyed everyone in Phys ed?

"Probably because you were pissed off," Rycon responded to my unspoken thoughts. He didn't bother taking a sip of his water as he handed me a glass. He wasn't even winded. "It's an adrenaline thing, grandmas have lifted cars to save their grandchildren when under stress. It probably affects you more considering your daemon blood." I nodded as I chugged back the water.

"Anyway, you need to run every day. I could hear your heartbeat as you...ran." He said it as if whatever I was doing couldn't be considered actual running. "Sounded like a wet balloon trying to inflate. Not great." He finished, in his usual cocky way. "Go sit down, the magick folk will be here soon. I told them to bring food."

I frowned. He had talked to Meredith and Conrad? He invited them over? He told them to bring food? What was going on with him? He hadn't been kidding though. I'm not sure why I was shocked that Meredith was a good cook. They had taken my house arrest seriously and brought bacon, eggs, cheese and butter.

"Don't want to use up all of Clair's groceries." Meredith said as she set up camp in the kitchen. I curled awkwardly into the couch, not quite knowing how to respond to this obvious act of kindness. I wished quietly to myself that Clair could have been here. She would have known what to say and would have had everyone laughing. Conrad flopped down on the couch across from me.

"Wi spoke tuh Kieran. He's coming from England. Should be here tomorrow."

I nodded. Rycon stiffened from where he was sprawled a few feet away at the kitchen table, but he said nothing.

"Should we eat outside?" Meredith asked from the kitchen.

"Godsdamnit woman, you're burning the eggs." Rycon snapped and got up from his place at the table to help. I almost laughed. Meredith made eye contact with me and shrugged. Who would have known? Rycon in the kitchen. He took over and shooed Meredith away with a wave of his hand.

Conrad, Meredith and myself piled out into the backyard to set up the seating area for lunch while Rycon flipped eggs in the kitchen. As Conrad and I stuffed cushions into the wireframes of patio furniture, Meredith seemed to stop to gawk at Clair's garden.

"Raven...wow." She gasped, looking over the work Clair and I had done the night before.

"Yeah, Clair loves gardening." I said forcing a cushion into its chair.

Meredith just pursed her lips before turning to pour waters from the plastic jug Clair kept filled with chunks of cucumber for just such an occasion. Rycon came out with a platter stacked with bacon, eggs and toast. We all sat together in the sun.

It was strange, this feeling. To have friends, to be happy. The fist around my heart clenched tightly as if to remind me that it wouldn't last.

38

Rycon had been appeased with my attempt at a workout, so the rest of my day was devoted to the magick folk. They had me perform exercises meant to stretch and use my aura.

"Is like a muscle." Conrad explained. He stood with his feet shoulder width apart, and his knees bent. His arms moved gracefully with his index and ring finger pointed towards the water fountain Jeremy had installed last summer. The water erupted from the stone basin and shoots of crystalline liquid flowed in perfect arcs around me, in tune with his movements. "Yuh has to constantly work at it or yuh will lose it. Mimic mi movements, but pull on di darkness dat makes up yuh aura. Make it follow the water streams."

I closed my eyes and tried to find the edges of my aura as I had a hundred times before. The once dark blanket that had swirled around me was dull, faded. I ordered it to move and follow the easy path of water that streamed around us. Wisps of smoke like energy separated and wobbled in an attempt to obey.

I struggled to dig deeper into that quiet place where I knew my power lay. I lost focus and imagined how Mrs. Serefini would have reacted if she could look out her window into our garden. Then, the memory of her being transported from her home by the paramedics hit me in the chest. My eyes flew open and the small wisps I had managed to conjure died.

I had almost forgotten that I had likely killed that poor woman. The guilt made it impossible for me to continue. Conrad let go of his stance and stood up to his full height, frowning.

"Rayven, yuh need tuh focus." He said, his voice uncharacteristically somber.

"I know. I know, I'm trying. It's just hard." I breathed.

Rycon, who had found a comfy place in the sun on the deck spoke up.

"She doesn't need to focus. You need to piss her off. All her power stems from her rage." Conrad glared at him.

"She needs tuh learn how tuh control her aura without di rage. She can't go through life being angry all the time.

"Why not?" Rycon asked with a smirk, "It's worked for me so far." Conrad shook his head at him, before turning back to me.

"Mi worried about di *triquetra.*" He said, scratching the back of his head. "Ever since wi put it on yuh, yuh've been getting increasingly weaker."

A small memory tickled the back of my mind. As if someone else had warned me about the charm.

"It shouldn't be dis haad fah yuh." Conrad continued, worry furrowing his brow. Meredith, who had been examining Clair's perennials, spoke without looking up from what she had been doing.

"If we remove it, we run the risk of alerting the entire Dominion of Sin of her whereabouts. We don't have the resources yet to protect her if they send an entire army. Her power is a stain, and they will smell it like a shark smells blood in the water."

"I'm not going to lie, it makes me feel like shit wearing it." I admitted, swallowing back against the wave of nausea that had overcome me after trying to do that small metaphysical exercise.

"Let's just wait until Kieran gets here and see what he says. If he thinks his coven will be enough to protect you, we will take it off." Meredith said, finally turning from Clair's plot. I nodded, still not fully convinced. I just couldn't shake the feeling that leaving the charm on might do more harm than good.

"We should go, Conrad." Meredith said, sending him a meaningful look, which usually meant they were communicating telepathically. "Raven needs to rest and we should bring our concerns to my father." Conrad nodded, and turned to me.

"Take it easy for the remainder of di day Rayven. Don't let that eediot make yuh overexert yourself."

"Who me?" Rycon asked innocently from his lawn chair, a small smile on his face. "Would I ever do such a thing?"

"Yes." All three of us quipped in unison.

"Take care Rayven, mi see yuh in di morning." Conrad winked at me. "Big day tomorrow." I tried to swallow back the lump of anxiety that had welled in my throat.

"Yeah. Big day."

The rest of the afternoon passed without any incident. Rycon left around two o'clock claiming that he 'needed a drink.' I expected Clair to come home ready to plant the sunflowers with me, but she was too tired from her shift. Her and I settled down to watch TV together and were asleep again by the time Jeremy made it home. I did not dream.

The day came like a bulldozer, and I woke gasping for air. The familiar fist of anxiety was clenched hard around my chest, and even the sunlight streaming in my window couldn't shake the nervous feeling coursing through my veins.

Was trusting Kieran the right decision? It was certainly better than the alternative. I couldn't sit around and wait for Amon to decide he was ready to abduct me.

Feeling as if I were backed into a corner, I heard the front door open downstairs. Both Conrad and Rycon's voices floated up to meet me as they called each other names like 'String Bean' and 'Sociopath.' One of those was accurate. I thought of Conrad's tall lithe form and bit back a smile. Ok. They were both close.

If I was going to meet this Kieran, I was going to do it in an outfit I felt comfortable in. What was it that Meredith had said the color black represented? Protection? Well, hopefully, she was right. I could use all the protection I could get. I pulled on my favorite black sweater and leggings before heading downstairs.

"Morning," I greeted them dryly, frowning as I made my way to the empty coffee machine.

"Morning Kitten." Rycon drawled. "You making coffee?" I glared at him as I went to grab the coffee grinds out of the freezer.

"I guess someone has too." I grumbled.

Rycon sniggered. "Someone woke up on the wrong side of the bed. Good. Hold onto that rage, you might need it later." I flipped him off and poured water into the back of the machine and turned it on. We really needed to get one with a timer or something.

"Dere's no need tuh be nervous gyal. Wi all going tuh be right dere with yuh."

"So, he's here?" I asked, leaning against the counter.

"Yeah, Kieran arrived early dis morning with a few other coven members, he at di Abbey's as wi speak."

"I'm not supposed to leave the house. I promised Jeremy." I pointed out. Conrad hesitated.

"Yes, mi know. Mi don't feel comfortable allowing dese strangers into the wards wi have set up here. In case tings get bad, mi want tuh be able tuh take yuh back here, where it's safe."

I frowned as I went to pull out three mugs from the cupboard. "How long will we be gone for?"

" 'Bout an hour. We'll have you back before Jeremy even knows yuh gone." Conrad said. Rycon scoffed. I chose to ignore both of them and poured us all some coffee. After a couple of sips, I was feeling more like myself. I looked up at Conrad over my mug.

"Fine." I said. "Let's get this over with."

39

The Abbey house welcomed me as I walked through the front gate. There wasn't really any other way to explain the warm caress against my aura, and the sigh it seemed to emit as I strolled up the walkway to the front door. Meredith's wind chimes prattled on as they always did next to the old worn out bench with the flaking paint.

The magick of the house turned from a soft warm sensation to a prickly uneasy burn as it brushed against me again. I tried to tell myself it was my nerves that made it feel like the house was trying to warn me about something. Conrad came up behind me and gave me one of his lopsided grins.

"Mi be right here with yuh Rayven, di whole time." He wasn't fooling me. His accent always got thicker when he was nervous. Rycon was hanging back, oddly quiet for once.

'I'm going to walk the perimeter.' He said into my mind, and disappeared down the side of the house. His tone had darkened into the mercenary persona I imagined he used when he was... working, for lack of a better word. I had no idea what he was looking for and didn't bother to ask. Maybe

he just needed an extra minute to prepare for this meeting. He had made it very clear how he felt about the Nightshades.

The door opened into the foyer, and I stepped in, kicking off my boots as I always did. To my left, in the sitting area was Meredith, Mr. Abbey and three magick folk I did not know. All five of them stood up as I entered. I could taste my heartbeat.

"Raven," Mr. Abbey greeted me warmly, and came to take my hands in his. "Come in, come in. I would like you to meet Mr. Kieran Nightshade and his associates.

"Hello Raven, it's a pleasure to finally meet you." The wizard who could only be Kieran stepped forward, and my heart stood still.

I'm not sure what I had been expecting, but whatever it had been, this man did not fit the description.

He looked to be in his late sixties and was merely a head taller than I was. His dark blond hair was shot through with silver and he had deep laugh lines that surrounded his kind, grey eyes. He was dressed handsomely, in a modest suit without a tie. Something about him was vaguely familiar. As if I had seen him somewhere before, but I couldn't put my finger on it. He shook my hand warmly and my weak aura prodded at him tentatively. I found no trace of malice, no indication of a threat. Just a warm, dry hand of a middle-aged man who had come to help me. His eyes fell to the *triquetra* and his expression softened.

"That must be making you a wee bit uncomfortable." He said, reaching out to tap it gently with his index finger. His soft English accent turned his words into music, and I jumped as I felt the *triquetra* warmed slightly beneath his touch. It felt as if he had left a tiny spark of magick on the charm. However, my aura was so weak, I couldn't be sure.

"A little bit," I muttered self-consciously, and took a step away.

"Aye. I would imagine so." He turned and gestured to his companions, or 'associates' as Mr. Abbey had called them. "Allow me to introduce to you to my coven members." The two strangers nodded in greeting. One of them was a tall, burly man with short dark hair and black eyes. He had a square jaw and was dressed head to toe in black, much the same way as I was. The other was a woman. She seemed to have been cut from the same cloth as the man, and was dressed in a similar fashion. Her dark hair was drawn back in a low, tight bun to mimic a military haircut, and her jaw was so sharp it looked like it could cut glass.

"This is Marcus and Maria." He introduced us to his coven members. "We have heard that you have been having some trouble with our friends across The Veil?" I nodded slowly, still not quite convinced. If it had just been this unassuming man, I may have been more easily swayed to trust him. However, the unfriendly looking muscle he had brought with him made me weary.

"Why don't we all sit down to have a cuppa? We can chat." He said kindly, winking at me. Meredith stood gracefully, her own eyes never leaving the silent Marcus and the serious Maria. Even Mr. Abbey, who had been smiling pleasantly throughout the encounter, had an underlying air of discomfort where the two dark magick folk were concerned.

"I'll go make us some tea." Meredith murmured, and swept from the room as Rycon finally appeared in the doorway.

What took you so long?' I snapped into his mind as he appeared, and he raised an eyebrow at me.

What Kitten? Did you miss me?' I knew it was silly, but I felt safer with him close to me. I watched carefully as Kieran observed Rycon's smooth and silent entrance into the foyer.

"Ah," The Nightshade purred. "You must be the shifter we have all heard so much about." Rycon's nostrils flared, taking in the man's scent. His eery yellow-slitted eyes dilated, and I knew immediately that he had sensed something he did not like. Rycon didn't answer, he simply watched the wizard as he sat back down in his seat.

Marcus and Maria followed suit. How such a small, pleasant gentlemen had been able to command such obedience from these obviously powerful magick folk was beyond me. Conrad took up his post to my right, and Rycon fell easily into the couch behind us. He sprawled out comfortably, seemingly at ease, however, I could feel his anxiety radiating through the bond.

The connection between our minds was alive and I could smell the smoke of his burning childhood home. I knew in my bones that the Nightshades had been behind it. My skin erupted in gooseflesh and I watched as Kieran's gaze seemed to follow the invisible line that anchored Rycon to me. I glanced at Conrad who tried to hide his discomfort with a smile.

"I would like to start by thanking you all for making the long journey here." Mr. Abbey said politely as he settled into his armchair by the window.

"As you know, Raven has recently been targeted by the Dominion of Sin. What they want with her is unclear at the moment, however, we have reason to believe that Ash Nevra has a contract out on her. Rycon, here, was hired to...take care of her. However, during the attack, Raven seems to have accidently bound herself to him. He cannot hurt her without putting himself at risk."

Kieran nodded understandingly. Meredith entered the room at that moment with several cups of tea on a delicate tray. They floated of their own accord around the room to their respective recipients. I noticed that Marcus and Maria did not take a sip.

Kieran observed Rycon over his cup, his grey eyes crinkling.

"Rycon?" He asked. "Rycon of Olkuyrbe?"

The shifter nodded minutely. I frowned.

"You are the son of Kallio and Rysa, no?" Kieran asked, casually stirring the hot tea in his cup. Rycon stopped breathing next to me. I could feel the rage coursing through his veins as if it were my own. "Terrible, what happened to them." Kieran said softly, never taking his gaze off of the young mercenary. A dark rumble erupted from Rycon's chest. The growl was so deep that the couch shook.

"That is enough." I seethed at Kieran, surprising myself. My own body was tense. Even Conrad looked pissed off at the way Kieran used the names of Rycon's parents to goad him.

"You are here by our invitation," Mr. Abbey spoke up from his place in the armchair, his face grave. "You will treat us with respect or you will be asked to leave."

I drew strength from Rycon's rage and my aura brightened beneath the oppressive spell of the *triquetra*. Kieran's eyes flashed and he smiled.

"You have inherited your father's uncanny ability to command a room." He said to me softly, falling back into his kind facade. I knew he was not talking about Jeremy. "My apologies. I only meant to express my condolences. Please know that I had nothing to do with the attack on the Olkuyrbe leap. That was one of the many reasons I chose to emancipate myself from the Nightshade coven."

I didn't know what a leap was, but I wasn't about to look ignorant in front of this strange man. I assumed it meant pack, or pride. I wondered briefly what type of animal group was referred to as a 'leap,' before my train of thought was interrupted.

'Yeah, right.' Rycon growled into my mind. *'He's lying. I can smell it on him.'* I remembered what he had told me about how it was impossible to lie to a shifter. My body went cold, it had been a bad idea to ask them here.

"I find it interesting that yuh claim to have emancipated yuhself from di Nightshades, yet yuh have not denounced di name." Conrad stated calmly. Kieran shrugged, and Marcus and Maria sat, stony faced as ever.

"Ah yes. Well, the goal was not to abandon such an old and powerful bloodline, but to change our ways." He responded easily. "Once I broke the blood bond, the rest of the coven followed, unhappy with the cruel and corrupt ways of the past. We rebuilt the Nightshades under a new credo. We follow the goddess' rule of three. Whatever we send out into the universe will return to us threefold."

'Liar,' Rycon hissed into my mind. Kieran's eyes darted back to him. I wondered if he could sense our silent exchanges.

"I have heard of you Rycon." He drawled. "From what I know about your ways, I find it hard to believe that you are happy to be bound to Raven. You seem the type to value freedom above all else. Would it make you more comfortable if we could offer you some reprieve from these invisible shackles that bind you to the daughter of The Origin?" He asked, gesturing towards his associates. The air seemed to have been sucked from the room. He had caught Rycon's interest.

"I'm listening." He said. It was the first time he had spoken out loud since he had entered the room.

Before I could say anything, Kieran held out a hand, his thumb, and forefinger about an inch apart. I jumped as I felt him metaphysically grip the bond between us. He slowly brought his fingers closer together, and it felt as if the bond was narrowing. The liquid pass of energy slowed as the edges of the channel closed beneath the Nightshade's grip. I gasped when his fingers finally met.

I couldn't feel Rycon anymore.

40

We had only been bound for a few days, and I had not realized how accustomed I had become to his mind existing within mine. My senses dulled back to a human capacity. I could not smell his rainforest aura anymore and I felt a deep swell of loneliness in my chest. I turned and stared at Rycon, my eyes wide and my heart pounding. I don't know why I expected his reaction to be the same. Why had I assumed he had come to care for me at all, considering he tried to kill me just days before?

Rycon did not seem to be experiencing the same sense of loss that I was. He was staring at me with a sense of awe. A slow, cat-like smile bloomed on his face. Rycon turned his head slowly away from me, and made eye contact with Kieran who had a disturbing smile on his face.

"Thank you." He breathed, flexing his hands before him, as if he could finally truly feel his own body. Kieran's smiled widened.

"Rycon," I said, my voice cracking. He stood up from the couch smoothly, barely glancing in my direction. He looked toward the window as if he was seeing the outside for the first time in years.

"Later Kitten," was all he said, and then he was gone. Everyone was silent. I was shaking. The hole in my chest where Rycon had been was getting larger by the second. My throat was closing and I felt my eyes burn. I would not cry. I would not cry.

"Well, that is one of your problems taken care of," Kieran said jovially, taking a sip from his tea. Mr. Abbey was frowning. He seemed concerned and shaken from the terrible display of power Kieran had just demonstrated. I knew that he himself would not have been able to block the bond between us.

"Now it is simply a matter of taking care of the Dominion of Sin. I have a few tricks up my sleeve for that as well."

My spoon was rattling in my teacup as I quivered. Conrad put his cup down and reached over to take it from me. Meredith's lips were pursed from where she stood silently in the corner of the room. Marcus and Maria looked...pleased. Something was very wrong. I needed to get out of here. Mr. Abbey spoke up.

"Yes. I believe that is an issue that might be addressed another day. We only intended for you to meet Raven today, and you have already done more than we could have expected." I had barely been there an hour, and I was already thoroughly terrified, and the Nightshades knew it.

All I could think about was that before they had blocked the bond, Rycon had told me that every word out of Kieran's mouth had been a lie. They were not here to help me. We all knew it. And I wasn't even sure that Mr. Abbey himself would be enough to protect me from this man.

'Conrad.' I whispered into his mind. 'Get me out of here.' Conrad showed no outward sign that I had spoken to him. He smiled at the Nightshades in his easy laid back way.

"Rayven's parents have asked her not tuh leave the house, and wi on borrowed time here. Mi promised mi would get her back home before her parents returned from work. Mi going to take her home, but wi should make plans to meet tomorrow and discuss how wi might protect Rayven from di Court of Lust and di Court of Pride." He stood, pulling me up with him.

"Of course." Kieran said, putting down his own cup. He stood with us and reached forward to shake Conrad's hand.

"Perhaps you, your associates and I can put together a plan today that we can present to Raven at a later date." Mr. Abbey said as he stood with us. I knew this was a tactic to ensure that the Nightshades did not follow Conrad and I home.

"That sounds like a wonderful plan." Kieran responded easily. He turned to me and held out his hand for me to shake. "It was a pleasure to meet you, Raven." I stared at his hand doubtfully. I did not want to touch this man ever again. Mr. Abbey saved me by intercepting.

"Have you seen our garden? Meredith is quite talented. Come, I will show you." Kieran's eyes flashed at the clear interruption, however he nodded and smiled graciously.

"I would love to see it. Come Marcus, Maria let's go outside." The three of them followed Mr. Abbey out. Meredith looked at Conrad and me.

"Do not let her out of your sight." She said quietly, before turning and following the Nightshades into the backyard.

Conrad grabbed my hand and hurried me out the front door. Rycon was nowhere to be found as we rushed to the Hornet. He was muttering spells in patwa the whole way down the front path. Enchantments that I assumed were meant to keep the Nightshades from tracing our journey home. He tucked me into the passenger seat before hopping behind the wheel and firing up the engine. My shaking had gotten worse. My teeth were chattering and I was colder than I had ever been.

"Bad idea dat to bring dem here," Conrad said.

"Before they did...whatever it is they did to our bond, Rycon told me they were lying. He hasn't emancipated himself, and he definitely had something to do with the death of Rycon's parents."

"Mi know," Conrad said. He shifted into first and shot off down the street. He made sure all of the lights were green on the way home.

"Conrad. I'm scared." I whispered as the car weaved easily in and out of traffic.

"Mi know," Conrad repeated, his eyes on the road. He was gripping the wheel so hard that his knuckles popped.

"What are we going to do?" I asked, still shaking violently. The hole in my chest where Rycon had been, was like a knife in my heart.

"Add more wards to yuh house. Mi a stay overnight. I'll style-up miself so Clair and Jeremy nuh worry. Wi should think about relocating yuh. Mi nah going tuh lie Rayven, mi worried dey will still find you."

"Me too," I said.

He pulled up in front of my little townhouse and ushered me through the electric blue door. He settled me in by the front window with a cup of tea and a blanket in an attempt to warm me up. He muttered spells and wards over me as I sat, wrapping me up in protective magick. When he was done draping me in spells, he headed outside and I watched him through the window as he weaved even stronger wards around the house.

Several moments later he returned, settling down next to me. I had calmed down a bit. The warm magick he had cast around me helped to still my pounding heart.

"Mi sent word to gran. Wi may need more backup. Mi neva seen somebody block a bond like dat before, so easy. Kieran is powerful, man."

"But I thought you said your grandmother shouldn't travel?" I whispered.

"Shi might have to. We can't face dis alone. Dis is escalating more quickly dan anyone expect'." He looked at me, his eyes sad. I bit my tongue. Rycon had warned me. He had told me this was a bad idea. I had a nagging feeling that someone else had to, but every time I tried to examine that memory closer, it slipped away.

"Mi so sorry Rayven. Mi should have known better. Dis is all my fault." He looked so defeated next to me. I put my hand on his.

"You didn't know. None of us did. Not for sure at least. All we can do now is stick together." He nodded and turned to look out the window.

"Wi in fah a long night." He said. I nodded.

Jeremy and Clair both came home around the same time, which was a rare occurrence. Conrad had shrouded himself in a no-see-me glamour, and as we ate dinner he sat in the living room keeping watch.

"Are you ok Raven?" Jeremy asked in between bites. "You're quiet today."

I nodded. "Yeah dad, I'm fine. Just a bit tired."

Clair was frowning at me. Her grey eyes filled with concern. "Why don't you go lie down honey, if you're not feeling well?" She asked softly, reaching out to touch my hand.

I smiled at her weakly. "Ok I will. Are you guys sure you don't need help cleaning up?"

"No, that's fine, Raven. We've got it." Clair said.

Jeremy nodded. "Go rest. I'm heading back out to the precinct after dinner, and I won't be back here until the morning. I'll make you breakfast."

"Ok." I conceded, standing up. Conrad got up from the couch, still hiding under his glamour. To my surprise, Clair glanced in his direction as he moved. I frowned. Could she see him? She shook her head slightly, and seemed to discredit whatever it was she had thought she'd seen.

"Have a good sleep. Let me know if you need anything." She said, standing to kiss me on the forehead.

"Thanks mom." I said softly before heading upstairs. I could feel her gaze on me as Conrad and I slipped away to my room.

As scared as I was for myself, I was even more worried for Clair and Jeremy. This was their home. If anything were to happen to them, I would never forgive myself.

Conrad waited politely outside my door as I changed. Once I was tucked into bed and ready for sleep, he settled in for a long night in my computer chair.

"Sleep good Rayven. Mi keep watch." He whispered a few words in patois, and my eyes suddenly felt too heavy to keep open. Almost immediately, I fell into a dreamless sleep, and I was grateful for the empty void that swallowed me whole.

41

The entire house shook. There was a groan and a snap. Conrad was shaking me violently.

"Rayven! Wake up!" He hissed. I was groggy and tired. What was happening? All of my furniture was rattling; books fell off my shelves and the tiny trinkets I kept on my desk crashed to the floor, shattering.

"What's going on?" I screamed as pictures fell off my walls.

"Dey found us," Conrad said urgently. "Quick, get dressed. Wi have tuh go," I held my hand to my head, swinging my feet off the bed. Conrad stood facing the door, ready for whatever would come.

The very walls of the house groaned around me as the wards bent and buckled under some unseen pressure. I had just managed to stand up from the bed as the door to my room exploded inwards. Maria stood in the frame, dark, serious, and terrible.

"Move, Obeah Man." She said, her tone was even and dry. I realized I had never heard her speak before, and I stood frozen.

Conrad raised his arms and the glass from the broken picture frames rose from the ground and hovered around us.

"Nah today," He snarled, and the glass shot toward the intruder. She waved a hand nonchalantly, and the glass turned to sand before my eyes. The house shook again. Maria held out a hand, and Conrad went stiff, his hands shot to his neck as if she had an invisible noose around his throat. She rose her hand and Conrad rose into the air with it, his eyes wide, and his feet kicking helplessly in the air. I watched in terror as he choked. Maria smiled as he struggled to breathe.

"Stop it!" I screamed. "Let him go!" I reached for my aura. It was so weak I could barely feel the burning of my tiny stars. I went to rip the *triquetra* from my throat, but it flashed and burned my fingers. I cried out in pain. My heart sank as I realized I couldn't get it off.

"Stop it! You're hurting him!" I screamed. Conrad's face had gone slack, and his eyes were rolling back into his head. He was going to die if she didn't let him go. Maria was laughing, she began to close her fingers into a fist and Conrad jerked under the pressure.

I didn't know what to do, I looked around the room desperately for a weapon, when suddenly Clair appeared behind the witch. Her hair was tousled from sleep and she was wielding a heavy wooden candlestick.

"Get the hell out of my house," Clair snapped, her voice unfamiliar and cold. She swung the candlestick back with both hands and smashed it into the witch's skull before Maria could react. I watched the dark witch crumble instantly to the ground, Conrad falling with her.

I ran to Conrad's side, sobbing. He was coughing violently, holding his throat. Clair stepped over Maria's prone form and joined me on the floor.

"Mom!" I cried. "We have to get out of here. I can't explain, but we have to go right now." Conrad was nodding with me, struggling to get up, unable to catch his breath. Clair held her hand over Conrad's throat and a soft blue light started emanating from her fingers. Conrad's breathing normalized immediately, his eyes nearly as wide as mine.

"There," She said, rubbing Conrad's back as he sat up. "That's better." He dropped his hands from his throat, staring at her, his usual lopsided grin spread across his face.

"Mi did know, man." He said, smiling at Clair. I was staring at both of them, shocked.

"I had a pretty good idea about you as well," Clair said kindly. "I was suspicious when Raven started wearing the *triquetra,* and I thought I felt new wards around the house when you started coming around. I wasn't sure until I caught you glamoured in the living room."

"What is going on? Mom, *you're a witch?!*" I gaped. Clair nodded.

"I used to be honey. It's complicated, and something tells me I don't have much time to explain."

"No. Yuh don't." Conrad said, getting to his feet. "Wi need to get Rayven out of here. Now." Clair looked at me sadly.

"I knew when I adopted you, this day would come." She said, reaching out to stroke my hair. She turned to Conrad as the house shook again. I could suddenly hear Meredith's voice outside shouting spells and what could only be a magickal duel taking place. Conrad looked relieved at the sound of her voice.

"Di wards were set tuh alert Walter Abbey and Meredith if wi were attacked. Dey should bi able tuh distract Kieran and Marcus long enough fah us tuh escape." He explained urgently. Clair's eyes widened.

"Kieran is here?" She gasped. I don't know why, at this point, that anything could still surprise me.

"You know who Kieran is?" I asked.

"Everyone knows who Kieran is," Clair said angrily, the way she said it, made my blood turn cold.

42

Clair looked invincible standing there in the doorway. Her lilac nightgown falling past her knees, the now bloody candlestick held loosely in her hand.

The wards to the house absorbed another blast and I cried out, ducking my head under my hands as more books spilled out of their shelves. She spun around to Conrad.

"We don't have much time," she said. "You're going to need all the help you can get to make it out of here." Conrad nodded earnestly. "Do you know the unbinding charm?" She asked him, her voice steady.

"Mi granny taught it to mi years ago. Mi think mi still remember it."

"I bound myself long ago, after I met Jeremy, and before I adopted Raven. I can still do small magicks, but I don't have enough access to my powers now to help you. You will have to unbind me quickly. I cannot cast it onto myself." Conrad set his jaw and stepped forward.

"Dis is going tuh hurt," he said darkly. Clair met his eyes without flinching.

"I know," she responded. "Raven. Stand back." I stood frozen.

"Mom, we don't have time for this. They're coming."

"I said stand back, Raven." This was not the Clair I knew. This powerful woman was not the soft-spoken, kind mother that had raised me. But to the core of my soul, I knew she would defend me to the end. I dipped my head in consent and stepped back.

Conrad laid his hands on either side of my mother's face. They both closed their eyes simultaneously, and my aura almost immediately reacted to the power that stirred in my bedroom. It started off gently. The air around them began to swirl. Where Conrad's palms touched Clair's cheeks, a white light began to grow.

"Mi hands belong tuh di goddess an wid dem hands yah, mi bring har pickney back tuh har."

The power built around them, the white light growing brighter and brighter. Clair began to scream as the magick entered her. Her body seized and I cried out. I took a step forward but a blast of energy threw me back into my desk, the corner hitting me in the back, hard. As the magick built, my own aura responded to it, reaching forward. I heard the words spoken back to me in English.

'My hands belong to the goddess, and with these hands, I bring her child back to her.' Conrad continued the spell, his voice rising to be heard above the whirlwind that was tearing my already destroyed bedroom apart.

"Wid di powah a di Maidin, di Madda an' di Crone, mi bring di dawta back a yawd."

My aura spread before me, the universe of my soul binding with the magick, allowing me to understand the words.

'With the power given to me by The Maiden, The Mother and The Crone, I bring this Daughter of the Moon home.'

And then I could see them. The Maiden appeared, her gown of white and gold flowing around her perfectly sculpted body. Her face was so beautiful it drew a tear to my eye. She walked towards Conrad, her transparent body layering itself over his. She rested her hands on Clair's face.

"I bring to you, Daughter of the Moon, the gift of strength, energy, and the uncorrupt nature of magicks."

Next came The Mother. Her belly was swollen with new life, her breasts supple and her face kind.

"I bring to you, Daughter of the Moon, the responsibility of motherhood and the ouroboros of love that accompanies it." She layered herself over Conrad and The Maiden, joining her hands with theirs on the side of Clair's face.

The swirling power expanded around us, and we existed in the center of the magickal storm. Tiny orbs of glowing light floated in and out of my aura's stars and planets. I could feel the earth as it spun on its axis. Clair's screams had died and her eyes had opened.

She stared through the ceiling, and suddenly I could see the night sky above us. It was so beautiful. Tears streamed down Clair's face and she held her arms out at her side, her nightgown whipping in the magick surrounding her. With her arms spread wide and her face tilted towards the heavens, she accepted The Crone as she appeared. The old woman came to us in a simple tunic. She was hunched over a twisted wooden cane, her arthritic hands were bent and hobbled with time. Deep lines that carved the contour of her archaic face were lit with burning internal light, and her milky white eyes settled on my mother.

"Daughter of the Moon." She said in her ancient voice, "You ask us to unbind you. All great magicks come at a price. Do you accept the conditions of these gifts?" I was filled with a sense of dread. What price? Clair smiled and beckoned to The Crone to come to her.

"I accept." She whispered. The Crone nodded solemnly.

"Then it is done." She floated towards Conrad, who stood beneath the ghosts of the Maiden and the Mother. She then laid her swollen hands on the side of Clair's face, and the twist and whorl of the energy reached a climax. Clair, Conrad, and I cried out as the power beat down upon us. I slammed my eyes shut as the world shattered. The three apparitions dissipated, and my bedroom darkened to its natural state.

Then... it was quiet.

I opened my eyes, to see Clair standing before me serenely. There was glow to her, that seemed to come from the inside. Clair smiled at me calmly and held out her hand.

"Let's go." She said. And we followed her out of my bedroom.

43

My house seemed foreign somehow, as if this was not the home I grew up in. Physically, it was the same, but the safety that I normally associated with the cream-colored walls and the carpeted staircase was replaced with a building sense of anxiety and dread.

Even my mother, who had always been a calm and serene source of comfort, was different. Though she was no less comforting. The woman who had come home in her scrubs, frazzled and smiling, now led us down the stairs, her feet sliding over the carpet soundlessly. Her shoulders were back and she was humming with an unearthly power that made even Conrad's oceanic aura seem like a trickling stream.

The nighttime separated before her as if it were the red sea. She was a beacon of strength, the leader of our sorry little party.

"We need to get them off of the property before Jeremy comes home." She said without turning around to make sure that we were still following her into the foyer.

The very fabric that built up the matter around her shuddered. "If they hurt him, there will be no survivors." Her voice was echoed by the Maiden, the Mother and the Crone. She stopped at the front door, and finally turned to face us. I trembled a little at her transformed face. She was both younger and older, kinder and stronger. Her silver eyes had bled to white.

"Stay close to me." She instructed us. Then she opened the door.

I couldn't believe any of the neighbors hadn't come out to see what was going on. Meredith was standing in a loose fighting stance before a figure that could only be Marcus. They were positioned in the middle of the street and the street lights were glaring down on them. The wards Mr. Abbey and Conrad had placed over the house glowed with a deep ultraviolet light as wayward spells struck them.

Watching Meredith duel was like watching a cross between a ballet dancer and a martial arts specialist. The trees that lined the street lent her their leaves, which turned razor sharp under her fluid movements and rained down on the dark mage like gunfire. Marcus, however, was no novice. The leaves turned to ash as a stream of fire jetted out from his palms.

His movements were much more abrupt than Meredith's, though they were no less deliberate. His actions were blunt and backed with power, while Meredith's were smooth, languid and accented with finesse.

He began to move forward, his stream of flame scorching the street. Meredith threw up a barrier, but the flames beat down, and her brow began to glisten with sweat.

"She's losing," Conrad breathed behind me. If he was trying to hide the concern he felt for his sister, he wasn't successful. Clair stood very still, watching the duel unfold. Both of the battling magick folk seemed oblivious to the fact that we had left the house.

"Yes. Go help her. I will get Raven out of here." Clair said finally. Conrad looked hesitant to leave us unprotected until Clair turned those glowing white eyes on him, backed by the force of the goddess. "Go." She said, that strange echo to her voice resurfacing. Conrad hovered for one more heartbeat before nodding curtly, and taking off in a brisk jog to join his sister in the street.

He couldn't have arrived at a better time, just as he approached, Marcus sent a rapid volley of fire streams toward Meredith, too fast for her to evade effectively. I watched in horror as she tripped. Time seemed to slow as a well placed stream of fire made its way across the street directly toward her.

"*Mer!*" Conrad bellowed, and he raised both of his hands. The grass from the lawns around us wilted as Conrad called all of the water from every plant within a hundred-foot radius within seconds. The trees that lined the street shriveled, their trunks empty husks. The green spring grass was leeched to brittle yellow straw. Conrad used the water to form a wall directly in front of Meredith, effectively blocking Marcus' fire blast.

Marcus turned to face Conrad, fire coating each of his hands. The water Conrad had called to him slid away from Meredith in a glistening stream and twisted around the Obeah Man like a great sea snake.

"Yuh wi nuh touch mi sista again." Conrad's voice was low, deadly. I almost couldn't hear him from where I stood. "Mi fi drown yuh where yuh stand." A shiver ran down my spine. Conrad, my friend, who was always in a good mood, always so positive, had just threatened to drown this man on dry land, and he had *meant it.*

I knew Conrad had magick, I had seen him use it in small amounts while we were training. But I had not been prepared for the cool, calculated, absolute control he had over the water he commanded. The now-dead lawns and brittle trees were the unfortunate casualties of Conrad's ruthless desire to protect those he cared for. All magick came at a price.

Marcus didn't speak. He responded by sending a searing burst of flame directly at Conrad. I cried out in alarm, but my friend barely flinched. With a minute flick of his wrist, the stream of water that had been flowing around him in a defensive ring shot out with crystalline accuracy. It slipped down the center of the fire blast, following it all the way to the mage who had cast it. The water sizzled and turned to hot steam as it broke apart the torrent of fire. Conrad's magic sucked it right back out of the air, to further power his watery attack.

Marcus was thrown several feet away as the water blasted him squarely in the chest. The force of the water felt as if it were strong enough to cut through stone, and I doubted the mage would recover from the hit.

Clair and I held our breath. The fire mage didn't move from where he had fallen, and Conrad didn't waste any time before running to Meredith's side. Clair turned to me, she laid a glowing hand on my face and I trembled.

"Mom, I'm scared." I whispered. Her expression swelled with a mix of sorrow and anger. I knew the anger was not for me, but for the people who had frightened me.

"I know darling. Let's get out of here." The way she spoke was so like the Clair I had always known. It didn't seem to fit in this new powerful body that she now seemed to inhabit.

"We can't leave them," I whispered, staring at Marcus' limp form. I swear I saw him twitch. Was he still alive?

"We must. They are risking their lives so we can get you to safety, if we stay it will be for nothing."

I frowned but knew she was right. This was all happening because of *me*. I was putting everyone in danger. Finally, I nodded.

"We are going to have to move very quickly. Try your best to keep up, but let me know if I'm moving too fast." I dipped my head in understanding.

"Ok. Let's go." She said, and I followed her down the street as we ran for our lives.

44

My mind kept going to absurd, desperate ways to solve the problem in front of us. All of the emergency reactions that had been drilled into my head since I was a child kept leaping to the front of my mind, only to be immediately shot down by the reality of the situation.

The reality was we were on our own. There was no one to save us. We could only save ourselves. I was in the cotton shorts and beer-branded t-shirt I normally slept in. I had been too dazed to heed Conrad's warning to change when I had woken up. Unlike Clair, I hadn't even had the foresight to put on shoes, and my bare feet slapped on the sidewalk as we ran.

Unlike the time I had forced myself to run with Rycon, I seemed to be tireless. I didn't feel the tiny stones that bit into the soles of my feet. Adrenaline was keeping me going, and I felt like I would never stop.

We turned onto Cornwall and were sprinting full force towards River Street. Clair spoke into my mind, not bothering to waste breath calling out to me.

'I know a safe place we can go until we can figure out what our next move is. We're almost there.' I nearly sobbed with relief. We were going to be ok. We were going somewhere safe. We were going to make it.

We peeled across Cornwall and even this late, there were taxis ready to honk at our reckless jaywalk. We hit the other side of the street and all but skidded into Oak Street Park. The slight patch of grass that it was, seemed like a tiny sanctuary and I felt myself relax as my toes touched the springy sod.

Then, up ahead, what looked like a swarm of bees began to crowd into a dark shape. Under one of the glowing, golden lanterns, one by one, the dark specs joined together to build the outline of a man. The way he was standing as he fully materialized with his back to us, reminded me of Amon. Was it Amon?

Clair ground to a halt in front of me, throwing her hand out to catch me in the chest as I almost stumbled past her.

"Don't move." She hissed, her voice catching in what could only be fear. The dark shadow of the man slowly turned to face us, before stepping into the light. It wasn't Amon.

"Hello, Clair." Kieran said, his voice coated in familiarity. I froze. My blood turned to ice in my veins as I looked into the face of my waking nightmare.

"Out for a stroll?"

To anyone else, it would have seemed as if Clair was smiling, but to me, it was more of a baring of teeth.

"Kieran." She said, her voice lower than I'd ever heard it.

"Kieran?" He asked, mock surprise in his voice. He took a casual step towards us. He was still wearing his modest suit. His hands were in his pockets, as if he were indeed 'out for a stroll.' The sickly rumble of his aura told me otherwise. The aura that he had hidden from me in Mr. Abbey's house. He wasn't hiding anymore.

His kind face was sharper somehow, his grey eyes flashed in the dimly lit park. "Is that anyway to greet your father?"

I turned to Clair, my eyes so wide I felt as if they might fall right out of my head. That was why he had seemed so familiar. His kind grey eyes, his dark blond hair...

"Mom..." I started, but she held a hand up, silencing whatever else I had to say.

'Do not say anything in front of him. You will only give him ammunition.' She warned in my mind, and I hoped that Kieran couldn't hear.

"Tsk, Tsk, Tsk, Clair. I expected more of you. Out here in the middle of the night, running around with this... *half-breed.*" He nearly spit out the last word, as if it were a malediction.

"I pray to the goddess that you don't sit up at night wondering why I emancipated myself from you, when you continue to conduct yourself as such a close-minded bigot!*" Clair snapped. Her voice shook, but the hand that she still held up, guarding me from him, never wavered. My mind was reeling. Emancipated? Slowly, the realization dawned on me. Clair was the Nightshade whose emancipation triggered my supernatural birth. How was it that she had come to adopt me? I was dizzy. This was too much.

Kieran was unhurried as he walked toward us, almost as if he were savoring every moment.

"You had so much potential, Clair. I had planned to groom you for leadership. You could have been my successor." He took another easy step forward, his hands still in his pockets, a sickly grin on his wicked face.

The power that reverberated through Clair made me catch my breath. The light that emanated from her, beat back the thick, suffocating energy that pulsed toward us as Kieran advanced.

"I never wanted it. I never wanted anything that you had planned for me, father.*" She said 'father' with the same disdain that he had said 'half-breed', as if it were a disgusting word. As if it was revolting for her to apply that term to the likes of him.

"You ruined my childhood, and you took my adolescence from me. I will not let you do the same to my family.*" She snarled. There was no other word for it. The raw pain in her voice and the ferocious desire to protect the ones she loved made my throat tighten. Kieran just smiled, now only a few paces away.

"We'll see about that," He sneered, and without any other warning, he fired a bolt of lighting at us. I screamed and ducked; but Clair reacted instantly, her right foot fell back behind her and her left leg bent. she held both hands forward and absorbed the bolt without flinching. Electricity jumped around her, sizzling the grass and singeing both of our hair.

"You're going to have to do better than that." She said dryly, standing back up, blue lightning still crackling across her skin. Kieran laughed.

"Oh, how I've missed that spirit!" He quipped and I felt his aura build.

'Run Raven. Run now.' Clair hissed into my mind. *'I'll hold him off.'*

'I won't leave you.' I said back, even my mental voice was breaking with emotion. *'I don't even know where to go.'* Her glowing white eyes broke away from Kieran to glance at me for a split second, before returning to the man attacking us.

'Yes, you do Raven. Follow your instincts. You'll know what to do.' She whispered back. The dark beat of Kieran's magick was growing and he began to laugh. He spread his arms wide as the power grew.

"Are you ready for this one, my little protégé?" He called out, his English accent drowning in his madness.

'This is not the time to be cryptic mom!' I was crying now, real tears streaming down my face.

'There's no time Raven. Go. Now!' She twisted the wrist of the hand that had been held out to protect me moments before, and a gentle gush of power pushed me several feet away from her. *'I will find you Raven. Anywhere is safer than here right now.'*

After one more moment of hesitation, I did as she asked. I turned back the way we came and cringed as the first of the spells were unleashed behind me. Everyone I trusted to protect me was risking their lives while I ran away. I've never hated myself more.

45

I was sprinting down the street, barefoot and lost in my own city. I didn't know where I was or where I was going. My mom had told me I would know what to do, but I didn't. I was lost just a few blocks from my own home. I knew these streets like the back of my hand but I couldn't tell left from right. I was nearly hysterical.

As I ran deeper into the city, I passed late-night pedestrians on the sidewalk. I couldn't ask anyone for help. I was sure I looked insane in my pajamas, running shoeless down the sidewalk. I finally ducked into an alley between a bar and a convenience store. My breathing was ragged from both the anxiety and the running. The adrenaline was wearing off and the sheer panic was kicking in.

I couldn't get a grip on myself. I was spiraling out of control. I sunk down against the greasy alley wall, squatting on the heels of my feet. I put my head in between my knees and let out an exasperated scream. The patrons of the pub smoking outside shuffled to the other side of the pub front, away from the crazy person losing her mind in the alleyway.

I had to think. *Think Raven.* Clair had told me I would know what to do, but I could barely reach my aura. The *triquetra* had somehow become even more suffocating since I had met Kieran. I tried to touch it again, to pull it off my neck but hissed as it immediately flared and burned my fingers. I wondered vaguely if Kieran had done anything to it in Mr. Abbey's house.

Where *was* Mr. Abbey? Could I call him? I didn't have my cell phone. The idea of me walking into the pub behind me and asking to use the phone was laughable. They would call the police immediately, especially the way I was dressed. I ran my hands over my face and my fingers brushed the cold spot on my chin where Amon had touched me in the library.

Amon. Should I call him? Would it make things worse? The thought of Amon right now did not terrify me the way meeting Kieran had. I had to trust my gut, I literally didn't have any other options at this point. Clair had told me I would know what to do. This felt like the right thing to do.

I reached a shaking hand to my chin and hesitated for just a moment before committing to pressing my finger against it. After a deep breath, I built my resolve. I was going to do it. I was going to call him. My fingertip brushed the cold point on my chin again and I focused.

'Amon. Amon, help me.' I breathed. There was nothing. Come on. I tried again.

'Amon, can you hear me?' Then there was a flicker.

'That charm is blocking me, I can't see you. Where are you?' His voice was very faint, barely a whisper. So quiet, I could have convinced myself I imagined it. I exhaled a sigh of relief, before I realized I had no idea where I was. I braced my hands against the sticky alley wall to help myself up.

I would run out to the street signs and tell him where I was and he would come get me, he wouldn't want me to die. I owed him a life debt, he would want to cash that in. Hope built in my chest again as I staggered to my feet. I rubbed my dirty hands against my thighs in frustration. I would get out of this.

I had taken my first step towards the street when I heard a dangerously familiar voice behind me.

"Hello, Kitten." Rycon said, as he dropped from the pub's fire escape. "You're a long way from home." He stood before me in his usual uniform.

Jeans worn through at the knees, motorcycle boots with a white t-shirt. His short leather jacket hung off of his lithe frame as if he had been born in it. I choked at the sight of him.

"Rycon," I gasped, relief flooding into my chest. He had come back. I wasn't alone. "We have to go. I'm going to call Amon, I think it's the only thing to do. You were right. These people are dangerous. My mom was the Nightshade that had emancipated herself. She's fighting with Kieran right now. It isn't safe." I stumbled towards the street and suddenly he was in front of me, blocking my way.

"Rycon? Didn't you hear me? We have to go. Do you know what street this is?" I asked, peering over his shoulder, trying to catch a glimpse of the intersection. He touched my shoulders almost gingerly, and finally, I stopped and looked at him. Really looked at him.

His expression was grave. His usual 'go fuck yourself' attitude was nowhere in sight. I searched his face, my eyes darting back and forth. I couldn't reach him through the pinch Kieran had placed on our bond.

"Rycon?" My voice was quiet now, barely a whisper. Realization was beginning to dawn on me, I just didn't want to believe it. His hands were still on my arms, and his strange yellow eyes fell down to his fingers as he played with the low-hanging sleeves of my t-shirt. I began to push away from him as I realized what was happening, and his grip tightened, holding me in place.

He pulled his unearthly eyes away from my shirt sleeves as if escaping some sort of dream, and met my gaze head on.

"I'm sorry, Kitten," he said softly. I think on some level he was.

"Not sorry enough," I breathed back, understanding now that the chase was over, and I had lost the race.

"No," Rycon said as he spun me around and bound my arms behind my back. "Not sorry enough."

46

If Rycon had just stabbed me in the heart with the knife I knew that he had hidden in his boot, it wouldn't have cut as deep as his betrayal. He'd slung me in front of him on a motorcycle of some sort, with my hands still tied behind my back.

The link between us was completely blocked, so it was through my human ears that I heard him take a deep inhale through his nose before he revved the engine and kicked off.

"Are you *smelling* where Kieran is?" I asked, disgusted. Rycon didn't answer. He easily balanced the weight of both of our bodies on his motorcycle as he navigated through narrow back alleys throughout most of the city.

It took us nearly an hour to get to our destination, the docks. Once we turned onto the docks, we were surrounded by a small city of shipping containers within minutes.

There was not a soul in sight, and I was sure if I screamed, Rycon would simply kill anyone who would come to my rescue. I was back in that weird loop where normal safety precautions didn't apply. He hadn't even tried to gag me. Rycon slowed as we approached the lake. The distant city lights were cast in star-like reflections across the mirrored black surface of the water.

"Rycon, what a pleasant surprise." Kieran's voice whispered. I was shocked. I had assumed this meeting had been prearranged.

"To what do I owe the pleasure?" Kieran continued. Marcus and Maria stepped up out of the dark into the dim light. I felt the blood drain from my face. How were they alive? I had thought for sure they had been killed.

What had happened to Clair? Where were Conrad and Meredith? *Please don't be dead. Please don't be dead.*

Rycon stepped off of the motorcycle and dragged me off with him. He smiled his usual salty grin, but I had seen the inside of him. I knew him. The smile did not reach his eyes.

"You blocked our bond earlier. If you break it now, I'll give her to you in exchange for my freedom." His voice hummed with anticipation, and his grip tightened on my arm. Kieran's face lit up with glee. He raised his arm and casually cocked his hand signaling Marcus to move forward.

"Stay away from me!" I hissed as Marcus approached. However, I was beginning to learn very quickly that I no longer had any say in what happened to me. An invisible force tore me from Rycon's grasp, and I was suddenly in Marcus' arms. I looked across the considerable distance that I had just flown to meet Rycon's gaze. I made sure he could see all of the hurt and pain in my eyes. If I didn't know any better, I could have sworn I saw the same feelings reciprocated in the shifter's gaze.

"You have her. Unbind us." Rycon demanded. His voice was low, and his fists were clenched.

"All in good time," Kieran said casually from behind me. "Bring her mother to me, and I will unbind you." My heart rate accelerated, and I began to sweat. Clair was alive then. Rycon's dilated pupils narrowed and his nostrils flared. Then suddenly he relaxed and fell back into his easy mercenary stance.

"Consider it done," he sneered from across the lot as he straddled his bike and kicked it into gear. I reached for my aura but the *triquetra* burned so brightly against me that I cringed in Marcus's grip. All I could do was beg.

"Rycon, no! Leave her out of this! Please, Rycon, *Please!*" I struggled against the fire mage, but his power just crushed me farther into him. The shifter paused and looked me in the eye. I felt like he was trying to tell me something, but our bond was blocked, I couldn't understand. I couldn't even find the strength to try reaching out to Amon again. These Nightshades were suffocating me.

"I'll see you soon, Kitten." Was all he said, before he squealed away, his back tire burning rubber on his way out of the pier.

Kieran appeared in front of me once Rycon's engine was nothing but a distant dream in the night.

"Alone at last." Kieran said, his tone filled with mirth. I struggled against Marcus again, but the more I resisted, the harder his magick beat down on me. I sunk to my knees on the cold pavement.

"Take her away," Kieran ordered, and Marcus dragged me off my feet, Maria a silent presence behind us. "It's time to find out what lies under that pretty skin."

Despite myself, I screamed as they dragged me across the asphalt. I hoped, for their sake, nobody would try to save me.

47

The Nightshades dragged me into one of the shipping containers that littered the lakeshore. I gave up struggling by the time the steel doors slammed shut behind us, blacking out the starlight. In the crippling darkness, my limp heels slammed against concrete steps that must have been dug out specifically for restraining someone like me.

The further down we went, the damper it got. I cursed myself again and again for not heeding Conrad's warning to get dressed when he had woken me up mere hours ago. Somehow, I doubted my captors would dignify me with a warm change of clothes.

Without Rycon's night vision, I existed in pure darkness for the agonizing trip to what I could only assume was meant to be my cell. I heard the drag of a heavy door against concrete and the faint light of a single bulb crept out as the opening widened. Marcus threw me into the bare, concrete room, and the heavy door shut behind me, with the click and tumble of what seemed like a thousand locks.

I was definitely past shock. I was freezing cold and shaking, my hands and feet were ice. Panic welled in my chest as I took in my surroundings.

The damp cement walls were grey and coated with mold. There were no windows or mattress, but there was a metal bucket in the corner that I assumed was so I could relieve myself. The humiliation of it all was overwhelming. Just as the anxiety began to peak into a panic attack, Kieran materialized in the center of my cell.

"Welcome, Raven to your new home," he said. He spread his arms and turned for effect, a hateful smile plastered on his face. I stood shaking before him, not from fear, but from the cold. I somehow managed a scowl.

"I understand that you are upset, however, I would advise you to think before you respond to my next query. You will not be able to retract your choice at a later date." I imagined that the snake wore the same smile when he asked Eve to bite the apple.

"Agree to surrender your power to us here and now, and we will promise you a quick death. Refuse, and we will be forced to take it from you," he gestured to my current surroundings. "Choose the wrong path, Raven, and I promise you, shitting in a bucket will be the least of your concerns."

I remembered Meredith telling me that Ash Nevra was after my power. She had told me that if I surrendered it, it would likely kill me. Of the two options Kieran had given me, there wasn't much of a choice.

I thought of Clair battling her own father in the park to protect me from him. I didn't know what had happened to her, Conrad or Meredith. All I knew, was that if they had given their lives for me, it had to mean something. I would not bend.

I didn't have it in me to give a sarcastic smile, as Rycon would have, or pull a nonchalant Conrad shrug. I had never been one to play games. I spat in his face and flipped him off simultaneously. It said something about his arrogance that he did not expect me to deny his offer enough to block such a pedestrian assault.

"Go to hell," I hissed. My aura tried to respond to my rage, but the stifling force of the *triquetra* was now backed by the dampening wards they must have placed on the walls of my cell.

Kieran wiped the spit from his face with a look of disgust.

"Primitive, and vial. Just like your mother." I wasn't sure if he was talking about Clair or my birth mother, maybe both. "So be it. No need to tell me to go to hell Raven. You'll soon find, that this is hell." He said softly, before disappearing. I screamed and spun, banging my fists against the steel door that kept me from the starlight. The sting of steel reverberated against my bones, and that pain was the only thing that kept me sane.

48

I had no idea how much time had passed before Kieran came back. It could have been hours or days. All I knew was I had given up attacking the steel door, and my wrists were covered in greenish-black bruises from the pounding. I switched tactics and focused on the *triquetra*.

I was determined to get the thing off my neck. It was preventing Amon from finding me and it was dampening my power. It wasn't that I trusted Amon any more than I trusted Kieran. I was just hoping that whatever plans he had for me required me to be alive. If I could get the charm off, I was sure I could get out of this awful place.

It didn't matter how hard I tried, I couldn't hold onto it long enough to pry it from my neck. Every time I tried to touch it, it burned white hot and buried its magical fingers deeper into my aura. By the time Kieran returned, I had curled up into one of the corners and had cried myself to sleep more than once.

As Kieran materialized in his usual swarm, it became apparent that he was not here to bring me food, which I had been hoping for. He did, however, bring me water. He passed me the bottle as Maria entered my cell.

I ripped the top off of the bottle and chugged back the life-sustaining fluid faster than I should have.

I ignored Maria's sneer at my desperation. How long had I been down here? It must have been at least a day for me to be this thirsty. However, it was hard to tell as I had never been deprived of water before. How long could a human go without water? Three days? A week? I couldn't remember. All I knew was it felt like bliss on my tongue, though it did nothing to diminish the chill that had seeped into my bones.

"Hello again, Raven," Kieran said, looking down his nose at where I crouched in the corner, trying to conserve my own body heat. I said nothing.

"Maria here is going to begin a series of...sessions that you will be undertaking, as a means of your conversion."

What did that mean? Still, I said nothing. 'It will only give him ammunition.' Clair had said that to me when he had first attacked us in the park.

"Alright," Kieran said, leaning back on his heels with his hands in his pockets. "I'll leave you to it then," he disappeared. Maria stood silently against the wall and...did nothing.

I frowned but stayed where I was. If her strategy was to get me to investigate, she would be waiting a long time. I had seen every horror movie in the book. No way was I going to go poking at the bad guy.

So we sat in silence, well, Maria stood. I crouched in the corner clutching my empty water bottle, fighting the urge to stick my tongue inside it to get every last drop. My stomach felt like it was eating itself, and I found myself endlessly scanning the barren room for something edible, knowing each time that there was nothing.

Finally, something happened. The steel door swung open, and I leap to my feet. I was slow even by my standards. If my plan had been to rush the door, I never would have made it. Be that as it was, the reaction had been involuntary, and I quickly sank to my knees as soon as I realized who it was that had walked in. It was Jeremy.

"Dad?" I asked, my voice catching in my throat. "Dad? Is that you?" He looked just like he always did. His soft weathered trench coat was folded up at the sleeves on his forearms. He had crinkles in the corners of his eyes that deepened when he smiled, and his hair was that charcoal grey that only came from men who had been born with dark hair.

I crawled toward him, delirious with hunger and hypothermia.

"Dad, you need to get out of here, she'll kill you." I choked, referring to Maria, but something was wrong. He didn't acknowledge Maria in her corner, and the way he looked at me was strange.

"Raven," he said, though there was no warmth to it. "Do you know how many nights I have laid awake, wishing we had never adopted you?" The comment was a blow I hadn't been expecting. I physically buckled, sinking further into the floor.

"What?" I gasped. Tears welled to my eyes for the first time since I had been captured.

"Do you have any idea how much of a burden you have been? The constant fighting. Pulling your mother and I away from work. Your mother was up from a promotion before she had to start leaving mid-shift to come and get

you." He was glaring at me and I was nearly sobbing. I had always known these things, but they had never blamed me for them. They had never made me feel worthless. I had always done a good enough job of that myself.

Jeremy had been my soldier, my beacon, my anchor. To hear him, of all people, confirm the worst of what I had always thought of myself... it was excruciating.

"Dad?"

"You're always getting into fights. None of those other kids have to go to therapy. Did you ever wonder if the problem might be you?" Jeremy sneered at me, his face twisting into something I didn't recognize.

"Dad. *Please.* I didn't mean it, I'm so sorry... I-I-love you so much." I was choking on my own words. I couldn't believe he was saying these things to me. I was a broken little girl, and no one wanted me.

My pride disappeared, my anger evaporated, and I crawled on hands and knees toward the only father I had ever known. I reached up to grab his jean-clad leg, as little Raven had done thousands of times before, begging, pleading for him to choose me, *forgive me.* My hand... passed right through him. I froze, but ghost Jeremy kept talking.

"You're a disgrace. You read all of those silly books, you're too old to be reading that crap. It's *embarrassing.* Your mother and I are *embarrassed by you."* I froze, clenching and unclenching my fist, watching my fingers pass in and out of the apparition.

My gaze snapped to Maria, and she was smiling. She was doing this. This wasn't Jeremy, it was an illusion.

"You bitch," I snarled, and lunged for her, but I hit an invisible wall. I bounced off of it and slammed into the concrete floor, the wind exploding from my lungs. Maria's laughter echoed around me.

"We couldn't have people over. No, no, no. You scared all of them away. We used to have friends before we adopted you. Now none of them want anything to do with us. '*Who is that creepy girl? Why would you adopt* that, *of all things?'* This is the sacrifice we made for an abomination like you."

I knew now why Maria had stood there for so long. She had been delving deep into my mind, finding my worst fears, so she could play them back to me through the mouths of people I loved.

Knowing that it wasn't real didn't make it any easier. Maria made eye contact with me and smiled and then, the concrete door to my cell opened again.

49

Conrad was next. He sauntered in with his cool and breezy attitude. He confirmed within minutes that he barely tolerated me as a friend. He put up with me because I was his ward, his mission. I was nothing more than a project for him.

Meredith followed, then Mr. Abbey, but the worst of all was Clair.

"You're not real." I croaked. My voice sounded broken even to me. I had lost track of how many minutes, hours, days, my loved ones had been telling me how worthless I was before Maria finally brought out Clair.

"Oh, but I am real Raven. Everything you've ever done to me has been real." She said, standing before me in her usual scrubs and ugly rubber hospital shoes.

"All I ever wanted was a daughter to go shopping with. Someone who I could enjoy the occasional latte with and gossip about boys. Instead, I got whatever you are." I sat there, staring at the apparition of my mother, and I couldn't keep the tears from rolling down my face.

"What did I do to deserve you, Raven? All I ever did was try to love you." I knew it wasn't real, but my heart was breaking. I had been enduring this for so long. They hadn't fed me. I was losing my grip on reality, and my mother was telling me she never loved me.

"How do you repay me? With violence, anger, constant fighting."

I was breaking. I knew that was what the Nightshades wanted. The last shred of the real me was hanging on by a stubborn thread. I wouldn't give in. I wouldn't break. But when Clair looked at me and told me that she wished she had adopted someone else, anyone else, I could barely hold on.

"Mom, all I ever wanted was to be someone you could be proud of." I whispered softly. Not to the apparition, but to the real Clair, wherever she was.

The apparition sneered at me, twisting my mother's face in a way I had never thought possible.

"Who would ever be proud of you? You're a monster." It said. And I felt my face crumble with emotion, despite myself.

I had started to dread the sound of the door opening. A sound that should have instilled rebellion, salvation, or even just a mere lust for sunlight. However, the Nightshades had been successful. When the door opened again, and Marcus stood before me, I was not disappointed. I was almost relieved that it was not another person I cared about that had come to tell me I was someone they wished they had never met.

50

There was no fight left in me, while Marcus dragged me out of my cell and strapped me to a heavy wooden gurney. The block on my aura was more and more suffocating every day. There was no point in struggling anymore. They would win the physical battle. My only hope now was my mind. If they broke that, I wouldn't be much use to anyone.

I watched as Marcus bound my limbs and Kieran materialized in this new unfamiliar chamber. Torches burned in iron brackets, and I tried not to laugh as my half-crazed mind tried to make sense of the byzantine interior design.

"So, you have proven to be as tough as everyone has formerly implied. Unfortunately for you, we must now turn to more medieval practices, if you insist on remaining so stubborn. I thought you would have consented by now." Kieran said as Marcus tightened the restraints. Despite my weakened state, my heart was beginning to pound against my chest. Being tied down was bringing back memories of the widowmaker. This time though, the *triquetra* had a chokehold on my powers. There was no escaping.

"I thought you said I wouldn't have an opportunity to revoke my choice once it had been made." I replied dryly, my vision blurring with repressed hysteria. Kieran smirked.

"That doesn't mean we don't want to hear you beg, my dear." He said before he disappeared. Marcus stood next to me and held his hands, palms down over my stomach.

"Let's see what's inside." He murmured. I looked into his eyes. I imagined he could slit my throat with that same serene expression on his face. I suddenly regretted not fighting harder to get out of the restraints.

"Marcus. Please. Don't do this." I begged. No response. I tried a different tactic; "I owe a life debt to Amon, I'm sure we can work something out." I was grasping at straws. I didn't even know if a life debt would give me any sway with Amon. I remembered his voice, the tang of worry when I asked him to come get me. "If you get me out of these wards, I can contact him. I'm sure he would pay you anything you want."

"What I want, is to see your insides." Marcus said, that razer point focus still on his hands, held just a few inches above me. Before I could interrupt again, he said: "Open." All my protests died on my tongue.

The pain started out soft, almost nice. I had been so cold for so long, that when my bones began to heat under the magick of his hands, it was the most comfortable I had felt since I had come to this godforsaken place.

The warmth didn't last for long. It was like watching a pot boil. For one long minute, the water is stagnant, only a wisp of steam skimming the top that suggests that the water is hot. Turn away too long and the water is foaming out the seams, burning on the stovetop.

Suddenly, my flesh was melting and I was screaming. Marcus was chanting *What's inside, what's inside, what's inside.*

My head slammed back against the wooden gurney as the white-hot heat flowed through my veins, up, up, up through my skin. The magick branded thin topical marks on my flesh from the inside out. The bloody burns healed almost immediately into whimsical designs of all the things I loved. Coffee beans and plants and passages from books. The scars faded with the heat, and Marcus seemed out of breath.

He was panting over me like some murderous primate. His beetle-like black eyes met mine, and once again I was struck by the emptiness in them, despite my terror.

"Again." He said, and I shrunk away from him as far as the restraints would allow. I could feel that fist in my chest, holding the molten core of power that lived within me. The fist that had been smothered by the *triquetra* for weeks. I could feel it close around that beating core of darkness, tighter and tighter, protecting it.

Marcus' magick burrowed deep into me, attacking the unintentional shield I had built to protect the daemon that lay dormant within my human body. He was trying to find it, that eternal darkness that would be the undoing of them all, if it were ever set free. I knew he would melt my bones and peel off my skin, strip by strip if he had to... and he would enjoy it. As another wash of liquid fire bubbled up from the marrow of my bones, I screamed. I could not think or breathe, and though I knew that they would never permit it, I prayed that I would die.

51

This became my new normal—a never ending cycle of psychological torture followed by physical torment. I took to cowering in the corner of my cell, away from the apparitions, with my hands over my ears. Maria made sure I heard them anyway.

I couldn't do much about my sessions with Marcus either. On the day's where Marcus would drag me away, all I could do was fight, tooth and nail, against the restraints. Over and over again, my flesh would burn from the inside as my bones turned white hot. My skull would scream on my molten spine. After enough times, the needlepoint scars that laced my body in vein-like patterns stopped disappearing.

On days when I was back in my cell, the two siblings would often gloat over my cowering form. They would take turns trying to pry my water bottle away from me. I had taken to cradling it in my sleep, just for the opportunity to hold something.

Sometimes they would simply stand in my cell, conversing, assuming I was too far gone to listen. I had come to cherish the idle chit-chat of my captors. Anything to drag my now broken mind away from the mental and physical torment I endured daily. I often tried to pull the triquetra off my neck when they weren't paying attention. Its suffocating presence no longer protected me from the bad guys. The enemy already had me. The charm would burn against my fingers. No matter how often I tried to free my aura, it would not budge. Struggling with it often left me feeling weaker and more deflated.

I couldn't even lose myself in happy memories, as every sunny afternoon I had ever spent with Clair in the garden was now ruined with her specter's words: *Who could ever love you?* Every ride in Jeremy's undercover cruiser was now buried beneath his cold, disgusted sneer. *You've been nothing but a burden.*

The day I had spent wandering around the city with Conrad, eating ice cream, had been snuffed out. *You're a chore. I wish I had never been sent to find you.* One by one, my loved ones became my tormentors, and after enough time had passed, I began to believe the things they whispered in my ears.

After one night of listening to Maria and Marcus discuss things that I'm sure they found mundane, I woke up on the concrete floor to the dreaded sound of the iron door opening. I slammed my eyes shut tighter, not wanting to hear what new horrors Maria would project to me from the depths of my own mind.

However, the voice I heard had not yet appeared in the apparitions. I opened my eyes in surprise. It was Rycon.

"Kieran needs you outside. We're being attacked." He drawled to my captors.

"Where have you been?" Maria snapped. "You were supposed to be guarding the lines."

"I was on special orders from the man himself, lady. That took priority." Rycon countered. "You going to make the boss wait, or what?"

"Why didn't Kieran tell us?" Maria argued. it was unsurprising to me that Marcus remained silent. I could see his cold dead eyes swimming. *What's inside, what's inside, what's inside...* I curled even more tightly into myself.

"I don't know. Do you think I asked him? He said go get Marcus and Maria. So here I am, getting twiddle-dee and twiddle-fucking dumb. Go kiss your master's ass, and don't shoot the messenger." Rycon snapped.

Apparently, Rycon's explanation was enough. I listened as my tormentors stalked out, Maria snorting with indignation. I didn't hear the iron door shut. Instead, I heard Rycon whisper.

"Kitten...gods, what did they do to you?" I stayed turned away from him, curled up, facing my corner. I could hear him step closer. He could just be another apparition. I didn't trust what my senses were telling me anymore.

"I was only gone for a few hours. What the-"

A few hours?!

That had gotten my attention. Spector or no, there was no way I had been trapped in this godforsaken place for less than a month. I uncurled my broken body and turned to face him. He took one look at my face and stepped back. I repeated the thought that had erupted in my brain out loud.

"A couple of *hours?*" I cried. What had Kieran done? Rycon nodded his olive skin paling. I didn't believe it. This was another trick.

Steps started sounding down the hallway. Marcus and Maria had left the door open, and my mother's all too familiar face appeared in the gloom. Now I knew it was a trick.

"You're not real," I croaked at the apparition. My voice had been used for nothing but screaming for more days than I could count.

I scuttled back on the dirty floor, the rags of my night clothes pulling at my throat as the waist of the t-shirt caught between my hips and the concrete. My back hit the unforgiving wall behind me. I'de had enough. I just wanted it to go away. The thing that was and was not Clair was too much. I couldn't take it anymore. I knew I was screaming nonsense, but I couldn't stop. Endless torture and humiliation had stripped me of my senses.

"*GET AWAY FROM ME! YOU'RE NOT REAL; YOU'RE NOT CLAIR!*" The not-Clair portrayed a convincing display of emotion. Its eyes seemed to well with tears, and it took a tentative step forward.

"Raven, It's me. I don't know what they did to you -" It said, holding its hands out, palms up. To try and calm me into a false sense of security. To make me believe I was being saved. It couldn't fool me. No one was coming to save me. I wasn't worth saving.

"LEAVE ME ALONE!" I half snarled, half sobbed, I whipped the half-empty water bottle I had been clutching toward the phantom, with my less-than-considerable might. It hit her in the chest and it bounced off harmlessly. I froze.

No one took a breath. All three of us sat frozen. Rycon and Clair waited to see what I would do. I struggled to gather my scrambling thoughts. The water bottle had touched her. She was solid.

She was real.

52

Slowly, I got up. My legs shook as I took a hesitant step forward. I think Clair was holding her breath as if she knew any sudden movement would send me into a screaming panic. One step at a time, I made my way across my cell, until I stood before her.

She stood, unmoving, before me, barely daring to blink. Her eyes were misted with unshed tears as she took in what I was sure was a terrifying sight. A tear finally escaped its watery prison and slid down her cheek. Her lip trembled. I reached forward and touched the small salty drop with my shaking, filthy fingers. The tear was warm against my freezing skin, and I was so overwhelmed with emotion I felt I might explode.

"Mom?" I asked, my voice hitching in my throat. She nodded gently, earnestly.

"It really is me, Raven." She reached out gingerly to cup my cheek. "I should never have let you go, I am so sorry." Her own voice was breaking. I shook my head, my face crumbling into tears that I had refused to shed during hours - no... *days* of torture. I collapsed into her and began to sob. She wrapped her arms around me and pressed me close. She smelled of lavender, and I knew she had to be real. Even Maria hadn't been able to capture her clean scent.

I don't know how long we stood there. She held me tight as I broke down. All the pain and fear leaked out through me. Sobs wracked through my body so hard I could barely hold myself up.

"Shhh, Shhh." She whispered, rocking me against her. "I'm here. You're ok. You're going to be ok." I didn't have words to tell her what had happened to me. I couldn't explain how much of a relief it was to be touching a real live person. Feeling her solid body made me quiver with unrestrained relief. She was made of flesh and blood. She had come for me.

"I love you, Raven, I am so sorry." *How could anyone ever love you?* The painful memory cut through my mind. I peered up into her beautiful face and knew she had no idea what it meant to me that she had said that. Even after everything, she had come for me. With my mental shields in ruins, she of course, could read my thoughts.

"I will always come for you, Raven." A fierceness in her eyes smoldered as strongly as the pain in my heart.

Rycon coughed awkwardly from where he stood a few feet away. He had tried to give us space, and I had completely forgotten he was even there.

"Not to break up the reunion, but we have a finite amount of time to get out of this shit hole," he said. Both Clair and I looked at him. Clair's expression said enough. We wouldn't have had to get out of here at all if he hadn't betrayed me in the first place.

"Why are you both here?" I asked. My voice was still rough from so much screaming. The shifter and my mother both understood what I meant. Why were they working together?

"I was trying to tell you in the shipping yard last night," Rycon said. Last night?

I still didn't understand why they kept saying I had only been here for a few hours. "Yes, ok... I originally brought you here hoping that if I did so Kieran would sever the bond. But he was lying when he said if I brought Clair to him, he would free me. He can't free me. He was full of shit. If he decided to kill you, I would have died with you, so...I went to get Clair."

"You are a disgusting creature." Clair spat over my shoulder. Rycon rolled his eyes.

"Tell me something I don't know, witch." He drawled. "Anyway. I couldn't leave you here while we're still bound." Did he have any idea what I had been through? What he had done to me? I glanced down at my arms, still covered in pencil-thin white scars from my 'sessions' with Marcus.

My entire body was covered in intricate scars from my neck down. He was sorely mistaken if he thought coming to save me would be his redemption. I could never forgive him for this.

"I still don't understand how It felt so much longer for me down here than you. I swear I have been here for weeks." I whispered, my voice still strained. Clair's face crumbled again.

"Kieran must have had you in a time loop. It is dark magick that makes time pass much more slowly for the target of the spell. Jeremy hasn't even come home yet in our time path. The fact that he had you trapped in a loop down here for weeks is...enraging. Even I didn't know he was capable of magick that powerful."

"Well, I think our pal Ash Nevra has something to do with that." Rycon speculated. "She must be siphoning power to him somehow." Despite her distaste for the shifter, Clair nodded in agreement.

Rycon turned to face the door. "Okay. Enough catching up. We have to go."

53

Clair's attention snapped to the shifter, her face filled with distaste.

"One thing before we go. This, I'm sure, will be the beginning of many punishments you will endure over the next little while to make up for your betrayal." Clair held her right hand before her face, her pinky and ring finger bent, her middle and forefinger pointing upwards, and her thumb resting against her chin. She blew lightly against her protruding fingers, and I felt a tingle in the line between myself and Rycon that I had declared dead long ago, at least in my timeline.

The block in our bond wiggled free and released itself with a pop, like a cork on a champagne bottle. Rycon's energy came roaring back, and even with the suffocating power of Kieran's enhanced *triquetra,* I felt marginally better. Rycon staggered with the release on the block, and I'm sure it was less enjoyable for him as the destruction and pain I had been through passed into his body. He was feeling what I had been feeling for the first time, and he did not like it. His eerie eyes flashed with a burning hot rage.

'Even I'm not this sick.' He hissed into my mind, and it was a relief to have his strength back, even after everything he had done. He shrugged out of his leather jacket and handed it to Clair.

"Magick this away somewhere safe. I don't want to have to come back to get it." Clair looked like she would argue until Rycon pulled his gun from the back of his jeans. He bent down and grabbed his jade-hilted blade from his boot, and handed both to me. "You'll need these more than I will. Any progress we made with your training is gone now. Once I shift, I won't be able to carry them anyway. Do you know how hard it is to replace a gun in Canada?" He mused out loud. I accepted the weapons for what they were, though I was in such a state of duress that I couldn't ever imagine using them.

"You'd be surprised," Rycon said, answering my half-finished thoughts. I realized as he stood before me, the suffocating humidity of his rainforest aura building, that I would finally see him shift. "You know how to use that, right?" He asked as pinpricks began to rub against his skin from the inside, pushing his flesh up into a million tiny tents.

Yes. I knew how to use a gun. Jeremy had taught me, though he had never kept one in our house. The gun felt heavy in my hand. Not sure if that was saying much, as the empty water bottle had been nearly too heavy to throw. I couldn't remember the last time I had eaten. Rycon was now stripping off his white cotton t-shirt, his face grave.

'I know I screwed you, but I promise it will never happen again. You can tell if I'm lying. Please save that jacket. It's all I have left of him.' His father. The jacket had belonged to his dead father. I knew he was telling the truth, and I knew Clair had heard his telepathic request, and the jacket misted away from her arms.

Rycon's yellow-slitted eyes crinkled at the corners in the closest thing we would ever get to a 'thank you,' and then he changed. It was unlike anything I had ever seen.

A ripple started like a pebble had been thrown in a lake, but it began from the inside of him. The ripples in his very skin grew deeper and deeper until they cracked at the seams, and nothing but black fur exploded from the creases. His bones were exposed, and I watched them shift and move with a sickening 'popping' sound as his flesh peeled away to make room for the ebony fur.

His nails grew and sharpened into claws, and his skull reshaped. Blood and puss spilled from the crevices as he changed, and his ripped blue jeans fell off the slim hind legs of the largest black panther I had ever seen.

Somehow, I didn't think they were supposed to be this large. His head came up to my neck, and his body was nearly two times the length of mine standing up. I gripped the butt of the gun and the hilt of the knife he had given me in each hand on reflex. Seeing an animal that large and wild was unnerving, even though I knew it was Rycon beneath all that fur.

His energy as a panther was the same but different. Wilder. Freer. I now understood why he had decided to trade me for his freedom. A beast like that did not belong on a leash. The bond I had forced on him was much more restrictive than any chain could ever be. I glanced at Clair, and she pursed her lips.

Rycon's still-yellow eyes met mine and he nodded his great head down once. It was an act of compliance. An apology. His jaw was open, and his canines gleamed in the light, each as long as my palm.

'Let's go.' Even his voice in my mind sounded different. More serious, authoritative. Once, the chief of his leap, a mantle he had given up a long time ago.

Rycon's muscular tail whipped behind him as he stalked silently from the room. I glanced at Clair. The idea of leaving this room after so long was oddly terrifying. The thought of being punished if I were caught almost outweighed the bleating cry for freedom that hummed through my bones.

"I will not let anyone touch you," Clair promised, holding out her hand to me. "Not again." I nodded and looked to the open door. It seemed to be shrinking before my very eyes. As if I needed to make a move soon or the opportunity would be gone forever. Despite the *triquetra*, I clung to the small part of Rycon I could still access and took a step forward. The energy I channeled through the bond was the only thing keeping my broken body upright.

"I will get that thing off of your neck as soon as we are safe." Clair promised. "It is a perversion of what that charm is meant to symbolize. Whatever Kieran did to it, is complex. I will need some time with it." I knew Kieran had tampered with it, but it had made me feel sick even before he arrived. It was a charm of protection, and the fact that it seemed to repel the very essence of my being, disturbed me. Maybe daemons and magick folk just didn't mix.

At some point during my internal ramblings, we had entered the hallway.

"See, Raven? We made it. We're out." Clair whispered to me, pride swelling with each syllable. I glanced behind us, into the empty room that was still lit by that single, bare, flickering bulb.

It was surreal to look at from the outside.

I was free.

54

Rycon was sitting with his back to us at the end of the hallway, peering around the corner into the darkness. His great tail was swishing behind him in agitation.

'We have company.' He said into our minds, as his feline mouth would not allow him to speak out loud. He folded into a crouching stance I had only ever witnessed on the Discovery channel before suddenly exploding around the corner and out of sight. We couldn't see what he had done... but we could hear the screams.

Clair and I waited by my cell. She gripped my hand so hard her knuckles turned white. I waited to feel afraid, but there was nothing left in me to feel. Some essential part of me had been broken in that chamber. Another thought that should have terrified me. Still, I felt nothing.

Moments later, Rycon emerged from around the corner, his jowls dripping in crimson.

'Clear.' Was all he said, before padding back around the corner, expecting us to follow him. I wondered how many situations he had been in before that had required him to use words like 'clear' to describe a hallway.

I continued to grip Clair's hand as we moved forward. She gently held me back and put herself before me, sheltering me from what was to come.

Though nothing she could have done could have prepared me for the four dead bodies sprawled across the hall. I didn't recognize any of the fallen magick folk, and another thrill of panic coursed through me. Where were Marcus and Maria? How many witches had Kieran brought with him? Would there be an army of Nightshades waiting to intercept our escape?

The fallen had their throats ripped out, and Rycon was sitting at the end of the passage, his tail swishing behind him and his eyes gleaming as only a cat's eyes could in the dark. I tried not to look to closely at the dead bodies, but I couldn't help but see their bared spines shining in the dirty light, where Rycon had eaten out their throats. One of them looked like he could have been my age. Now he was dead. I wondered what Kieran had done or said to him to recruit him. Had he known what he was getting into when he had joined the Nightshade Coven?

'Move faster,' the panther hissed into our minds. Clair spoke for me.

"She will take as much time as she needs. We will handle what comes." Rycon sent a metaphysical shrug down the line.

'Whatever you say,' he stood up, his perfect panther form was silent on the impermeable floor.

Then I felt him. I felt Marcus before he appeared around the next corner, and I understood why Rycon had urged us to hurry. I would never be able to rub the stain of Marcus' aura from my skin, and my blood ran cold as I felt his power fill the damp space.

We were one corner away from the stairs to true freedom if I remembered correctly. I could hear the stars singing my name. The broken planets in my aura reached toward the fresh air, and I cringed as they smashed against the suffocating membrane that was Marcus.

I buckled. I couldn't move.

Clair pushed me further behind her.

Marcus appeared to materialize from the shadows as he turned the corner in his characteristic black garb. His expression was the same as it had been when I first met him. The same as it had been when he had tortured me.

"Move," Clair said, that strange triple echo of the moon appearing to back up her threat, but it fell dead on Marcus' ears. I had learned that he was not one to be intimidated, bribed or threatened. He ran on his own dark path and only had eyes for me.

A cruel smile slid across his face. Clair maneuvered herself between us, but I could still feel those two soulless pits burning like coal. *What's inside, What's inside, What's inside...* A twin pair of yellow irises flared behind him, and Rycon launched himself at the mage's back, quieter than a whisper.

But Marcus knew. Of course, he knew. He blasted Rycon out of the air with a lick of fire and the entire chamber reeked of burnt fur as Rycon slammed into the staircase that separated us from freedom.

Everything was moving in slow motion. Rycon tried to stand from where his massive feline body had hit the stairs. His shoulder blades rolled under his muscled furred form and his paws slipped out from under him. Clair began the quiet build of power given to her from the goddess. It was painfully slow. I couldn't wait. Suddenly, I remembered lesson number three.

Bullets are faster than magick.

Marcus was advancing on Rycon as the cat shook his great head, peeling off the ground to stand on his four paws again. The beast's claws unsheathed and scraped against the ground, a snarl erupting in his throat. His black lips pulled back to bare his ivory-white teeth.

I was outside of my body. I remembered that in my right hand, I still clutched the Beretta 92FS. Jeremy's lessons came back to me. I was sighting down my arm before anyone knew what I was doing. Clair's build of power staggered as she glimpsed at me over her shoulder. I had one eye squeezed shut, the other eye on my target.

There would be a recoil. This gun was much too large for me. If I fired, I would hit higher than I aimed. My arm floated down.

"Raven. No..." Clair pleaded. Jeremy had been anti-gun my entire life. *Guns kill more friends than enemies.* He had always said. The memory almost made me lower the Beretta until Marcus' black eyes met mine.

There would be a ricochet if I missed.

The antechamber to the stairway was behind Marcus on an angle. I drifted right. If I missed, the bullet would get caught in the stairway and not hurt anyone on my team.

It wasn't a conscious thought. My finger curled around the trigger, and I fired. *Low.* Said a voice in my head. The blast erupted like a shock wave through my arm, jamming my joints into one another. I felt the bullet leave the barrel like a punch to the chest. I had been aiming for his torso, but the force of the bullet sent my arm up and to the right, and it hit Marcus in the side of his neck.

Blood exploded from the wound, and I watched it arc through the air as I took a step forward. The gun was still held before me, in a straight-armed stance. His eyes showed the first spark of feeling I had ever seen.

What had felt like weeks of torture, digging through my skin, and scarring my body beyond repair. He met my eyes and didn't beg. He smiled.

I fired again.

55

The next bullet caught him in the chest. He went down as I continued to inch forward. He tried to sit up on the backs of his elbows to face me, and I fired again.

I reveled in his inability to gather his power. I could feel his burning aura sputtering like a candle. It was how I had felt when he had belted me down against that gurney. He was already on his back when I fired a fourth time, now nearly shooting point-blank into his still body. His limp form jerked as I continued to fire. My finger kept pulling the trigger. Over and over again. I lost myself in the deafening bangs that echoed against the dripping stone of the dugout.

Someone was screaming as I repeatedly pulled the trigger on the man who had raped my soul. I watched his face turn to gore and the incessant screaming I was hearing was interrupted each time I sobbed. I realized it had been me screaming, as my finger continued to pull, firing the now empty clip into the already well-dead fire mage.

Something soft touched the back of my left hand, which was still gripping the jade hilted knife. Rycon's massive panther head pressed against my hip and into my hand, avoiding the blade easily. Clair came up on my right side, and looked down at the ruined face of the man I had just shot to death.

'*He is dead, Kitten,*' Rycon purred into my mind as we stood over the wrecked body of the man who had violated me.

He was dead. I couldn't kill him a second time. I hadn't solved anything. It didn't feel like it was enough. All it had done was add a name to the list of people I had killed. Mrs. Serafini, Marcus. Who was next? I was unraveling. Glancing at the massive panther and my mother, I had no words. Clair curled an arm around me.

"Let's go." She said, as if tomorrow, we could explain this all away.

"Take me home." My voice was as dead as I felt. Looking at her, I knew that I would follow her to the ends of the earth.

She gave me a sad smile.

"Let's go home." She reaffirmed. We all turned to the staircase before us. A rumble from outside told us that the battle had just begun. I should have known Kieran would not just let me leave. I dropped the now empty firearm to the stone floor with a clatter, not caring that it would be a pain for Rycon to replace. I needed one hand free. The other one was still gripping that jade-hilted knife.

The ordeal with Marcus seemed to have taken more of a toll on me than I had thought. Walking up the steps to the outside world was painful, and difficult. Clair had one arm behind me, and the other one supporting my left wrist. My hand still clutching Rycon's knife like my life depended on it. Rycon himself flowed up ahead of us, despite being thrown against the wall by a blast of witch-fire.

'*Shifters are naturally resistant to magick,*' He explained as I struggled up the stairs. I think he was trying to distract me. I hadn't realized how hurt I was. Both physically and psychologically. '*It can still kill us, but it takes longer, and way more power than that douchebag had.*' I didn't have it in me to respond.

After what seemed like forever, we made it to the final plateau. We paused to allow me to catch my breath, and then... the very shadows themselves began to come alive.

My bones constricted in fear, pain flared down the translucent white lines that now coated my body, thanks to the mage I had just murdered. I stood, shaking, waiting for Kieran's signature swarm to appear. Clair's hands tightened on me and she pulled me towards her, but Rycon remained still.

Instead of Kieran, Amon materialized before us. I had never seen him dressed for battle before. Even when he had come for the widowmaker, he had worn a collared shirt and charcoal slacks. Today he stood before me, Prince of the Court of Pride, armed and ready for war. Ornate silver raven-shaped fastenings held a bolt of midnight fabric to his shoulders. The ebony cape draped around him to the ground, fading into night where it swept his booted ankles.

The rest of his body was plated in close-fitting matte black metal, and that sword made of pure nighttime rested at his hip. Up close, the blade seemed to gobble up the light around it. My aura strained towards that empty black sword, and the *triquetra* burned until my core quieted. The daemon's face was serious, and those piercing green eyes met mine, even as Clair stepped in front of me, gently pressing me behind her again.

"I have been trying to reach you since you called." He said to me, his voice flowed like liquid over my bare skin, cooling the fire in my scars.

"They had her in a time loop," Clair stated. Amon's gaze jerked to her as if noticing, for the first time, that she was there at all. Let alone acknowledging the fact that she was the only reason I was still standing. He nodded toward her, in the closest thing to a bow a prince could make.

"Clairafine," he said simply by way of greeting. She tilted her head in return. Clairafine? When this was all over, Clair had some explaining to do.

"Prince Amon," She responded, and the side of his mouth twitched up in a half smile before he turned the full attention of his gaze back to me. Of course, she knew who he was. I seemed to be the only person who hadn't known how the world really worked until a few weeks ago. Well me, and probably Jeremy.

"Can you walk?" Amon asked me, almost gently. The burn of his gaze told me that if I needed help, now was not the time to try and be a hero. There was another great rumble and the very bricks around us shifted. Once we went outside, things would move very quickly.

I did a quick scan of my body. I was weak, but with Rycon's bond back, I could draw enough energy to get away, especially if he guarded me. Mentally, I was in shambles. I was wrecked enough that I wasn't questioning things like how Amon had known I was here, or why it seemed like he and Clair had met before.

He had asked if I could walk, not if I could run.

I nodded.

56

"Good." Amon said. He turned to Rycon, who had been waiting indifferently at my side.

With Amon's entrance, the panther had pressed himself against my hip, but remained silent.

My mind was still moving too slowly. I could barely register Amon as a threat. I was just glad he was there and seemed to be on our side for the moment. I couldn't take any more surprises.

"You," Amon spat the word at Rycon like he knew what he had done to me. I wondered how much he had seen through the touch-based tracker he had placed on my chin before Kieran had taken me underground. "You will get Raven out of here. If you fail, Rycon, I will make sure you spend the rest of your life, praying for death." Watching a cat roll its eyes was strange, but it happened.

"Stay behind me," The daemon prince ordered and turned to open the door to the outside world. It seemed he was used to giving orders, and even more used to having them obeyed.

His cape of night brushed against me as he moved and my aura reacted to it, only to be slammed down by the *triquetra*. I bit back the gasp of pain that shot down my spine as my stars collided with the planets that orbited them. The daemon in me poked its nose out from between the fingers of the fist I kept around it. Kieran's magick dug down into my raw skin trying to find it. To draw it out.

Without warning, Amon opened the door to the world and my iris' constricted against the new light. Rycon leapt from my side into the early morning sun and Clair formed a shield of glowing energy before us. Amon looked back at me once before drawing his blade of midnight. All I could do was grip my jade hilted knife tighter, and I knew now, that I would use it.

The docks were cloved in a fuschia-cerulean light. Was it the sunrise of the morning after I had been incarcerated? No. I wouldn't let myself think about that.

I remembered the day when Clair had found me on the chesterfield, and we had a dirt war in the backyard. That day now felt like it had been so long ago. When this was all over, we would go back and plant those damned sunflowers. I pushed the image of that little sack of seeds that were waiting for us into her mind. She smiled at me and squeezed my hand as we stepped out onto the pavement.

'*Yes, as soon as we get home.*' She said to me. I blinked against the light. So different from what I had been exposed to for what had felt like months underground. I blinked and couldn't get my bearings. I staggered and Rycon's soft, hard body was there when I thought for sure I would fall over.

I bit back the choking scream in my throat and gripped a tight fist into Rycon's fur. *I can't see, I can't see, I can't see...*

Amon's mind pressed into mine. '*You are ok. Your eyes just need to adjust. You still have all your other senses. Use them.*' As his aura brushed against me, the *triquetra* weakened. My eyes struggled to adjust. I used my aura to feel out the scene before me. I could sense the auras of Kieran and his dark army and the familiar energies of my friends. They stood in a neat line before the impossible wall of sickly Nightshades.

Conrad's salty ocean aura, humming before the itchy parasite that was Maria. Meredith's leafy green energy was facing Kieran's venom. There were also auras I didn't recognize on both sides.

On our side, there was an aura that I immediately recognized as Mr. Abbey. He was strong and steady. I realized now that he must have walked around with a damper on his power. His energy was formidable. There was a woman with him, she was older, wiser even than Mr. Abbey himself. She had the steadiness of the tide, and Conrad's turbulent, playful storm seemed to derive from hers. Was this Patricia?

Then there was another female, who felt as volatile as the weather. Her power shifted with her mood. She was a chameleon. She was accompanied by a male, and he was strong as a mountain, his power hot like a cracked desert. I knew when he laughed, valleys would crumble beneath the weight of his will.

Our war had summoned gods, and I needn't have opened my eyes to witness them.

57

My vision came back in phases. I followed Amon's deep, rich aura of purples and velvet greens into the center of the fold.

'RAVEN LET'S GO!' Rycon's voice reverberated in my mind as I finally was able to see again, just as Kieran shot a bolt of lightning at me. Clair threw up a blue-gold shield and the lightning crackled against it. The shield held, but I heard it groan under the pressure.

My vision, which had just been starting to come back, faltered again under the glare. I felt, more than saw the pavement crack beneath our feet as Meredith sent roots up through the ground to try to ensnare Kieran. I heard Rycon's roar and the *whoosh* as Kieran evaded his two attackers.

'Focus. You are bound to Rycon. If you cannot see, use his eyes.' Amon's voice was in my head, and I knew what to do. I followed the line of power that bound the shifter to me, and I blinked, finally seeing the battlefield before me with crystalline clarity.

The docks were filled with witches and daemon's alike. Both Conrad and the wise, elderly woman, whom I could only assume was his grandmother, were drawing water from the nearby lake. I watched as Conrad used the water to drown two advancing witches, forcing the water in streams down their throats. I shuddered at the violence that was so out of character of my happy-go-lucky friend.

Kieran was laughing, his hands above his head. Power grew like an invisible knife cutting through the air behind him. To my horror, several daemons walked out through the gap he had created.

The Veil.

These daemons must be from Ash Nevra's army. The army that was too big for even Amon to overthrow. They were spilling into the Toronto docks by the dozens.

Meredith turned her attention from Kieran to face the oncoming mob as I stood still from under Clair's shield. Mr. Abbey came to her side, followed by Amon, and the two other people I had sensed during my initial blindness, but hadn't recognized.

The male who had reminded me of a mountain, fit the description I had originally given him in my mind's eye. He towered over the rest of our team, and his biceps were easily the width of my waist. He wore the same close-fitting black armor Amon had on. His dark hair was long and tied back in a low ponytail.

He drew twin sabers that were crossed behind his back and smirked at the oncoming army as if they were merely an inconvenience. In contrast, the chameleon daemon at his side had short cerulean blue hair braided on each side of her head in two Dutch braids. She seemed diminutive next to him, but if I had to go up against one of them, I would have chosen the Mountain. Her aura was so powerful that it was only matched by Amon himself.

She was dressed in the same matte black armor, but she bore no weapons. She faced the oncoming swarm of daemons with empty hands and the same challenging look on her face as the Mountain that towered next to her. She almost looked like the idea of fighting this onslaught of daemons and magick folk was her idea of a good time.

I started to see double and realized the vision in my own body had returned. I pulled out of Rycon's mind and back into my head. The daemons kept coming through the tear Kieran had made in The Veil. Without counting Rycon and Clair, we had only seven people on our team, facing a steadily growing army. There was no way we stood a chance. I began to shake. It was hopeless.

"Wait," Clair said softly, feeling my building terror. "Watch."

The dark army that was filled with beautiful, deadly, faces stood before our tiny team, and nobody moved. *Yuh soon find out, Rayven, usually di most beautiful tings, are often di most dangerous.* Conrad had said that to me once, and facing this onslaught of daemon's, I finally understood what he had meant.

Kieran stood before his dark army, his face filled with triumph. Amon's expression was irreverent, almost bored, as he stood only a hundred feet away from the wizard that had made every single one of my nightmares come true.

"Last chance, Kieran," Amon said casually as if he were betting another man on a good poker hand. Kieran regarded him scornfully.

"When I bring you home to my queen, she will make me into a god," He sneered. The blue-haired girl rolled her eyes dramatically as if all this banter were a bore.

"Are we going to fight? Or exchange pleasantries all morning? I haven't even had a coffee yet." She muttered.

Conrad and Meredith were the palest I had seen, staring at the wild blue-haired creature with wide eyes. I realized they were scared. Why weren't these daemons that had accompanied Amon scared? Kieran raised his eyebrows, still grinning like a cat with a mouse. He gestured towards our small squadron politely.

"Please, after you." He invited. The blue-haired daemon's smile widened.

"With pleasure, asshole." She retorted. Her left leg fell back into a fighting stance and her right hand shot forward, pointing at the group of daemon's directly across from her, shaping her fingers to mimic a gun.

"Bang, bang," she quipped lazily before a dozen daemons were immediately vaporized. The blast that erupted from her fingers was so white that the sun seemed to dim. The skitter and smash of the energy tore through the air and rumbled through the shipping yard like a sonic boom.

My jaw must have hit the floor, and the opposing army immediately mobilized, enraged. Both Blue Hair and Mountain ran fearlessly into the melee, taking the opposing daemon's down effortlessly two, even three at a time.

Amon followed his team. His aura encompassed the entire battlefront and I writhed against it. He made the daemon in me soar.

With a flick of his wrist, the elongated shadows created by the army of daemons in the morning light peeled off the ground and came alive. I watched in awe as the shadows turned on their own counterparts and attacked them.

Amon himself went after Kieran.

58

The Prince of Pride and the head of the Nightshade coven shot into the air above the battle, and my magick folk friends crowded under them, each using their unique gifts to beat back the seemingly endless swarm of opposition.

Mr. Abbey stomped the ground, and an entire slate of asphalt launched into the air and shot forward to pulverize a slew of Nightshades.

Conrad continued to drown his adversaries on dry land while his grandmother, Patricia, pulled so much water from the great lake I thought it would empty, then she shot the water into the sky to create a small but deadly, hurricane.

Meredith was dashing. Her power over plants was urging the earth to bend to her will. Plants, that I hadn't even known were trying to grow in this barren wasteland were erupting through the concrete and tripping up any daemons at risk of besting Amon's team of two.

Watching Amon battle Kieran mid-air was one of the most mesmerizing things I had ever seen. They both moved so quickly it was hard to keep track of them.

'That asshole is definitely bound to Ash Nevra. No wizard can move that fast or even hope to come up against someone as strong as Amon. Not without funneling power straight from the hell-bitch herself.' Rycon said into both Clair's and my minds. Clair nodded.

"We should get out of here," she said finally. Rycon dipped his great head in agreement.

Clair smiled at me, turning away from the battle. Everyone was so distracted with destroying each other that no one noticed us as we slipped away.

Clair placed her hand on each side of my face. "We have some powerful friends now, Raven." I knew she was referring to Amon and his team. I wasn't sure I was ready to call them friends, but I wasn't in any position to turn away willing allies. "Let's go home," she continued, smiling. I had never wanted anything more in my entire life.

'CLAIR!' Rycon roared. His voice in my mind echoed against his panther's scream. Clair's body jerked, her hands tightening on my face, before loosening completely. Her eyes widened and she staggered backward.

"Mom?" I asked, startled. "Mom, what's wrong?"

She was staring at me, stunned. Then finally she glanced down, and my gaze followed hers. Blood was seeping down her front at an alarming rate. I glanced behind her and saw Maria with her hands out, an evil look on her face.

My mind couldn't process what was happening. Clair's knees buckled, and I rushed forward to catch her, but she had become dead weight, and my weakened body couldn't hold her up.

"MOM!" I was screaming now, sobbing. I sank to the ground with her as more and more blood spilled from her chest from a wound born of an invisible weapon. "MOM!" I repeated, still screaming.

I could feel Maria building another blast of power now, but I didn't care. Rycon launched himself at her and took her down. I could hear the two of them engage into a fight, but I couldn't tear my eyes away from my dying mother's face.

I was on my knees now, and Clair was lying down, her head and shoulders in my arms. I curled around her, rocking her back and forth.

"Meredith can fix you," I sobbed. "She can fix this. No, no, please, stay with me. Meredith... she has herbs, just hold on I'll get her..." I started to get up to do as I said, but Clair touched my face weakly.

"No," she whispered, she coughed, and blood erupted from her mouth, staining her lips. "Just, stay here. This is what I owe the goddess for granting me my powers back. I knew that my time was limited. I just didn't think it would be this quick."

She tried to laugh, before coughing again. I wasn't sure if the battle had literally stopped behind me, or if I had just stopped hearing it. I felt the rage and sorrow begin to pour off of Kieran from where he hovered above me in the air. He was an evil wizard, but I didn't believe he wanted Clair to die.

"Mom." I sounded like a broken record, but I didn't know what else to do. I pressed my hand against the hole in her chest and tried to hold the blood in fruitlessly.

"Mom, no, don't give up. We still have to plant the sunflowers. *Please. Please don't leave me.*" My voice was breaking. She closed her eyes and patted my cheek softly, choking almost delicately on the crimson still spilling from her mouth. I tried to sit her up more so she wouldn't drown in her own blood.

"Raven. You have to win. You have to protect Jeremy. You are the balance that this world needs..." She opened her eyes and smiled at me. She weakly rose a hand to brush my cheek.

"You have always been... a fighter."

And then, she was gone.

59

The battle had stopped. Everyone stood frozen as Kieran's daughter, and the only woman who had ever bothered to love me died in my arms.

"Mom?" I whispered. I shook her. "MOM!" I heard a drum beat start from somewhere. It began slow, and the deep rhythm methodically increased. I looked into Clair's face, her eyes wide and her face as beautiful as ever. Frozen now, forever in death.

Boom, boom, boom.

"Hey hun, want me to fix you a snack? Clair was smiling, in her scrubs, already half in the fridge just as she got home. Whether I wanted a snack or not, you knew she was making something.

Boom, boom, boom, boom.

The kids at school had thrown rocks at me, and I came home bleeding. I was sitting on the closed toilet seat, and Clair was bandaging me up. Her face was grave. *'Sometimes, Raven, people are just afraid of things they don't understand.'*

Boom, boom, boom, boom, boom.

'Raven, you're a fighter. You always have been. Whatever you're going through, I'll always be here to fight with you.'

But she wouldn't be. She was dead. *Maria had killed her.*

Boom, boom, boom, boom, boom, boom.

I suddenly realized the drumming sound was coming from inside of me. Even Rycon and Maria had stopped fighting. The giant panther padded over to me, and I met his large, yellow eyes. It was the first time I had ever felt anything close to sympathy from the panther, and the memory of his burning childhood home flashed in my mind.

'When they kill someone you love, and trust me, they will; I'll ask you to put that aside, and we'll see how easy it is for you.' That conversation had just been days ago. But, now I understood his pain, his rage, his hatred. He bowed his massive ebony head, and I knew what I was going to do.

Boom, boom, boom, boom, boom, boom, boom.

My daemon was awake now. She forced her head out of the fist I kept her smothered under. She would hide no more.

The *triquetra* burned hotter than it ever had, scalding my flesh, but I headed it no mind, and the daemon in me forced my body to stand. Clair's limp corpse slid off my knees to nestle on the ground.

I was going to kill them. I was going to kill them all.

The drum in my chest built to a crescendo, and the *triquetra* dug its fingers into my aura, holding on for dear life. My ring of ravens that I had worn my whole life, suddenly seemed to wake up. The tiny pendant that Meredith had told me was the symbol of my heritage vibrated against the *triquetra* and loosened the hold it had on me, almost gently prying the magical fingers out of my aura.

With half a thought, the cursed thing ripped from my throat and shot so fast from my body that it embedded itself into a nearby shipping container. I turned slowly to face Ash Nevra's army. Kieran and Amon still hovered above me, both watching me. Maria was nursing her wounds from her scuffle with Rycon off to the side.

Without the *triquetra* to dampen my powers, I felt like I was seeing the world for the first time. My planets and my stars were spinning with purpose, and I could see the creatures around me as they moved, but it was like my mind saw their movements before they themselves even committed to them.

I could smell the blood beneath their skin, hear their thoughts, and see through all of their eyes simultaneously. Tiny, metaphysical threads jumped between every living thing around me, even the small plants that had managed to climb through old cracks in the docks. The sickly fish in the polluted lake had tiny life arcs tracking them as they moved through the water. Even the beetles and ants couldn't hide from me.

I took a step towards the now frozen army, my bare feet slicing open on the field of shrapnel that lay before me, only to immediately mend under the enormous hum of power that now beat freely from my core. I could see myself through every being's eyes, and my thin, wreaked body stood as if held up by a single string that ran down my spine. My eyes had been swallowed into blackness, and my head bobbed as hot tears streamed down my cheeks.

Kieran floated down from where he hovered above me, his face, for once, appropriately grave. He looked at his dead daughter, who now lay behind me.

"Raven, my intention was never to kill Clair,' his voice almost sounded strained.

The daemon inside me hissed, but I did not move. The beat of the drum in my chest continued, and with each pulse, the steel shipping containers that littered the docks around us vibrated.

Kieran turned to Maria, who was covered in scratches from her scuffle with Rycon. She looked terrified.

"How dare you." He snarled at her. She may have feared him, but she shrugged, holding her ground.

"Ash Nevra ordered her death." I felt the build of power as Kieran's rage, and grief took him over. I raised my left hand and silenced him.

She was *mine.*

My head turned and bobbed on its own accord to face Maria, who paled and stiffened under my midnight gaze.

My aura was pulsating with each beat of that eternal drum. It grew and surrounded me in an obsidian orbital shield, and my bloody feet drifted off the ground. I hovered in the air in the center of my atramentous armor, my loose, dirty night clothes floating around my wafer-thin body.

The witch could do nothing but watch as I hovered in the air, above her, my dead mother lying beneath me. The small sack of sunflower seeds danced across my vision. They would never be planted now. We would never garden together again.

I felt a sob build in my chest. It started small, then turned to a scream.

Boom, boom, boom, boom, boom, boom, boom, boom

I didn't have time to think about building power, all my lessons with Conrad and Meredith flew from my mind. *I was power.* And it was immediately available at my fingertips. The hand that still held Rycon's jade hilted knife rose of its own accord. I sent it through the air like a dart, and I knew I would not miss. I watched it impale Maria through the neck, and it felt *good.*

But it wasn't enough.

A quasar erupted from the palm of my hand, following the path of the ancient knife, and I felt Maria's bones as they melted. I drank up her poisoned soul as she died. Turning, I dragged the dark beam of energy with me as I screamed, tears spilling down my face. I felt each death as the endless stream of power literally liquified the daemons and witches alike who stood before me. My screams of grief and rage turned to manic sobs as each soul climbed up the river of oblivion spilling out of me and continued to fuel my power.

'*Shit,*' Rycon exclaimed before leaping towards Conrad, Meredith, Mr. Abbey, and Conrad's grandmother. '*Get the fuck out of the way. She'll never forgive me if I let any of you die,*' he snarled, but I didn't care.

I was going to burn this fucking planet to the ground.

60

The magickal storm I had summoned tore through the wasted docks beneath me. With each passing second, I lost more and more control. Clair's smiling face hovered just behind my mind's eye.

I love you, Raven. How many times had she patched me up? How many times had she held me when I had been afraid? My rock, my pillar, my strength. And now she was *dead*.

The beat of the drum in my chest ran even faster. Daemons from Ash Nevra's army weren't even pretending to fight anymore. They were running.

Running from *me*.

The daemon in me smiled. I pulled their life threads together and knotted them in my hand as they ran. Closing my fist around the knot, I allowed the hatred, the rage, and the grief inside of me to flow down their spools, and I relished as they all dropped to the ground. Dead. Like the birds. Like Mrs. Serafini. This time I wasn't afraid. This time, I called for the reaper and invited him in like an old friend.

I spun on an axis, my planets and stars orbiting around me with purpose. *Kieran, where was Kieran?* I finally found his life thread, which he desperately tried to conceal with magick as he gathered his powers around him.

I blinked, and I was in front of him. In shock, he nearly jumped out of his skin as I hovered motionless before him, my hair whipping in the storm that raged in my translucent orb of power. The beat of the drum in my chest sped up to a climax as I faced him, toes pointing towards the ground, my all-black eyes glued to his face.

"You killed her," I no longer needed to use my mouth to speak. I'm pretty sure every living being heard me project those words. I wasn't even bothering to try to contain my rage. The very ground beneath me splintered, and the asphalt broke apart.

"No, I didn't," Kieran snapped, his voice faltering against his growing anxiety. I could taste his fear on my tongue, and it pleased me. Before I could react, he slipped through a hole in The Veil and simultaneously closed all the remaining gateways behind him.

No.

My rage built higher at his escape, and the beating drum hammered along with my heartbeat. My scream alone was deadly, and any glass in the immediate vicinity shattered. I could hear police sirens and feel Rycon hiding my allies behind a nearby container.

The planets in my aura whirled faster, and the midnight in my heart expanded, blanketing the docks and plunging us into darkness. That drumbeat was relentless. Faster and faster it built, the black hole where Clair had been was growing and sucking me down. I knew the power would consume me, and I would die amongst the thousand corpses I had just created.

I did not care.

Suddenly Amon was before me. As a reflex, I threw up my hands, ready to incinerate him as he hovered near my impermeable aura. He didn't so much as flinch.

"You need to stop, or the power will consume you," his voice was low and even. It was a testament to my advanced senses that I could hear him at all over the storm of energy that was continuing to build around me.

I didn't need to tell him I was ready and willing to accept death. My grief had consumed me. The torture had broken me. The quiet would be a relief. I hovered before him and waited as the power around me continued to build. He did not look sympathetic. His face hardened.

"That is *enough*, Raven."

He floated forward toward my shield. I pushed him away with my considerable might, but he waved a hand and deflected the blow. Okay. He *was* very powerful.

He forced his way into my shield. The energy tore at his silver hair. I pushed against him, but he continued to compel himself into the inky orb I had formed around me. Finally, he was hovering with me over the wasted docks in the eye of the storm.

"Raven. You need to stop." He repeated. My heart was crashing against my chest, and my energy literally started to crush several nearby shipping containers as if they were tin cans. The police sirens were getting louder.

"They killed her," my voice cracked. I sounded odd and far away. Despite the raging storm outside my safe little orb, I had unintentionally preserved Clair's body. I could still see where she lay among the ruins, protected by a small domed shield I had created around her without realizing it.

"I know." He said as he floated closer. Without the *triquetra* to separate us, he reached out a hand to touch my face, which was still soaking wet with tears. His touch immediately caught the attention of my daemon. "We will avenge her, but we cannot do that if you die here, now."

I thought of all the souls I had collected, and the many, many more, that could still be held responsible. I thought of Ash Nevra. A daemon I had never met, who was responsible for all of my pain. She was probably sitting comfortably somewhere, relishing in Clair's death, hoping I would follow my mother into the afterlife. Another memory hit me like a hurricane.

I was a child again, sitting in the office of my elementary school. Jeremy had just finished a shouting match with the principal, who had expelled me. The kids that day had shut me in a locker. That had been a bad idea.

The ringleader of that particular prank ended up in the hospital shortly after I got out.

'*Of course, she would lash out at them,*' Jeremy had shouted at the principal of that school. What did she expect from a child being tormented day in and day out by her peers?

'*You're placing the blame on the wrong person.*'

The woman had smiled at him smugly and told him there was nothing she could do. Her hands were tied. She had been happy to be rid of the angry little girl with dark hair. I hadn't known then that my aura had been poisonous enough to turn her against me.

During the drive home in his cruiser, he had looked at me, and I hadn't understood why he had been so angry. I had always assumed he had been angry with me.

'*When people are so horrible to you that you want to give up, remember, that's what they want you to do. Don't give them what they want. Don't ever give up.*'

My rage flared, and I felt more power bubble up from within me. I felt it score through my bones and wrap around my frantically beating heart. Amon was right. If I died now, Ash Nevra would win. Clair's death would have been for nothing. I couldn't die. Not yet, but I didn't know how to make it stop.

61

I reached out and grabbed his arm, the matte-black metal of his armor crinkling like paper beneath my touch. The metal felt like nothing I had ever touched before. It was otherworldly. He raised his eyebrows at the display of strength but said nothing.

"Help me," I gasped. He nodded and pulled me in close. I winced, waiting for him to knock me out or blast me with some kind of magick. Instead, he leaned in, touching his lips gently against mine.

The shock of the kiss wrenched me out of the downward spiral I had been headed towards. His energy rubbed intimately against me, and my daemon sighed softly. My blood was on fire, but my skin went cold with exhilaration. His lips were soft and dry, and his scent enveloped me. My mouth flooded with the warm taste of cinnamon. I felt myself soften, and my body began to melt into him before I realized what I was doing. Then... I slapped him.

His head snapped to the side, and I was impressed for a moment that he had managed not to be thrown right into the ground despite the amount of power I had put behind the slap. The storm that had been raging died down to a whisper, and the drum in my chest fell silent.

"What the hell was that?" I snarled at him. The planets and stars in my aura were slowing, and I realized suddenly that we were still suspended in the air, and as my power died, so was my ability to hold myself up. Fifteen feet was a long way to fall, half-daemon or not.

Amon touched his cheek where I had hit him, and the corner of his mouth twitched upwards.

"It worked, didn't it?" He asked, sliding forward to hold me, so I wouldn't plummet to the ground. The shock of the kiss quickly wore off, and suddenly I was tired.

So, so tired.

Maybe it was the grief or the amount of energy I had used to wipe out our enemies. Either way, suddenly, I could barely keep my eyes open. I collapsed into Amon, and he hoisted me into his arms before lowering us both to the ground. His left arm was under my knees, and his right arm supported my back. Despite myself, I allowed my head to rest against his shoulder.

With my rage gone, the docks were now a silent wasteland. My small band of friends emerged from behind the now slightly crushed shipping container. I knew now I hadn't imagined the police sirens. I could see cruisers racing up around the bend.

Amon's feet touched the ground close to Clair's body, and tears welled into my now normal eyes. The sight of her wrecked me to my core. Rycon padded forward, followed by the magick folk, Blue-Hair, and the Mountain.

"We don't have time," Amon said before anyone could speak. "I am taking her across The Veil. Anyone who would like to join us is welcome to come." The latter was directed at the small coven of magick folk I seemed to have adopted over the last couple of weeks. I was still in his arms and too exhausted to be enraged by the fact that he had made this decision for me. To my surprise, everyone nodded.

'I obviously don't have a choice, then.' Rycon said, stepping forward on silent paws.

Amon gave him an icy look. "No. You do not."

Conrad stepped up next. "Mi coming."

"Me too," Meredith said.

Mr. Abbey and Conrad's grandmother exchanged glances.

"We will stay here to manage The Board and relay today's events. We will contact you as soon as we have news." Mr. Abbey said. Amon nodded. The police cruisers were pulling into the docks now, tires squealing on the pavement as they surrounded us where we stood by Clair's preserved body. The rest of the corpses had been destroyed beyond the point of recognition by my energy storm.

Mr. Abbey and Conrad's grandmother shimmered away. Blue-Hair and the Mountain came to stand beside us as Amon opened a hole in The Veil. I glanced down at Clair's broken body before we stepped through, whispering a silent goodbye to her in my mind. Moments before we passed into the daemon realm, I glanced up, and my eyes met with Jeremy's as he stepped out of an undercover cruiser at the forefront of the fleet.

I saw, more than heard, him mouth my name in confusion as he took in the sight of me wrapped up in a strange man's arms with a larger-than-life panther, Conrad, and the rest of our party.

Amon stepped through The Veil just as Jeremy's gaze fell to take in Clair's silent form, his face paling. As the door to the new world closed behind us, I made eye contact with him one last time and mouthed the words, *'I'm sorry.'* And then, we were gone.

ACKNOWLEDGEMENTS

I would like to express my heartfelt gratitude to the following individuals without whom this novel would not have been possible.

First and foremost, I owe a debt of gratitude to Lori-Ann Drecketts, my editor and sensitivity reader. Her insights, feedback, and guidance have elevated this book beyond what I could have achieved on my own. I highly recommend Lori-Ann to anyone looking for a developmental editor or a sensitivity reader for a Jamaican character. Her handle on Fiverr is jamsoulsinger, and she truly is amazing.

I would also like to extend my thanks to Michele Chivers, my mother, who has been my unwavering cheerleader since I first began drafting The Origin's Daughter nearly ten years ago. She has always been Rycon's number one fan, and I am thrilled that she can finally see him grow as a person in these pages. These books would not be where they are today without her.

To my husband, Michael Gural, thank you for your unwavering love and support. From listening to me read chapters I was struggling with to providing feedback when I needed it most, you have been my rock throughout this process. Your encouragement and willingness to pick up the slack at home when I fall into an ADHD fueled writing rage have been invaluable. I love you more than words can express.

I would also like to give honorable mentions to my besties: Kelsey Cheyne, Milica Godberson, and Steph Bruns. Thank you for being my support system, listening to my word vomit about my characters, and providing encouragement along the way. Your support means the world to me.

Lastly, I would like to thank myself. Little Alex would be so proud of me for finally bringing Raven, Amon, Conrad, Rycon, Meredith, Kasha and Dossidian to life for the rest of the world to meet. I am grateful to have had the opportunity to tell their story, and I am proud of what we have accomplished together.

DON'T MISS BOOK TWO OF

THE ORIGIN'S DAUGHTER SERIES:

THE DOMINION OF SIN

AVAILABLE NOW ON AMAZON!

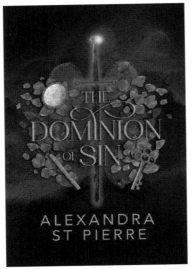

Raven wakes up in the Court of Pride, to find that it is not the fiery hellscape she had expected it to be. However, she is a prisoner, trapped by her life debt to the Dark Prince of the Court of Pride, Amon.

She is still reeling from the torture she has endured at the hands of Ash Nevra's dark wizard, Kieran, and the murder of one of the only people she had ever loved weighs heavily on her heart. The idea of serving this daemon prince who has ensnared her in an unbreakable magick pact feels impossible.

Despite the crippling grief that clutches her heart, Raven quickly learns that she has bigger problems than Amon. Ash Nevra has not only taken over the Dominion but has been enslaving daemons for centuries. As Raven trains to face the looming threat of Ash Nerva, she discovers powerful artifacts and long-buried secrets that could turn the tide of the oncoming war.

In a world where the enemy is always one step ahead, and not everything is as it seems, Raven must tread carefully to protect those she loves.

Full of romance, new friendships, action, adventure, and mayhem, this thrilling paranormal and urban fantasy romance is sure to keep readers on the edge of their seats. Will Raven be able to save her loved ones, or will the evil forces triumph? Find out in this heart-pounding story.

ARE YOU AN ARTIST?
DO YOU LOVE THIS SERIES?

Tag @theoriginsdaughter on Facebook, Instagram or Tiktok in any fan art you create for a chance to win a signed hard copy of The Origin's Daughter and The Dominion of Sin!

One winner will be selected by the author and announced on official The Origin's Daughter Facebook Instagram and TikTok accounts at the end of each month until April 2024. Winners will be asked to DM their preferred mailing address to the official accounts of The Origin's Daughter.

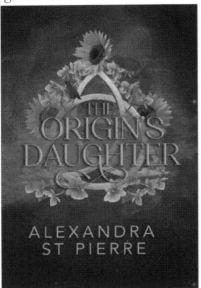 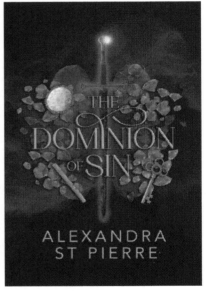

@TheOriginsDaughter

Don't miss the next installment! Follow us on Facebook, Instagram and Tiktok for updates, contest winners, and more!

Printed in Great Britain
by Amazon

27277955R00146